Spencer Hill Press

Contact: Spence City, an imprint of Spencer Hill Press, PO Box 247, Contoocook, NH 03229, USA

Please visit our website at www.spencecity.com

First Edition: October 2013.
Kendra L. Saunders
Death and Mr. Right: a novel / by Kendra L. Saunders – 1st ed.
p. cm.

Summary:
The agent of nightmares is fired and stranded in modern Boston. With the help of a pretty thief, he strives to get his job back and overthrow a shadowy governing body of immortals.

Cover design by K. Kaynak
Interior layout by Marie Romero

978-1-939392-04-6 (paperback)
978-1-939392-05-3 (e-book)
Printed in the United States of America

DEATH AND MR. RIGHT

Kendra L. Saunders

SPENCE
CITY

This book is dedicated to
the folks at the Concord, NH Starbucks.
You have no idea how much
those delicious chai lattes meant to me.

CHAPTER ONE

Today was the firing kind of day.

Death, the agent of nightmares (and youngest agent in the entire system), made his way through the halls with a smile on his face and a bounce in his step. Firing days held a certain electric charge in them, a potential for a little bit of much-needed inner-office drama.

No morning was ever complete for Death without a stop by the coffee machine in Mandy's office, both for the caffeine high and the snatches of gossipy conversation he was likely to hear.

Death leaned against Mandy's desk, and then rose to his tiptoes. Mandy's desk was a bit on the tall side, and Death was, well, a bit on the short side. But he was pretty sure it was a scientific fact that brains stunted physical growth, which he believed explained a lot about his own particular vertical challenge.

Mandy cast him a mindful nod. She was busy on the phone with what Death assumed to be an irate coworker from a different division, judging by Mandy's repeated requests along the line of "Well, can you just stop talking and let me connect you to Malcolm?"

Death saluted Mandy and carried his coffee cup away, propelling himself down two hallways and into his tiny office.

Death's office might have been better suited for a hamster, both because of its small size and because it had a tendency to be papered from wall to wall, although hamsters don't usually decorate with charts, graphs, reports, and notes. Oh, and books that had never been read or, in most cases, opened.

When it all boiled down, Death loved his job. He just didn't like reading about it.

"Death?"

He raised his head to find Malcolm in the doorway. "Hey, Malcolm. Mandy's got a live one for you on the phone."

"Right. Listen, get your assignment done soon, would you?"

Death blinked at his supervisor. "I'm not behind schedule."

"Yeah, that's cool," Malcolm said, as if Death had never spoken. "Get it done by tonight, would you? Thanks."

Now, everyone in the office had their opinions about Malcolm. Death happened to be of the opinion that Malcolm was a miserable bore with a propensity toward unwise facial hair, but such things probably shouldn't be said anywhere other than on the anonymous notes sometimes found in the men's bathroom on Level 3 of the HQ building. (The particular note that Death had glimpsed there last month had said something along the lines of "MALcolM IS a DisGraCE to the COMPanY!!!")

Death liked to keep his opinions about Malcolm to himself, and maybe to Mandy. And a few friends.

"Is something wrong?" Death asked, wading through the clutter of his office so he could stand a bit closer to his supervisor. "I've actually topped our nightmare numbers from last year by 3%. So many people had nightmares this week that I had to scale back to keep the balance from getting skewed." A smile broke over Death's face, despite how much he tried to stop it. "One of the nightmares from last week made it into the mortal news realm. It was this baseball guy, kinda famous, and I gave him a nightmare. He was interviewed the next day on TV and he actually *mentioned* it because he was so disturbed. See, in the dream, he was standing in a field at night and all of his teammates were wearing these glowing clothes and they were floating, headless—"

Malcolm cleared his throat behind his hand and gave Death a pinched-lipped nod. "Just get your assignment done." With that, Malcolm slouched off, his hands pushed into his pockets and his posture taking on the weird slug-like appearance that it always seemed best suited for.

Death shrugged to himself, took a few more generous sips of his coffee, and then exited his office.

The second floor of HQ housed the rather intimidating mail system of the agency. Letters, messages, and assignments filled the second floor to the brim and employed countless people whose names Death still couldn't remember. He liked to visit the second floor, if only for the possibility of meeting new people.

Death caught the elevator just before its doors closed, then realized with a start that he wasn't alone. His elevator mate was none other than the pretty redhead who worked up in one of the larger, fancier offices on one of the top floors of HQ. Death had seen her a few times from a distance, but had never had any direct contact with her.

"I'm going down. Uh. I'm going to the second floor," he said.

She nodded, absently pressing the button for the second floor and then staring at the little readout as it cheerfully announced they were on their way up to the 9th floor.

An important part of being an agent was agreeing to play by the "Sacred Laws." A few of those particularly serious Sacred Laws included not stealing things and not falling in love. Love was a forbidden tangle of emotions and it wasted time, according to Them, the mysterious hierarchy of beings to whom everyone at HQ submitted. (Death had never seen Them and had no idea what They looked like, but if he thought long and hard about it, he pictured Them as unpleasant beings with a lot of tentacles, like something from a Lovecraft novel.)

Falling in love was the sort of half-romantic but incredibly foolish thing that all agents sometimes talked about, but very few were stupid enough to act on.

Feelings of adoration were kept private, and gestures of devotion were policed.

All of that being said, Death had never thought a little good-natured flirting had to be out of the question. And he'd gone through enough of a dry spell in that department during high school, right?

Death leaned his weight against the wall of the elevator, crossing his arms and planting an enticing smile on his face. "So," he said, as the elevator doors chimed open and the red-haired beauty disappeared from sight, back to her fancy office on her fancy floor.

Oh, well.

The elevator breezed back down to the second floor and Death strolled into the mail room, the red-haired lady already forgotten in lieu of the excitement of letters, deadlines, and yelling shift leaders. A paperboy nearly ran into Death as he sped by with a white cart of inter-office messages.

Death reached the assignment kiosk eventually and searched out his name in the messy filing system. His newest Assignment Card had his name printed at the top and then a very simple assignment...transport some paperwork to Boston and hand it off to another agent. No big deal.

Certainly not a big enough deal for Malcolm to act so nervous over.

Death collected the small parcel of paperwork that he'd be transporting and headed back to the elevator.

This time his elevator-mates were two of the tallest and most intimidating-looking Wings that Death had ever seen. That was saying something, considering that all Wings were tall and intimidating. One of them was fair-haired and fair-skinned, and the other was dark-skinned and red-haired. Both of them had the frightening all-white eyes of their kind and, of course, the carefully folded feathered wings.

When Death had first been promoted, he'd been informed a dozen times that Wings were not to be crossed or questioned and should never be touched without permission. Their wings were strong enough to allow them to fly, but also coated with various poisons and other dangers that could kill even an agent. Some rumors said that Wings shot lasers from their eyes, but Death wasn't sure if he believed that.

"Find the jar," one of them said, in a voice laced with centuries of justice and bloodshed. The Wings looked at each other silently, as if communicating through their minds, and Death found himself pressing closer and closer against the wall to avoid accidently touching either of them.

The elevator stopped and the doors chimed open. "This is my stop," Death said. "Sir. Sirs."

Both Wings turned their grave, majestic heads toward Death, fixing him with their gauzy white gazes. "What is your title?" the fair-skinned one asked.

"Death."

"And what is your name?"

"My name? Uh, it used to be something else."

The Wing's eyes narrowed slightly. "What is your name?" it said, this time without the slightly more friendly questioning lilt.

"Kelly Gold."

Where he usually heard a snicker or detected a sneer on the part of anyone who heard his name for the first time, this time Death only received a creepy blank stare in return and then, after what felt like an eternity, a slight nod.

"Go on your way, Kelly Gold," the Wing said, stepping aside.

Death almost tripped in his hurry to get out of the elevator. He only turned once he was a safe distance away from the Wings, as he watched them disappear into the swallowing mouth of the elevator.

A sense of painful foreboding shook Death as he headed back to his office, gathered a few of his belongings, and left HQ for Boston. Wings never paid him any attention, and he didn't particularly want that to change. Wings and reapers had a remarkable way of ruining someone's life—or afterlife—simply by existing.

And Death rather liked his life.

CHAPTER TWO

It wasn't every evening that Death and Mr. Right found themselves in such close quarters, but this was March the 32nd and people liked to say that it was a day when anything could happen. Except the postal service behaving efficiently. That was prophesied as something that would never happen.

"You working tonight?" Mr. Right asked, in his customary soothing voice.

Death, who had been staring at the sunset as if it might open up and burst on him, shook his head and finally angled himself toward his companion. "There's something bigger than me out there tonight." He pointed at the sky. "See that? See the red?"

Mr. Right rolled his eyes heavenward. "I suppose."

"That's the tide coming in."

"Your cohorts?"

"No, no. No, this isn't agents." Death sighed, digging one boot into the ground and twitching his gloved hands impatiently. "What about you? Did they give you the night off?"

It had been exactly 254 years since Mr. Right had been given a vacation, but he smiled politely as he answered. "I'm on break."

"How long?"

"An hour. Standard break time."

Death quirked an eyebrow. "They overwork you. Isn't there something in the manual about that? In the sixth chapter. I'm pretty sure there's a whole section in the sixth chapter about break time and holidays."

"We're not exactly a union." And that was true. To create an intense yearning, a passionate feeling, a mutual attraction, a love so powerful that it filled every textbook and musical note...it wasn't easy. It required time and energy and countless hours on the clock. Many times, it required a day without any break at all. Many times it required a devotion that could wear thin for even someone as patient and hardworking as Mr. Right.

"I wish I was working tonight!" Death said, wheeling around and tossing his hands with a dramatic flair. He looked like some sort of piece of confectionery, his short hair arched upward on top and tinted as blue as a paint splatter. "I specifically requested to be kept on tonight. We're up on nightmare ratios, but not as much as I'd like to be." He paced, all exaggerated movements and snarled upper lip, then motioned skyward. "But there's that, all of that up there, you know. They want to hurl a bit of lightning around and show off."

Mr. Right chuckled. "You're the prince of showing off."

"I'm the prince of many things."

"So…what are they doing up there?" Mr. Right asked, raising a Thermos of coffee to his lips. Coffee was one of approximately three mortal inventions that bordered on divine brilliance. Gluten-free cookies came in at a close second behind coffee.

"How should I know what they're doing? Not my department."

Mr. Right pretended not to know any of the rumors that circulated at the monthly donut-and-discussion meetings.

"It's not because they transferred me," Death said, peering suspiciously at Mr. Right. "They haven't transferred me. It's just not my department."

"Oh."

"Don't bother pretending that you haven't heard about it, I know everyone has." Death paced again, this time pushing his shoulders back, his chest out. He looked a bit like an angry bird, courtesy of his small stature, but Mr. Right was polite enough not to laugh. "It has nothing to do with that girl!"

Mr. Right smiled. "Ah, romance."

"There was no romance. She stole something from me and I'll get it back. Until then, I will continue my work as usual."

"And avoid pretty girls."

Death's finely featured face erupted in a crimson blush that spread clear to the tips of his ears.

"Well," Mr. Right said, "I think it's a bit melodramatic of them to let you go, no matter the reason. It's not like you broke any of the Sacred Laws or killed someone."

"Killed someone? No, I'm not the Reaper," Death said, dropping his voice to a practiced whisper. Speaking of the Reaper too loud was a good way to land in trouble fast. While Death's duties included creating a feeling of foreboding, constructing nightmares and generally making mortals have a lametastic day, he was forbidden from extinguishing any mortal life. That task was left to the Reaper and his cronies, who were endearingly referred to as "reapers" with little r's.

Well, maybe not endearingly.

Mr. Right nodded silently to himself, glancing once again toward the horizon and the red clouds that had settled there.

"Even if anything happens, it'll be a transfer. They can't let me go unless I break one of the Sacred Laws." Death stopped pacing. "I've never stolen anything from the Wings division, I've never opened the Box, and I've never spelled 'they're' without the apostrophe."

Laughter burst from Mr. Right and he nearly fell off the cement block he'd been sitting on. "You…you do know that's not actually one of the laws, don't you? Oh, you didn't. You didn't know? Malcolm was only joking about that one. It's a pet peeve. It's not really one of the Sacred Laws, though I suppose a lot of professors wish it was." Mr. Right wiped away tears and grinned at his companion.

"Malcolm," Death muttered, after a long pause. He narrowed his eyes.

"Now, now, don't look so murderous, or you'll break a Sacred Law anyway."

Death smiled then, all gleeful malice and ill intent and pointy teeth. "Gary was telling me the other day about how much Malcolm hates spiders. I think I'll make Malcolm a nice little nightmare about furry spiders with fangs as big as his face…"

Mr. Right checked his watch, noting that he still had fifteen minutes left of his break. His next task was of vital, world-changing importance, but no need to rush it. Fifteen minutes wouldn't make much difference in the course of history, so Mr. Right took another long sip of coffee.

"What else has he lied about?" Death asked.

"Lied? He doesn't lie, really, he's just sarcastic, and you don't detect sarcasm."

"Well, what else was he 'sarcastic' about?"

"It's true that you're not allowed to murder, to open the Box…"

"Steal office supplies."

"…steal things from the Wings or any of your other superiors. And don't mess with time. That's a big one with the higher-ups. They have the schedule for a reason."

Death rolled his eyes.

"And of course, no falling in love."

"Ah ha! See! I haven't broken any of them."

Mr. Right shrugged, taking another sip from his Thermos.

"I didn't fall in love with her! Don't you see? It's a gray area. There's a difference between seeing someone or…or liking someone a little—NOT THAT I DID!—and loving them. There's a huge difference. You know what happens when you're in love? You get all stupid and giddy and you say dumb things and you act different. I barely even spoke to this girl. I can't help if she's attractive, and I can't help that she's a crazy thief who stole something from me. It doesn't mean anything."

About a hundred times a day, Mr. Right heard people say things along those lines. The amount of denial in the love game was always amusing, especially from the men. He'd learned to just sit back and wait out the little fits and tantrums, because no one ever wanted to admit to being in love. Love was too confusing and traitorous to the self. Too dangerous.

"When I get those papers back, this will all be behind us," Death said, resuming his frantic pacing.

"What exactly did she steal from you, anyway?"

Death twitched. "Uh. A list of names."

"Names? Like the names of the damned?" No answer. "Oh, Death."

"I'll get it back!"

The names of the damned were all-important documents that were for no one's eyes other than the Wings. Even reading them could result in immediate exile. Mr. Right couldn't help feeling confused about why Death would have been given an assignment that involved *touching* the documents, never mind transporting them.

Mr. Right sighed and glanced at his watch again.

A flash of red lightning tore across the sky, chased by thunder. Mr. Right winced. The poor mortals. They never fared well during these sorts of things, especially since they struggled with the concept that their scientific perceptions were just a lot of comforting drivel that kept them from feeling small and vulnerable. The sky wasn't blue because of water molecules or whatever had been written in school books. It was blue because someone wanted it to be blue, and if They were in the middle of a squabble about the color, it might change without warning.

It had changed already six times in the last thousand years, but memories had been wiped so that everyone assumed it had always been green or purple or, most recently, blue.

Now and again, children were smart enough to ask, "Why is the sky blue?" And then their parents would fumble with the answer, slipping around the implanted memories for a few seconds before deciding that yes, yes, the sky was most certainly blue and yes, it was most certainly supposed to be that way and yes, there was a very easy and scientific explanation for it.

"I love this weather," Death said. "And March 32nd. It's my favorite day." He tapped his fingertips together.

"March 32nd, the day that doesn't officially exist. It's a bit disconcerting."

"I like that word! Disconcerting." Death rolled the word around his mouth and grinned. "Next meeting, I'll use that in my description sheet for the badges." He stopped pacing. "Who do you think they'll fire today? Last year they fired three people, but I think this year they'll just get rid of Giddiness. He's had his head on the chopping block for a long time and he doesn't even see it. I saw his chart, and his numbers are down 20%

from last year. And they didn't issue him a new pair of boots; you know what that means. Oh and Jessica. They'll get rid of her for sure! No one likes her. She's weird and she gives me a headache whenever she's around."

Mr. Right shrugged.

"I don't understand how they don't see it coming. It's always so obvious, especially last year with Despair. I guess he didn't adjust to mortal life, either. I tried sending him some letters and he hasn't answered."

"Most of them don't want to be friends after they're exiled," Mr. Right said, a wave of melancholy settling over him.

"I heard about that one Wing, what was his name? The tall one with the different-colored eyes? Mandy said he drove himself off a *cliff*."

That story had been repeated a hundred times, changed, like a bad game of telephone, until the details were a bit exaggerated. Or very exaggerated, according to some sources.

After a while, Mr. Right checked the time again. Break would be over in three minutes, and then he had the big assignment.

"Has anyone ever known what you were?" Death asked suddenly. "I mean, any of the mortals. Have they noticed you?"

Mr. Right considered. "Sometimes they're clever enough to see our auras, but not usually." He pointed one finger at his companion. "You, for instance, give off a lot of aura."

"Ooooh, I do?"

"That could just be your ego, though, old friend."

"That girl noticed my aura," Death said. "She looked me in the face and said 'You are something strange.' But with an accent. I can't do a Boston accent."

"You're not good at any accents."

"True, true. So what are you doing when your break's over? Anything exciting? I should join you. All this standing around is making me crazy. Maybe we could head to London like we did that time when you got the wrong assignment from Malcolm's assistant. That was fun."

"Break's over now," Mr. Right said, and let out a heavy sigh. "So, Death, tell me something. What was that girl's name?"

"Lola." As soon as he'd said it, Death froze. The twitch in his fingers lessened and his face relaxed as his eyes focused on the horizon. "Lola…her name was Lola."

"Yeah? What's she like?"

Death turned his gaze to Mr. Right. "She understands things. And she's so beautiful," Death said, as if he had just remembered something very important and then lost it again.

"I bet she is."

"No, she is! She's beautiful." Death nodded to himself, perching beside Mr. Right on the concrete block. One foot dangled below him as he pulled the other one up and tucked his knee under his chin. "She's probably thinking of me right now. We had something special, I think."

Mr. Right patted his old friend on the back and whispered his apologies. Death's bright blue aura faded to nothing, and somewhere in the sky over them, papers were signed for the demotion.

For a few remaining minutes, it was March 32nd. Anything could happen on March 32nd, the day that doesn't exist.

CHAPTER THREE

Boston was a nice city to visit, so long as you hadn't just been exiled from everything you'd ever known and stripped of all of your basic powers. And Boston was, of course, the place that all of the exiles were sent.

Death wasn't exactly sure how he ended up on a train; maybe Mr. Right had directed him there, or maybe his dazed mind had worked just long enough to seat him next to a smelly old guy in a bright orange hat.

But really, Death didn't become aware of his surroundings until the train halted for a millionth time and the aforementioned old guy fell over into him, yelling "haaaggagagabaja!" in his ear.

"What…what stop is this?" Death asked aloud, attempting to untangle himself from the orange-hat-man. His attempts were unsuccessful, though, as the old guy seemed more interested in falling asleep across Death's lap. Yuck. With a complicated move worthy of a comic book hero, Death freed himself and stood up.

A teenage girl tapped at her cell phone keyboard and cast a withering stare in Death's direction. "This is Government Center. You here for the convention?"

"Convention?"

"Costume freaks."

Death frowned. "Why would I want to go to a convention for costume freaks?"

The girl rolled her eyes. "Look, I'm not into it, but who am I to judge? My ex liked wearing mascot costumes for fun. Good luck." Just then the train lurched forward again and Death lost his balance, hitting his knees a bit harder than he'd ever want to admit.

At the next stop, the doors slid open and the girl stepped off the train without a backward glance, leaving Death no choice but to scramble to his feet and race after her. Maybe if he could catch up to her, he could ask her some questions. The first, most important survival tactic for anyone in a new environment was to make a friend. Or, at least, Death had always believed that.

Crowds of silent, grim-faced men and women pushed him apart from the girl, though, and soon Death realized he was standing at the base of a grubby flight of stairs…and was about to be trampled by hordes of commuters. He threw himself into a wall to keep from getting crushed, all the while struggling to gather his wayward thoughts. Up, up and out. He needed to get out of this train station. The air hung heavy and suffocating with recycled breath and anguished business-brained people. Death had never smelled so much depression in his entire existence.

And pressing his face against the wall left him feeling infected with about six million types of germs.

Why did people even live like this? Travel like this? And why was that man over there wearing khaki pants with an undersized shirt? Death twitched a little. Horrors.

Death attempted to push away from the wall and walk up the stairs, but a young woman stepped in front of him, grinning and motioning to her camera. Before he could say anything, she'd snapped a picture directly in his face, temporarily blinding him. "You rock music?" she asked, as he blinked away stars. "Big rock music star?"

Now, a man doesn't have blue hair and dress like a dandy if he doesn't want attention, but Death had never felt less prepared for attention than he did in that moment. "I need to get out of here," he said, but the woman had already turned away from him and torn up the stairs, waving her camera around like a choice prize.

Death gripped the railing as he climbed the steps, praying he could get out of the claustrophobic underground as quickly as possible, but he found himself stopped again…this time by a sound.

It started out quiet, like a whistle carried on the breeze from far away, but then the sound increased and increased until it sounded as if someone was slicing Death's brain open with a high-pitched scream. He slapped his hands over his ears and crouched down to keep himself from losing his balance. The noise increased even more and he ground his teeth against it, leaking tears from the corners of his eyes.

All at once, the noise stopped and he slowly stood back up.

He'd read about that sound. Apparently it was a banshee scream, bottled and then released when an agent was in some kind of danger. The description "ear-shattering" did it no justice.

Things weren't much better on the street level, unfortunately, especially since it had started to rain. Death covered his head with his hands, but that did little to protect his hair. By the time he'd made his way a few streets over, he'd given up on that and was concentrating mostly on not getting run over by any rogue, homicidal vehicles.

Did these people know how to drive?

All along the way, pedestrians pushed by him, jostling him from side to side or nearly stabbing him in the eyeball with their umbrellas. And the cell phones, the cell phones! When had people become so attached to their cell phones? Death was almost certain he spotted a toddler, pigtails and all, chattering away on a tiny pink cell phone.

And then there was the subtle blue-black haze that enveloped so many of the strangers, illuminating their lingering nightmare essence. Death had to force himself not to get distracted by the wayward negative images, fears and evil energy of dread that so many people carried with them.

"Hey, you got some money?" a voice asked, and Death jumped. He turned around to find a young man smiling at him, hand extended. "Listen, my kids really want to see me and I want to get home for my daughter's birthday but I got no money for the train. You got money for the train? Even just some change. It'd be so nice to see her on her birthday, you know. But I've got this broken leg, you know? I can't really work like I used to."

Death hesitated. Usually he carried money with him just in case he needed to blend in or get one of those sugary drinks in the silver cans, the ones for rock stars. Those always made him feel pretty good (even if a little shaky and sometimes dizzy).

"Uh, let me see…" he said, reaching into his back pocket for his wallet. He'd barely taken it out when the stranger snatched it and ran away with surprising agility for someone with a broken leg.

Any other time, Death might have laughed off the whole thing and vowed to send the man the worst nightmares of his entire life, but…well, that just wasn't an option right now. So he took off after the thief, muttering and cursing under his breath all the way. He really ought to have signed up for that 3K marathon, or whatever it was, that the Wings had put together last decade, because he was pretty sure he was going to die from wheezing.

Oh and the roads were slippery from the rain. Especially for a guy in boots with two-inch heels.

Death dodged the zombie-faced pedestrians and umbrellas, made an impressive leap over a puddle and crossed a busy street without looking both ways. He'd almost given up on catching the thief when Death spotted him again. With one last burst of energy, he overtook the thief, snatched the wallet back, yelled in triumph…and promptly fell into the street.

A car horn blasted just behind Death, sending prickly, evil memories into his brain like needles. *GET UP, GET UP, GET UP!* He scrambled blindly to regain his feet, to move out of the way of approaching cars.

"You're crazy, man," the thief yelled, shaking his head before running away.

Death gasped and threw himself onto the sidewalk before anything could run him over. He'd gotten the wallet back, which was the important part. And he hadn't gotten hit by a car. Sure, he'd fallen into a puddle and his lungs felt like they were going to explode in his chest, but that would go away. And maybe eventually the revolting smell of wet rubber and sick smoke would dissipate. Right now he needed something to drink and a dry place to rest.

If the streets of Boston were crowded and dangerous, the cafes weren't much better. Death had to fight his way to the counter of MojoBoy Cafe, and a long, squinty perusal of the menu board showed that something as simple as a cup of coffee had changed in the last 30 years. Most everything had fancy, big-word names and cost a small fortune. Death's request for water was met with a frown. "I…I guess I'd like this too," he said, picking up a banana from a basket by the register. He opened his wallet only to discover that his money was gone.

"Are you going to buy the banana or not, sir?"

"No," he said, snatching up the banana and making a run for it. And just like that, he had to add banana thief to his resume of evil deeds committed.

Death wasn't sure how long he ran, but eventually he slowed his pace, gasping, and then stopped altogether to eat the banana he'd worked so hard to acquire. It was a disappointing banana, on top of everything else, bruised here and there and a bit too ripe for his taste.

With a groan, Death glanced heavenward.

When Fashion got word that he was being demoted, Death had stayed up all night culling information and putting together a six-page report on why Fashion should stay. He'd run it to the 8th floor himself, handed it to the secretary and insisted that it be given to Fashion's supervisor immediately.

Death had even stopped by Malcolm's office and hadn't stopped listing off reasons for his friend to stay until Malcolm had called for security to bodily remove Death from his office.

So why hadn't Mr. Right done the same thing? They were friends, after all, old friends. Why hadn't he gotten his orders and said, "I respectfully decline" or whatever sort of stupid, polite, and stiff thing he would say? It didn't make any sense.

Death would just have to find that Lola girl and get his papers back. He wasn't in love with her, of course. That had been some momentary flash of infatuation, some artificial nonsense created by Mr. Right and his love potions. With the rescued papers in hand, Death would have every right to reclaim his job and go back to creating beautiful mayhem the world over.

A lot of running and thievery was going to have to be involved, though, for this plan to work.

And maybe new boots.

CHAPTER FOUR

Headquarters had changed since Mr. Right had visited last, and nowhere more remarkably than the giant office on the top floor. What had once been a very dark and depressing room full of stacks of unread papers and ancient books had been replaced with a rather cheery color scheme and a few exotic potted plants. Windows peered out on the gorgeous cloud city of Alantis—not to be confused with that famous city that had been sunk by uneducated city planners—and pleasant music filtered down from invisible speakers all around the room.

"Mr. Right!" Malcolm said, leaping up from his chair and shuffling around the desk. "It's finished?"

"Yes."

Malcolm's gummy face switched to a smile then, a real smile that lifted the bags around his eyes and gave him a halo of creepiness. "You sent him on his way?"

"I put him on a train. He was a bit dazed," Mr. Right said. "You'll send his things to him, though?"

"His things? Oh. Yeah, his things."

Everyone kept their belongings in lockers on the tenth floor of headquarters, though a few of the more colorful agents kept things in hiding spots throughout the world. Death was one of those agents, mostly because he was scatterbrained. Many times Death had bragged to Mr. Right that he kept money in various banks and kept clothes in various buried chests, so that he was prepared for anything.

As far as Mr. Right had seen, though, the buried chest deal came about because Death irritated a pirate who ordered that he be buried along with all of his belongings and also some girl in a coconut bra and pink hot pants.

"You'll send Death's things to him, won't you? At least the ones he keeps on the tenth floor, I mean."

Malcolm nodded. "Hey, listen, since he's not really in that position anymore, we're not going to refer to him that way. You know what I mean? So from now on I'd really feel a great deal more comfortable if you'd just call him Kelly Gold."

Mr. Right considered this. Calling Death by his given name was a bit like punching a kitten in the face. The noise was ferocious, but the claws weren't that painful. Especially for Mr. Right, who stood about a head taller than Death and considerably wider across the chest.

"I can take his things to him, if you want," Mr. Right said.

"What? No, no, I'd rather you have no contact with him. New policy, dunno if you read it. No contact with exiles. Last week we had an exile and this other guy and they were plotting and...hey, look. We'll take care of it, okay? I'll make sure Kelly's things are given to him."

"Not to question your methods, but it would seem that sending some money, at the least, would be rather standard procedure. You know how he is. I doubt he carries much human currency with him."

Malcolm snorted. "Or anything of any use."

"That being noted, perhaps you should send him some provisions right away."

Malcolm's face took on that smile again and he motioned for Mr. Right to sit down. "You know, speaking of new policies, we've thought a lot lately about the competency levels around here. One break in a line can ruin the whole thing. One guy tap-dancing the wrong way can...well, you get the idea. Kelly Gold was not only blowing off his responsibilities, but he was beginning to place danger and strain on everything we're fighting to accomplish."

The smile didn't slip, even for a moment.

"He's irresponsible sometimes, but he means well," Mr. Right said. "He lives for his job."

Malcolm shifted in his chair so he could lean across the desk toward Mr. Right. "You know, every agent lives for their job, because they died to get it. Keep that in mind, Mr. Right. Dedication is required by definition."

"I understand."

"If someone wants to fall asleep in meetings and pull pranks on their supervisors and show up late to check-ins, they might as well let someone more serious take their place. We don't hand these jobs out from the kindness of our hearts. We hire according to skill and commitment. Kelly Gold was severely lacking in the latter."

"He's…done quite well with numbers. He's always spouting them off to me."

"Numbers can only do so much, Mr. Right, and we both know that. Anyway. How are your other projects? Do you need anything from us? I'm more than prepared to give you a bigger budget after that mess in Singapore last month."

Mr. Right had never been much of one for small talk, if only because he operated better in theories, in feelings and concepts. He much preferred body language to this kind of thing, but he perched on the edge of the offered chair and turned sleepy eyes toward Malcolm. "You're in charge of budget now?" he asked.

"I've always been in charge of budget. I'm in charge of a lot of things," Malcolm said. He was precisely the sort of man who could be handsome and likable if he wasn't himself. "Speaking of which, Jessica is taking over the Death position."

Jessica arrived on cue, which could only mean she'd been lurking just outside the room for an undetermined amount of time. She crossed the room in long, easy strides, and stopped just beside Malcolm's chair. She'd always been intimidating to most of the males at HQ, because she was taller than them and because she carried several visible holsters on various parts of her body. No one had been stupid enough to ask her what was in the holsters, except one intern named Benny who never returned to work afterward.

"That was fast," Mr. Right said.

Jessica nodded, sweeping a few strands of her brown hair behind one ear. "His position couldn't be left unfilled."

"No, I meant…you arrived in the room in a speedy manner."

Malcolm leapt out of his chair. "So, uhh, Mr. Right, I think we'll wrap this meeting up now. Do you need anything else? Anything at all. Listen, write it all down and submit it to my assistant and I'll get back to you, how about that? Hey, and if you can't get a hold of me or my assistant, don't hesitate to talk to Mandy."

No one ever talked to Mandy, because Mandy's entire purpose at HQ was sneaking calls to various friends and gossiping about secret lunch meetings between coworkers and members of the Wings division. Her office walls were smothered in old calendars and faded pages from magazines with articles like "WHAT IF HE'S AFRAID TO TELL YOU THAT YOU'RE FAT?" She was also known to wear criminally awful sweaters to holiday parties and then judge everyone else for any fashion mistakes they might commit.

Jessica smiled, staring directly into Mr. Right's eyes. "Mr. Right, you've been with us for such a long time. Six hundred years is nothing to laugh at. I'd like to make sure that you're happy here and satisfied with your position."

"Were you thinking of replacing me, too?" Mr. Right asked with a sigh, standing up. His head pounded, and he found himself rubbing his temples. "I've been at it so long that it might be more difficult than you think."

"Of course not! Goodness, no."

Mr. Right shook his head. "All right, then. Perhaps I should get back to work. You'll make sure Death gets his belongings, right? He gets carried away easily and he's scatterbrained, but he's not a bad guy. Getting demoted…well, he's going to take it really hard."

"Don't worry, we'll take good care of Kelly, I promise."

Mr. Right said his goodbyes to his superiors and slumped out. With the way of the world lately, everyone had to hold onto their jobs. And yes, sometimes it meant axing someone else, but Mr. Right would have to just accept that fact. Besides, Death would eventually find his footing out there, right? He was young. It wouldn't be so hard for him.

Mandy waved to Mr. Right from her spot behind her desk, all brightly colored shirt and overly coiffed hair. "You hear anything about Death?" she called, and Mr. Right paused. Did she already know? Mandy knew everything.

"He's been demoted," Mr. Right said at last. Better to just tell her the truth to start with, because it would only get twisted once it hit the rumor mill.

"For falling in love?" Mandy asked, rather breathlessly.

Mr. Right swallowed hard and then nodded.

"I see," Mandy said, though it was obvious she wanted to say a lot more.

"He'll be all right."

"Yes, of course. He's a resourceful boy. Figured out how to open the door to Jared's office when it got stuck. Climbed under something to get in, I think. Very resourceful." Mandy nodded. "Fell in love! Poor boy. So young. That's the one that always gets the new hires. Strange, though. He seemed so focused."

Something like guilt nagged at the back of Mr. Right's mind and he pushed away from Mandy's desk. By tomorrow the stories would be circulating throughout the delicate little system of communication that their kind reveled in. Death fell in love! The new kid, the *weirdo*, fell in love and got himself exiled.

"Is he going to find the girl and marry her?" Mandy asked, a hint of suspicion in her tone.

"I don't know."

"Well, you're Mr. Right. And if he loved her so much, wouldn't he marry her? You know how attached he gets to people."

"Perhaps it would be best if we respected his privacy and didn't talk about this."

Mandy nodded, muttering an agreement even while scribbling a note on a scrap of paper. Forget tomorrow. Everyone would be talking about this tonight.

As Mr. Right headed to the elevator, he passed a hooded creature. Judging by the average height of the figure and the glowing yellow of the eyes, it was one of the Reaper's cronies.

Mr. Right shuddered and hit the button on the elevator. There was no reason for the Reaper or his cronies to be out and about... unless something was very wrong.

CHAPTER
FIVE

Lola Lane had been known by many names before her 18th birthday, and then a hundred or so names in the two years after. Her current identification card called her Lola Lane and featured a photograph of her crooked, exuberant smile and natural light-brown hair. As she strolled into Mystery Ship's World Traveled Books, though, she was just Lola, the girl with the long pink hair. The girl who could snatch, steal, borrow or overhear anything.

The aisles of the bookstore were crammed with large and small books alike, most of them the sorts of things that no one would ever want to read. A small desk stood as lighthouse, guiding visitors through seas of unwanted reading materials. Lola stepped over a fifth edition of *Jeremy's Almost Diabetic Recipes for Baby Boomers* and a battered copy of *Building Birdhouses From Household Materials*.

She stopped just in front of the desk.

"I got the book you ordered," came a voice from somewhere behind the ancient computer and mismatched books that sat atop the desk. "It wasn't out of print, just difficult to find." The store clerk dropped a heavy, hardbound book in front of Lola. "Now, I'm not one to be nosy, but what's a nice little…girl… Well, why on earth do you need a book about the uhhh…" He paused, squinting down at the book cover, "'*Secret History of Cat Fights in Brazil?*'"

Lola offered a huge smile, the kind that melted most men into a puddle of goo. "School project!" she said. "I just want to graduate, sir."

"You're not in high school," the man said, apparently immune to dimples.

"Neither are you."

The clerk raised an eyebrow and Lola reminded herself that she was supposed to be a sweet, stupid schoolgirl. She smiled even bigger and dug the toe of one of her black boots into the ground.

"I'm not averse to ordering odd books, of course; it's all part of the business. I just don't usually get requests like this." The clerk tapped the top of the book with one finger, naming his price.

Lola fished into her backpack—one of those really worn-out kinds of backpacks that would like to retire but can't seem to do so quite yet—and found her wallet. She handed over payment and then hugged the book to her chest. "Thank you, sir. You have no idea how much I appreciate your time."

The clerk shook his head and disappeared behind his computer once again, leaving Lola to pick her way out of the store and force her smile not to slip until she was outside and around the corner.

Ugh, she hated Sunday jobs.

Lola's employer operated out of a café on West Florence Street, just behind the abandoned theater. The theater was famous because its owner had gotten really wasted one night and set the house piano on fire. It was a crime born of jealousy—his flapper girlfriend had two-timed him with a handsome Frenchman—and had resulted in a good deal of destruction inside the theater and a couple deaths. No one had ever bothered to fix the building or get rid of it, so it had remained in the same condition since 1927…injured, ugly, and a little haunted.

The café, however, was famous for absolutely nothing except mediocre coffee.

Just before entering the café, Lola slipped off her pink wig and shoved it deep inside her backpack. She straightened her brown hair and stood up a bit taller, pressed her lips together into a thin line. Her employer thought her to be 23 years old and from a wealthy family. No need for him to know that she had just turned 20 last month, and was the orphaned child of traveling gypsy-like actor parents. Some people just looked askance on that, especially when they hired you to steal things.

Jason Wellington, Lola's employer, was a displaced Englishman. He was always dressed as if he had somewhere important to go and his teeth were of the David Bowie variety, though a tad less scary. He'd make a hot professor, especially when he was displeased about something. His stern tone and defined jawline didn't seem very at home in a bad café on West Florence

Street, especially when he was telling a customer to enjoy her coffee or to go stuff herself…but maybe that was precisely why he'd gotten into the crime business. He never had many customers.

"He wasn't able to get the book?" Wellington asked as soon as he spotted Lola.

Lola handed him the book. "Three days."

Wellington tore through the pages, inspected the cover, weighed the book in his hands. After a lengthy pause, he shot Lola a smile. "It's the book."

"If you say so."

"This means he's working with Stolfeger."

Lola shrugged.

"I knew he and Stolfeger were in it together. I knew it." He turned the book over again, clicked his tongue. "Explains how he got his hands on that first edition of Lodley's book. And those maps." He looked at Lola. "Oh darling, you don't care about the details, do you?"

"Not really."

Wellington smiled and walked away from her, placing the book on a countertop. "What would you like? Coffee, tea?"

"Coffee."

A few seconds later, Wellington returned with a cup of milky coffee, which he placed in front of Lola. He waited for her to take her first sip and wince, as she always did, and then he handed her an envelope of money. "I'll have another job for you soon."

"How soon?"

"Perhaps by tomorrow night, if all goes as planned." Wellington leaned against the counter, on his elbow. "How late were you out last night, my crazy little friend?"

Lola slurped the coffee down, considering her answer. The truth was that she'd been out until after four AM, because one of her favorite bands had reunited for a short tour and had played a show at Ballard's. Ballard's! It had been a sweat-and-tears show, all standing room and squirming fans, cheap alcohol and memories of concerts that Lola was too young to have attended. She'd left Ballard's on a concert high and bruised from top to bottom, only to run into the enchanting Juicy Bed songstress just outside. What had started as a few words of admiration had turned into a long conversation, especially after a famous English artist named Leonidas Bondi had joined them and suggested they all go out for drinks. "A bit late," she said.

"How late is that? Two AM, three? Come now, Lola, you know you can tell me anything. It was your favorite band or something, right? Juicy…"

"Juicy Bed, and yes, it was late." Lola shifted her backpack on her shoulders. "When should I return for my next assignment?"

"Actually, I know how much you love music, and I've devised a rather ingenious plan. I met this hippie kid who has the hair like those… what are they called? Emos? Emus? Well, anyway, he came round earlier and asked about a gig tomorrow night. And of course I told him he could set up in the back if he wanted, so long as he stayed out of the way and didn't play anything that would scare away our business."

Lola glanced around the empty café and then back at her employer.

"You should come to his show, that's what I'm saying. I know you love obscure music. You don't get much more obscure than...hold on." He reached into his pocket and withdrew a crumpled piece of paper, unfolded it. "Twee Waterhouse. Huh. Good gods, what a name." The last part was muttered to himself, but then he was smiling again, all shark teeth and barely hidden tension. "What do you say, Lola? Bring some of your friends?"

"That's not a job, and I don't have any friends."

Wellington bent, disappearing behind the counter, and when he straightened again, he held a stack of off-white papers. "Pass these flyers around and give us a packed house tomorrow night. I'll pay you double the normal rate."

There were a million reasons why Wellington might want to help some obscure indie hippie-emo artist, but Lola couldn't think of a single one. "All right," she said at last, taking the papers from him and shoving them in her backpack.

"You look so displeased, pet." Wellington laughed. "Would you rather be distributing anarchist materials and flyers for your beloved Juicy Woman?"

"If you're paying me, it doesn't matter. You *are* paying me, yes?"

"Of course."

Lola nodded. "I'll get you a full house, then." She saluted and turned to walk away, only to hear him calling after her.

"Where are those papers, Lola? The ones from the other day?"

Lola's mind flashed back to the crowded city street, the tourists, the shock of blue hair that had caught her attention. She'd been informed that her target would have blue hair, but no one had quite explained to her that it would be the same color as a cerulean paint splatter. They also hadn't mentioned that his eyes would be the same color, to the shade. Snatching the contents of his bag had been easy. Saying goodbye to him had been the hard part.

"They're at my flat. You told me to hold onto them until Wednesday."

Wellington hesitated, but then nodded. "All right, but don't lose them."

"Have I lost anything before?"

"I'm not saying that you have, but you absolutely must not lose them." His tone turned serious, and his eyes darkened. "They're worth a bit more than our usual bid, you understand me? We could find ourselves in a spot we wouldn't like, if they're lost."

Most of Lola's jobs involved spying on competitors, stealing small items, spreading false information, and carrying bundles from place to place. None of it was particularly legal, but neither was it dangerous or important. She couldn't help feeling a seed of nervousness in her belly at the sudden rigidness in his stance.

"I won't lose them," she murmured, and his face transformed into a smile again.

"Good, good. I'll see you tomorrow evening, pet."

Lola bought herself some candy and then headed home through the back streets and secret passages. She hadn't been followed yet, but the possibility was always open when you earned your living in the manner Lola did. Sometimes people didn't like being pickpocketed or two-timed, which was understandable.

Thankfully, no one was nearly smart enough to track down Lola Lane.

CHAPTER SIX

Bill didn't live in his mother's basement, unfortunately. What he did live in was a two-bedroom apartment in Allston downstairs from a musician who kept strange hours and had a lot of German art-house parties. Death had to pick his way over a crying girl wearing a dress made entirely of soda cans before he could reach Bill's door. He knocked and found a red haired girl beside him, tugging on his sleeve. She was definitely drunk.

"The party's upstairs," she said in a stage whisper. "But it's bad luck to go up there alone. Do you know him? Will you take me up there? You'd think he was Gatsby or something!" She shrieked with laughter and Death winced, all the while attempting to pry her fingers off his sleeve. "Hey, do you have any of those pills? The ones that make you feel better? Everyone takes them, you know. Everyone. *Everyone*. Even my grandma. I like your blue hair. Are you an existentialist? I've never even seen a silent film, ha ha! But don't tell anyone!"

Death was fairly certain this girl had recurring nightmares about a monster swallowing her whole, and that he'd aided at least a few of her bad dreams over the years.

Thankfully, Bill opened the door just then, and Death flung himself inside, minus the red-haired girl.

"How did you find my address?" Bill demanded. He was definitely not drunk.

"You brought me here. Twice."

Bill blinked back at him.

"I slept in your bed," Death said and they broke eye contact, cleared their throats.

"That's uh…I don't…remember…uh…"

"I wasn't in it at the same time as you! It was after the trip to Texas and we were all tired, so I fell asleep in your bed. You weren't even in the same room."

Bill nodded. "Thank God."

"Yeah."

"What do you want?" Bill asked, pulling his hands out of the depths of the pockets of his creaseless gray slacks.

"I need some stuff."

Upstairs, a loud crashing sound set off a roar of laughter and applause. The lights in Bill's apartment flickered.

"What kind of stuff?" Bill asked.

Death shrugged. "Passport, ID. The usual."

Agents liked to use Bill because he was good at not asking too many questions. Such a trait was rare enough that Bill's collection of hyperrealistic pink-haired pixie dolls and OCD tendencies could be overlooked. (In

Death's opinion, it was Bill's pastel cable-knit sweaters that really threatened their business relationship, but there was little that could be done about that).

After a few heart-thumping moments of silence, Bill nodded. "Sit down and we'll take your pictures. You're paying the usual, right?"

"Uhhhhhh, yeah," Death said, forcing a grin that was probably more terrified than confident. "They'll send it to you in a couple days, as always." Oh gods, that was a big lie. Death would have to make sure never to encounter Bill again, lest he end up meticulously skinned and refashioned into a mostly life-sized blue-haired doll.

Bill took about 80 pictures of Death's face, with the brightest flashbulb known to man. And each time something was "off center" or a hair was in the "wrong place" or Death's nose was crooked.

Death decided against complaining, mostly because of that whole "getting skinned and turned into a doll" thing.

"You haven't been around here in a long time," Bill muttered, moving the camera a bit closer. FLASH!

"Uhhh, yeah. I was in Europe."

"They've got a lot of flu over there right now. People coming down with it left and right. It's all the public transportation. Disgusting." FLASH.

Death blinked against the millions of stars dancing in front of his vision.

"You should make sure to wash your hands when you're over there. If you think you've already been washing them too long, keep washing. No one ever washes for long enough." FLASH.

"Say, Bill...? Uh. I need glasses."

FLASH FLASH FLASH. "Glasses? I don't make glasses."

"Do you know where I can get some? Somewhere kind of...well, somewhere discreet." Death winced through a few more flashes. Maybe he should just skip the glasses, since he'd be blind anyway.

"There's a place near Government Center, next to the florist. Has a red awning. It's called Cat Eyes Optometry and they're open until late. They're not recommended."

Death nodded, rather pleased with himself for understanding that last statement. So this place would be super sketchy and weird and possibly illegal. Perfect.

"Do you mind if I head over there while you, uhhh...do whatever it is that you do?" Death asked as Bill finally put the camera away. It was always best to ask Bill before doing anything, including opening the refrigerator or entering the bathroom. The latter especially.

"Go on. Be back before 8pm, though, or I won't let you in." Bill hunched over his work and Death slipped out of the apartment without another word.

He'd made it a full three steps before a girl offered to drink his blood.

Death ran for the door.

*

The optometrist's office was every bit as shady as promised, starting with the graffiti on the door that said

BET YOU DIDN'T. Death frowned at the door for a few seconds and then pushed inside.

"Can I help you?" a voice called, from behind the front desk. Death had to tear his eyes from the giant dead tree that stood just beside the desk. It looked as if someone had forgotten to water it for about thirty-five years.

"Errr, yes, I need glasses," he said.

The girl behind the desk eyed him from toes to hair spikes, and then back down again. Her gaze worked over him a third time, slowing on certain tour stops. "Do you have your prescription?" she asked at last, rather breathlessly. He wasn't sure if she was breathless from staring at him or the physical exertion it required for her to propel her rather large figure around the desk and toward him.

"Uh, not on me. It's been a while since my last appointment."

She took a deep, deep breath. "Follow me," she whispered at last, and Death decided he would be safer with the faux vampire German art freaks back at Bill's place. Too late now, though. He needed those glasses. "Sit here," the girl said, motioning at a bench seat in front of something that looked a bit like a torture device that he'd won in an illegal raffle on a backstreet in London. He'd never gotten to use the thing on anyone. Too bad, really.

Death sat as instructed, and the girl forced him through a complicated set of somewhat unethical and increasingly uncomfortable feats that included having air shot into his eyeballs, staring at a blurry barn, and holding still while a stream of drops were poured into his eyes. By the time it was over, Death was pretty sure he was crying, but the eye drops made it difficult to know for sure.

"I need you to sit over here, now," the girl said, motioning at something that looked vaguely like a chair, but with more torture devices on it.

Death sat and silently recited every prayer he'd ever learned.

"It's okay, you know," the girl whispered from behind one of the torture devices. It made her appear to be a somewhat ambiguously motivated bug monster. "It's really all right. I won't tell anyone."

"Tell anyone what?"

"That you're a...you know. A rock star." The girl whispered the last part and giggled. The giggle felt somehow even more uncomfortable than the high back of the chair Death was pressed into. "We get them sometimes. A guy from Black Glitter was here the other day, picking up glasses. We don't tell anyone."

"You...just told me."

The girl sighed. "Well, we don't tell anyone ELSE. We're very respectful of your privacy." She asked him a series of questions, each leading him to feel more blind and stupid than the last, and then finally removed the torture devices from his face. "What band are you in?"

Death tried to think of something. His eyes felt as if they were going to melt out of his head. "I might have played with Alice Cooper once," he said finally. "You know, no big deal."

The girl stared at him as if he was insane.

"Alright, the bad news is, you have really, really bad eyes. In fact, I've seen newborn babies with better vision," the girl said. "The good news is, we have your prescription in stock. I can make your glasses today, if you…" Here she paused, meaningfully, heavily.

Death counted to five and felt the hair on the back of his neck stand up as he considered just what the "if you" might end up being. If you'd wash the floors? If you'd carry this package of drugs to a drop point and collect the money? If you'd put on a black tutu and pink lipstick and dance for me in my secret basement in front of a camera and a few of my friends from downtown?

Thankfully, she finished the sentence a bit more reasonably than he'd feared. "If you can wait. It shouldn't be more than an hour."

While Death knew that an hour would likely feel like six years, he agreed to the deal. After all, he needed those glasses. Without his aura, his vision had finally settled fully back to what it had been in his mortal days.

The wait certainly did feel like six years, and it left Death with nothing to do but flip through a few glossy magazines and stare at faces of people he didn't recognize. The world had changed a lot since he'd spent any great amount of time in it. From what he could gather, everyone was now fascinated by a lot of orange-tanned people in bad clothing.

And Tom Cruise looked old. REALLY old.

Eventually, the glasses were finished and handed over to Death for inspection. They were pink and black frames, clearly women's glasses, but he liked the way they fit, so he paid up just the same, smiled nervously, and hurried out of the office. He needed to get back to Bill's place before 8PM.

Death made it back to the apartment with ten minutes to spare, but a man in heavy black eyeliner stopped him just outside Bill's door. Judging by the two girls hanging off the guy, he must have been the musician from upstairs.

"You should join my party," Musician Guy said, all breathy and self-important. "I like your hair. Join our party; we'll hide you somewhere and then we'll find you. Then, who knows what."

"I'd like to, but I can't. Maybe after I get my aura back," Death said and the musician nodded.

"An aura is an important thing to have. Good luck, bluebird. Good luck."

Death rushed inside Bill's apartment the very instant the door opened.

"You won't believe those people! They're all crazy. How can you live with them?" Death demanded, even if a part of him was rather impressed that he'd been picked out of a crowd by a bunch of cool German art-house types.

He tripped, and fell into a table, knocking over one of the creepy pink-haired dolls. Bill turned around and snarled, "If you break anything, I *will* kill you." Not an idle threat.

In the end, Death got his fake identification, but he was pretty sure about 300 years had been taken off his life.

At least he had the necessary documents to travel, should he ever need to, and earlier he'd stolen enough money to keep him going for a while. No Wings had shown up with his personal belongings, which left Death certain of one very important and rather frightening piece of information—he was on his own.

CHAPTER
SEVEN

With all this rain, it was no wonder people were so depressed.

Wellington pulled his gray jacket tighter around himself and shifted his weight from foot to foot, standing under a large awning and staring skyward with increasing frustration. He hadn't thought to bring an umbrella the short walking distance from his café to the Walking Turtle Restaurant, where his client had insisted they meet. As fate would have it, dark clouds had crowded overhead like laughing minions and poured out the most drenching and oppressive rain possible.

"Crazy," someone muttered, and Wellington glanced to his right. A half dozen other men and women fidgeted and complained into their cell phones about the sudden downpour. "I haven't seen this much rain in Boston since I was a kid." The speaker was a rotund man with remnants of brown hair haloing the back of his head. Definitely one of the types to use nasty weather to press unwanted conversation on innocent bystanders.

"Yes. You'd think I was back in England," Wellington said.

"England, huh?"

Oh, no. "Yes."

"My cousin loves England. What brought you here?"

Wellington stared at him. "Not the conversation, that's for certain." With that, he propelled himself out into the rain and powered through the four blocks to Walking Turtle.

Now, Walking Turtle was not the sort of place that Wellington normally bothered with, because it was expensive and it was full of boring people. But business was business, and Wellington had certainly taken part in business dealings in shady places, so why shouldn't he occasionally do so in an establishment that housed a fountain in the lobby?

Two pretty girls asked for his jacket as he stepped inside. Wellington ran a hand over his soaked hair, regarding the manicured nails and unwrinkled white shirts of the girls before shaking his head. "I'll keep it, thank you," he said. "I'm here to meet with Jessica Parsley." Or was it Parson? Person? He couldn't remember. "I'm Jason Wellington."

The taller of the two girls eyed him, her upper lip curling a little before she let out a clanging laugh. "Follow me." She led him deep within the belly of Walking Turtle, a belly that turned out to have quite a few low-hanging chandeliers and lush red carpeting.

Wellington caught sight of a senator, tucked away in a booth with his wife or girlfriend or mistress or something.

Wellington had no use for politicians. Unless he was stealing something from them.

"Ah, Mr. Wellington," a voice called, and Wellington turned his eyes to the tall, dark-haired woman who stood up to greet him. He'd never met Jessica, but had spoken to her a few times on the phone. She stood as tall as he, easily, and her false smile more than matched the edge that perpetually lived in her voice. "Please sit down."

"Is there anything else I can do for you?" the hostess asked, still shooting Wellington a lot of accusatory and judgmental looks.

Jessica shook her head. "No, thank you, dear." She sat down at precisely the same moment Wellington did, and turned that fake smile back to him. "Caught in the rain?"

What sort was she? He tried to trace the inner workings of her mind, but found himself hitting some kind of wall before he could make any assumptions. "Easy enough to get caught in the rain lately," he said finally. "Weather's been strange."

The fake smile widened, and Wellington felt the uncomfortable burn of Jessica's gaze fixing on his own. "You're not the type to fall prey to a little bad weather though, are you, Jason Wellington?"

"I was raised in it."

This time the smile reached her eyes, which glowed a little. "That's good. Because I hear it's going to rain a lot."

Wellington wanted to laugh, but felt as if it would be impolite. And maybe impossible.

Their waitress arrived with menus and fancy glasses of water with lemon slices bobbing merrily inside. Wellington glanced at the prices and couldn't stop a snort of disbelief. $45 for a plate of pasta? They'd better serve it with a side of gold bullion or something for that price.

"Oh don't worry, Mr. Wellington. I'll take care of this meal."

Good. Pasta it was.

Jessica smiled when their waitress returned and she placed her order with an ease that almost tricked Wellington into thinking she'd never spoken at all. As soon as the waitress was gone again, Jessica withdrew a small book from her handbag and laid it open on the table. "You told me on the phone that you specialize in locating things."

Wellington sat up straight. "I won't brag, but I was the one who found Hindgurd's 'Novel Song and Cycle.' And the golden baby seal statue that used to belong to Franny Korb. That was said to be impossible, if I may remind you."

"Ah."

"And the little blue man with the papers. I got the papers for you."

At that, Jessica's green eyes flickered and widened a bit. "You'll continue to keep those somewhere safe and hidden for me, won't you, Mr. Wellington?"

"Of course, of course. I'm very professional with all of this. When I began my business, four years ago, you couldn't find anything in Boston. Now I have a profitable, efficient system, capable of acquiring almost anything that a person could want. Between myself and my associate, we've taken on countless projects of impressive nature."

Actually, the most impressive thing Wellington had ever done, aside from finding the baby seal statue, was to create a bowl in primary school pottery class. Even that had been a happy accident on account of another student switching projects with Wellington just before their bowls went into the kiln.

"Associate? The little pink-haired girl?"

Wellington considered this question. Was Lola currently pink-haired? "Lola Lane, yes. She changes hair color rather frequently." He realized how this sounded and cleared his throat. "It's a professional thing. Spies change their hair color all the time, as you know."

Their meal arrived.

"You've probably heard the phrase, 'Hell was built under Boston,'" Jessica said.

"Hmm. I hadn't heard that, but it sounds reasonable."

"What do you know about the stories of the Gray Agents of the Middle Ages?"

"Something about them, I guess."

"In the old days, before anyone understood simple things like cleanliness or personal safety or biology, they would blame everything on mysteries of legend. Perhaps a reaper had taken their wife, or a faerie had snatched their baby from its crib. These stories seemed more likely to most than the alternative."

Wellington nodded. "That makes sense. Now, it's just the government, huh? This is good pasta."

"The point I'm making, Mr. Wellington, is that the people of the past were genuinely afraid of the monsters they believed in. They lived with respect for beings more powerful than themselves and this, in itself, allowed for a simpler world."

Personally, Wellington had always believed antibiotics and hand soap were pretty cool modern inventions, but he nodded anyway.

"Over time, the great monsters and creatures of the past were forgotten or pushed into storybooks." Jessica put down her fork, fixing Wellington with another of her uncomfortable stares. "We're all disbelievers now, aren't we, Mr. Wellington?"

After a reasonable pause, Wellington said, "I believe in a few things."

"I would like to see belief return to this world."

So, she was crazy. Oh well, there'd been crazier clients in Wellington's years in this business. He nodded. "What can I do to help?"

"You're such a good, simple man," Jessica said, and it didn't feel like a compliment. "I want you to help me find something. It's been lost for two hundred years."

Finally, something good! Wellington sat up a bit straighter in his chair. "I've found old things before. What sort of thing is it? A book? A necklace?"

Jessica smiled, and this time her smile seemed incredibly genuine. "You're going to find me a jar."

CHAPTER EIGHT

Tourists.

Most of them wanted to take pictures with Death, which he was more than happy to allow. He couldn't really blame them for being fascinated by his good looks, impeccable fashion sense and creative hair color.

But even that got tiring after a while.

After about two hours and a much needed stop at a little café for food, Death found himself at the spot where he'd first met Lola. He remembered the spot in detail, because he and Lola had sat together at the reflecting pool and the sun had been very bright, and she'd pretended she was reaching up to shade his eyes and had actually pushed him backwards into the water. Though it was very shallow, falling on your back into the pool left you fully submerged. By the time he climbed out of the water, soaking wet and shuddering, Lola had been innocently smiling and asking if he was all right. He couldn't be sure, but he guessed that she'd used the unwanted underwater exploration time to steal his papers.

The crowd today held no sign of the evil girl, though. No pink hair or striped stockings. Of course, Death *was* rather short, so he couldn't always see much in a crowd.

Death asked around about Lola, but eventually his feet ached and his head hurt and the crushing exhaustion of mortality caught up to him. He settled on one of the benches lining the reflecting pool and gazed at the Romanesque church across the shallow body of water. Something about the building seemed peaceful, if only because it was over a hundred years old and still managed to find its place in the modern world.

What if he could find Fashion? Everyone said that Fashion had taken his banishment hard, had become a hermit in some tiny Russian town, but Death doubted that. Fashion hated cold weather! He'd probably worked his way south until he reached a fancy island or something, and then taken up residence on a beach. He was probably enjoying banishment. If Death could find Fashion, they could start a little bar on the beach like Tom Cruise in *Cocktail* and live comfortable lives with pretty tourists.

Good Lord, Death missed Fashion.

"You're one of those agent things, aren't you? The ones that fall from the sky?"

Death jumped a bit.

"Whoa, careful there, or you'll end up back in the drink like when the pink-haired girl pushed you in," a voice said, though it didn't appear to be coming from anything but air. "You're just gonna sit there? Really? Nothing? All right, well, doesn't surprise me. I don't have that whole 'living' thing going for me, and people can't help but discriminate." Slowly, a shape formed to match the voice, starting with a head and working its way down in shimmering lines.

Now, Death had conjured his fair share of ghosts for the nightmares he constructed, but he'd never really encountered many before (except that very nice one who haunted an ice cream shop in a rural Georgia town and liked to tell incredibly long stories about her father's farm). This particular ghost looked just like a man in his early 30s, if a man in his early 30s were transparent with a slight blue tint.

"I don't know. At this point, I'd almost rather have people run away and scream. This whole ignoring me thing? It gets old fast." The ghost shook his head and then fixed his gaze on Death. "I used to work for this company that was…well, we did good things; we made an impact on the world. Poor kids, hungry people, the homeless…you'd think that would count for something now." The ghost shook his head again. "So, what's your name?"

"Death."

"That's a weird name. But then, that last one said his name was Despair."

Death turned so quickly that he almost fell off the bench. "Despair? You've seen Despair?"

"This is exactly what I'm talking about. Not to get off on the wrong foot by confronting you about this issue, but you didn't even ask my name. Do you have any idea how that feels?"

"All right, what's your name, then?" Death demanded.

"No, see, now that was forced. You don't really want to know, you're just asking because I mentioned it."

Death shrugged. "Yeah, you're right, I don't really want to know. When did you see Despair?"

"My name is Michael," the ghost said. "My boss decided that I would be better working in Boston, which was completely absurd. I'm an Ohio boy, you know? Born and raised. The fields, the cows, the tractors, the game nights, homemade food, you name it. Then the boss says, 'You know what, Michael? You belong on the east coast. You like baseball.' Which, by the way, I didn't like baseball enough to move to Boston. You can watch baseball on TV in Delaware, Ohio, thank you very much. 'You belong in Boston,' he said, and then he told me about this job that he had for me out here and how much I'd love it and…"

Death stared at him. "Okay. When did you see Despair?"

"Aren't you a little short to be an agent, though? I don't mean that offensively, I'm just observing. And why did you get exiled? Oooh, did you have an affair with someone you weren't supposed to?" Michael the ghost asked, translucent eyes widening in excitement.

"No! I didn't fall in love with her!" Death said, a bit louder than he intended. "Where is Despair?"

"Oh, he's wandering around. He's not called Despair anymore, and he sings really embarrassing sort of depressing stuff. It's not like the Smiths, you remember the Smiths? I liked the Smiths. I think even

Morrissey would kill himself if he made the kind of music that this guy is making now."

"But he's around here?"

"Yeah, he sits here sometimes and talks to me. Not a bad guy to hang out with, I guess, as long as you're already dead."

Death considered all of this for a few seconds. Despair had always been smart and capable, and if he was being perfectly honest, Death used to be a bit jealous of him. "I'd like to see him. Where can I find him?"

"Some girl was walking around handing out flyers last night and this morning, because he has a show tonight. I don't understand how he got one, though, considering how miserable his music is, but…well, I've never really understood art."

"All right, where's the gig, then?"

"Some coffee place." The ghost thought for a few seconds, face turned upwards. Just as Death was coming up with clever threats, Michael clapped his hands together. It made no noise, of course. "It's the place on West Florence Street, right behind the abandoned theater. You know that place is haunted? I tried to hang out with some of the ghosts there, but they were all cliquish and none of them understood English. I think they were French. You know how the French are."

Death stood up and had taken about three steps when Michael called after him.

"You're just gonna leave me here? Do you have any idea how boring it can get to be a ghost in this place? There's no one to talk to, for one thing, and a man can only watch so many people fall into the fountain before it's not funny anymore."

Death turned back toward the ghost, slowly. "When I get my job back, I'll speak to Malcolm about getting you some kind of job, how about that? I know we've employed ghosts before. Not in my division, but...I know a guy who worked with one," he said, waving one hand a bit. "It'll probably be a desk job. I'm not sure what your skill set is, but it's better than nothing. How's that?"

"Were you responsible for that truck hitting me?"

"No, that was the Reaper," Death said, lowering his voice as always. "I have to go now, though. Despair can probably help me get my job back, and that would be in your favor as well as mine."

Overhead, the sky had taken on an ugly, bruised purple tint. Death stared up at it for a few seconds and then hurried on his way. He knew just where the abandoned theater was because he and Lola had walked there together, after the fountain incident. They'd picked their way through rubble and snuck their way inside, and Death had sat at the old piano and Lola had sat on top of it and just before they'd said their goodbyes, he'd kissed her. And she'd kissed him back. And then they'd fallen back into one of the walls in a feverish passion and eventually had to untangle their lips and limbs so he could leave.

Oh, when he found that girl...

CHAPTER NINE

By the time Twee Waterhouse sat down to play his first song, Lola had managed to pack the café almost to capacity with hipsters, tourists, and a couple of twitching weirdos. Hey, no one had specified where she had to find the crowd. And, after all, what was an acoustic hippie-emo performance without a few drug addicts and flannel-clad European snobs?

Lola watched everything from the safety of a spot in the back, sitting atop one of the wobbly tables. She couldn't help feeling curious about Twee Waterhouse, especially given his long golden hair and California Ken doll good looks. Something about his glowing appearance and the miserable sounds coming out of his mouth didn't seem to match up, and never more than when he started rapping about being exiled and forgotten and abandoned and unloved. Lola winced and snickered to herself at the same time.

Wellington worked his way to her, a cup of his miserable house-brew coffee in hand. "Great work, pet, great work." He handed over the coffee and motioned at the crowd. "And you know, I think a few of them are actually enjoying it!"

"The deaf ones, yes."

"Well, he's quite depressing, isn't he?" Wellington asked. Twee Waterhouse must have sensed this proclamation because he launched into a mournful note that slipped in and out of key and ended in a sob. "Reminds me a bit of the stories my Mum told me when I was little, about the angels of sadness. Liked to say that's what was wrong with her." Wellington shrugged. "Really, she was just an alcoholic tosser."

"When do I get paid?"

"Ah, yes. Let me take care of my customers first and then I'll be back with your money." Wellington slipped his mobile from his pocket and glanced at the readout. "Enjoy the show." He hurried away, phone pressed to his ear and head down.

Enjoy the show? That wasn't going to be possible without earplugs, but Lola slurped her coffee and tried to entertain herself anyway. Her eyes fell on various members of the audience, stopping briefly on some beardy kid in plastic framed glasses and a bow tie, and then on a young woman wearing a bright yellow hat, and then on a young man with bright blue hair and—

Wait. Blue hair?

Lola sat up straight, nearly dropping her coffee cup. Oh, she certainly knew that hair from a thousand paces away. She tried to look away from him, to duck and cover, but found herself tunnel-visioning him in the same manner as when one can't look away from a car accident. He didn't appear to be headed in her direction, or anywhere in particular. He just jostled for a spot in the crowd, glanced at Twee Waterhouse a few times, rolled up on tiptoe for a better view, and then jostled in the crowd a bit more.

Well, at least he hadn't seen her.

Just then, though, he turned his nose toward the air like some weird blue bird. He danced around on tiptoe and, before Lola could jump down from the table and escape, he'd made eye contact with her.

Then he walked toward her.

"No fountains for you to push me into this time!" he said, advancing on her more quickly than she could have predicted. He pointed one gloved finger at her, all scowl and tiny lines around his weirdly blue eyes.

She climbed down from the table. "I don't need a fountain. That was just part of the show."

"Really? What about kissing me in the theater? Was that just part of the show, too?" he demanded, so loudly that a few people turned and stared.

Without hesitation, she reached out and grabbed hold of his shoulder, turning him around and shoving him back into the crowd. She used her very slight body weight to propel him closer and closer to the door, smiling and nodding to people in the crowd all the way.

They finally burst outside and she pushed him into a wall. "What do you want?"

"I want my stuff back," the blue-haired guy said, and to his credit, he didn't seem afraid of her. Most guys reconsidered their choices when a woman dared to push them around a bit.

Of course, she'd pushed him into a wall during their last encounter too, but for entirely different reasons.

"You can't have it back."

"Give it back to me, or…or…" He glowered, the little lines around his eyes deepening slightly. "Don't make me finish that sentence, Lola Lane."

"I'm so intimidated right now, because you used my first and last name in a sentence," Lola said in a flat tone and saw a flash of triumph in her opponent's eyes.

"Good, then hand over my stuff!"

"I was being sarcastic."

His mouth turned down in a pout. "Oh. I don't detect sarcasm very well."

"Yeah, I can see that." Lola stepped back just enough that their bodies weren't touching, but not enough that he could run away.

"I lost my job because of your thievery."

Boston was a big enough city that Lola never feared running into one of her former targets. Plus, she had loads of disguises to keep her safe. So having to listen to the sob story of some office lackey who couldn't hold onto his stuff around a pretty girl? Not the most entertaining thing. "Go get another job," she said. "Not everyone can sit behind computers all day in nice offices and type names and phone numbers. Some of us have to survive by different means."

"Office?" The blue haired guy blinked at her from behind girl glasses. "I don't work in an office. They don't let anyone with a 5.0 rating in Aggression work in the offices. That's for the nice people like Mandy." He paused. "Well, she's not exactly nice, but she guessed Gabe and Horror would break up well before it happened. Maybe like, two months before."

Lola tapped one foot. "I'm sure your telemarketing company can buy some new lists of names."

"No, no, no. You don't understand. Those lists are very important. I got fired because I lost them."

"How much did it cost your company?"

"About eight hundred years. I don't know the exact figure without looking at the schedule, but eight hundred years is an educated guess."

The guy was weird, that was for sure. Lola had noticed that when she'd encountered him before, but right now he seemed about ten times weirder than ever. Maybe it had to do with the girl glasses or the earnest/angry expression on his face. "Look, you should…you should be more careful next time." She hesitated. "I hope you find a new job."

"There's no new job! I have to take those papers back to Malcolm. They're very, very important." This time his words were laced with something close to desperation. "Unless I get those papers back, I'm stuck here forever."

"In Boston? Join the club. There's worse things, believe me."

"There's nothing worse than this. I've been exiled, okay? Usually when an agent gets exiled, he turns up on the news a week later as a suicide case. We don't make it very long down here. It's not our world."

Lola couldn't stop the laugh that escaped her. "Oh, you're an agent? For what, a party shop? A circus?"

"Only if you are, too, Miss Pink Hair!" He pointed at her again. "Well, not pink right now, but you were last time!"

"How did you find me?" Lola demanded.

"I didn't mean to find you. Michael the ghost sent me here."

This just kept getting better and better. "Ohhh, Michael the ghost. Of course."

"You know him?"

He hadn't been kidding about the missing out on sarcasm thing. "Why did the ghost send you here?"

"Because Despair was exiled, too, and he's—wait. It's none of your business!"

Lola let out an exasperated sigh. "You're crazy. I'm sorry you lost your job, but there's nothing I can do about it now. I completed my mission and it's in someone else's hands now. Have a good life." She walked away from him, making it nearly five steps before he called after her.

"You have nightmares about your parents dying!"

Lola froze.

"And about puppets, especially ones that remind you of a play you saw as a little girl," he said, that flash of triumph lighting his eyes again. "There was this one big puppet that wore an eyepatch—"

Lola marched toward him, grabbed him by the throat and pushed him into the wall once again. "How do you know that?"

"I know a lot of things."

"This isn't *It's A Wonderful Life.* How do you know that?"

He peered back at her, his mouth twisting up into a smirk. "My job is to create nightmares, feelings of dread, rain when you don't want it, miserable birthdays, fear of what's under your bed... Oh, Lola Lane, I know things about you, and everyone else, too."

"But you lost that job?" she asked, rolling her eyes.

"It's not funny! Yes, I lost the job!"

"And now you've lost all of your magic powers and you're doomed to walk the face of the earth forever as some lost prince of the sky."

"Actually, that's pretty accurate."

Lola searched her mind for anyone who had ever been quite this crazy without a lot of alcohol, and came back with a blank. But his mention of her parents and the puppet thing...that was eerie. She never talked about her parents with anyone. She'd better keep an eye on this one until she could determine what else he knew and who he worked for. Maybe he was some sort of undercover agent, sent to find her and haul her back in chains. Doubtful, considering he stood about two, maybe three inches shorter than her and was approximately the same weight, but you never could tell.

"What's your name?" she asked.

"Death."

"Your real name."

He hesitated. "Death."

"I don't care what cosplay or video game or LARP you're into, I need your real name." When he still didn't answer, she leaned a bit closer. "I'm not going to help someone who won't even tell me his name."

"Help?"

"What's your name?"

His lips curled back from his slightly crooked teeth in distaste, and he scowled up at her. "Kelly," he muttered. "Kelly Gold. But call me Death, or I'll hurt you."

The laughter that bubbled up within her overflowed freely. "Kelly?"

"Call me Death!" he said with a hiss. The hiss sounded a bit like an unhappy kitten, which just served to make Lola laugh even harder. Eventually she took mercy on him and stopped.

"All right, Death it is." She walked away from him, and this time he fell into step beside her.

"You said that you would help me. Are you going to give back those papers?"

Lola's mind clicked through possible answers until she finally found one that seemed satisfactory. "You can stay with me tonight, and I'll see if I can track down your papers. How about that?"

Of course he agreed, and with that, they were headed back to her place.

Give her one night and she'd know every single one of his secrets.

CHAPTER TEN

Mr. Right stopped by his office and picked up the pile of assignments that had accrued in his absence. You take five sick hours and suddenly everyone in the known universe needs to fall in love with someone else. It almost made Mr. Right wish for the days of Cupid and his army of baby minions…almost, but not quite. The babies had been notorious for getting really drunk and telling people that they weren't babies after all, which only served to scare a few famous artists into painting wild representations of what they thought they'd just witnessed.

Mr. Right flipped through the notes, feeling his headache coming back. Maybe he should just ask for the rest of the day off, too, and see what would happen. If he were being honest, Mr. Right wouldn't mind retiring altogether and sitting on some quiet beach forever, far away from humans and all of their fights, divorce rates and crappy marriages. Love wasn't what it used to be, and Mr. Right wasn't sure if he cared anymore.

"Hey, Mr. Right?"

He turned and found Malcolm in the doorway.

"Jessica and I were discussing things, and I know you've been a bit under the weather. Anyway, we were thinking you should cut back your work load a bit, you know? Don't worry about all of that. In fact, I have an assignment for you, a real easy one. You can just handle that one for now and leave the rest."

Leave the rest? This was a bit like someone suggesting Mr. Right stick his entire head in the jaws of a hungry dinosaur. "I'm already a few hours behind."

"Of course, of course, but we know it's because you're sick. Everyone gets worn out and we really don't want you to turn into one of those guys who never gets a break and then one day he shows up at work with a handful of ninja stars and kills everyone."

"Ninja stars."

"It's happened." Malcolm handed him a piece of paper. "Just take care of this assignment and don't worry too much about the rest. We'll get some interns in here for the day."

Mr. Right sighed. "Last time you brought interns in, they turned the entire fourth floor into a rave. I think the janitor is still trying to scrub the glow paint off the walls and fix that hole in the roof."

"Well, we got new interns."

The thing about Malcolm was that you couldn't really argue with him. He'd been born into a position of authority, since his father had been head of the Council for about 300 years, and he'd picked up his father's irritating habit of not listening to the suggestions or advice of anyone around him. That very trait had ended in the old man eating poisonous eel in a batch of suspicious-looking sushi, yet Malcolm still rejected reason. (He did, however, avoid sushi. To a psychotic level).

"All right," Mr. Right said at last. He shoved the paper in his jacket pocket without looking at it.

Malcolm smiled. "Hey, thanks. I'll see you at the next meeting."

Mr. Right followed Malcolm out of the office, closing the door behind him and then falling into step with his boss. "Why are the Reaper's cronies wandering around HQ? I ran into one on my way up here and I can't help thinking they're a big part of the headaches and such."

"Really? Odd."

"Not odd. Everyone has bad reactions to them, unless they're already dead. Maybe we should have them stick to the shadows and creepy crawly places like before. I don't like it," Mr. Right said, and Malcolm came to a halt.

"I would think you, of all people, after working here for so many years, would understand."

"Understand what? They don't belong here."

Malcolm reached over and patted Mr. Right on the shoulder. "Better get used to it, Mr. Right. Things are changing around here. It's for our safety, all right?" Malcolm walked away, his feet shuffling noisily as he moved.

Mr. Right suddenly understood why Death had never liked Malcolm.

Whenever Mr. Right had a new assignment, he liked to stop by his locker. In the old days, it was because Death liked to play pranks, to leave moldy sandwiches in Mr. Right's locker or something.

Ah, Death.

The familiar pang of guilt struck Mr. Right as he opened his locker, and he wished for one strange moment that he would find a half-eaten sandwich on top of his papers and personal belongings. No such luck, though, as Death was far away and exiled to a horrible life among the modern servants of fate. He'd looked so lost and confused when Mr. Right had placed him on the train and patted his shoulder and wished him the best. In fact, he'd looked catatonic, but…well, of course he couldn't have been. He'd just been in a daze.

Poor thing.

Maybe it was the guilt and memories, but Mr. Right found himself down by locker 1197, the one that had the cryptic message "DON'T OPEN OR ELSE" finger-painted across it in neon glow-in-the-dark lettering. Death had never revealed what "or else" entailed, but he'd been quite proud of his work, anyway.

But wait…was his locker open?

Mr. Right poked at the door and it creaked, swung open slightly. Why wasn't it locked? Death was notorious for *needing* to lock his locker, lest piles and piles of odds and ends explode from within. He was a bit of a packrat, and not in the good way, either. So what was going on?

Oh, maybe they had taken all of his things out and put them in a box and someone had delivered the box to him. Yes, that must be it. After all, that was standard procedure regarding exiled agents.

This would have been a great explanation, had it not been for the fact that Death's locker was still mostly full. It looked as if someone had rummaged through it, yes, but they hadn't taken much. Death's good luck charm (a hideous little monster figurine that he'd found in a dumpster) and that weird belt he liked to wear—the one he claimed was made for men but clearly wasn't— were still in his locker, along with a lot of other personal items.

Something was wrong.

It wasn't until Mr. Right left HQ that he glanced at his assignment.

Lola Lane and Jason Wellington.

CHAPTER ELEVEN

Death had never particularly trusted anyone who lived at the top of five flights of stairs, especially when an elevator wasn't in the picture. Lola lived on the 5th floor of a building on Newbury Street, and the elevator was definitely broken.

"For how skinny you are, you're not in great shape, are you?" Lola asked as they reached her door.

With a bit more huffing and puffing than he was proud of, Death said, "I'm in great shape!" and flung himself into her apartment. He struggled to regulate his breathing as she closed and locked the door behind them.

"Maybe if you didn't wear three-inch heels, it would be a bit easier for you."

"They're not three inches."

Lola turned around and faced him. "This place isn't huge, so you might as well understand that now. My roommate has the bedroom. You can sleep on the couch tonight."

Couch. Death glanced at the couch and determined that, while it would fit him quite reasonably, it wasn't going to be very comfortable. In fact, he was pretty sure he could see springs and coils poking out from all directions. Hmmm.

"Well, where do you sleep?" he asked finally, glancing around the apartment.

"Usually I sleep on the couch, but tonight it'll be the floor, I guess."

Somehow, he thought he was the one doing her a favor.

"Is your roommate here?"

"No, she's hardly ever here."

"You could sleep in her bed, then," Death said. "You know, so you don't have to sleep on the floor."

"No way. I've only been in Cara's room once and it was because she invited me."

Death tried to imagine what a Cara would look like and his mind only provided him with a vague image of a big-chested woman wearing an Oktoberfest costume and yelling at everyone to stay out of her things.

"So, Kelly—"

"Death!"

"So, Death…you used to create nightmares and whatever," Lola said, peeling off her jacket and setting her backpack down. She slipped off her shoes and then walked over to the counter and sink that made up her kitchen. "What kind of weird job is that?"

"It's not weird. I'm the agent of nightmares! It's my job to kill happiness, to create emotional death. The death of hope! I mean, what if everyone was just happy all the time? Or running around being all cutesy, lovey-dovey?" Death asked. "I love my job. And I'm really good at it!" His fingers twitched at his sides as visions of some of his former jobs swam through his mind, and he cackled. "Someone called me Prince of Nightmares one time, because I constructed a dream that was...well, it was so awful that the guy ended up going to a therapist for years!"

The "guy" had been one of those football types (Carter Reed) that everyone likes and talks about in the local newspapers and gives discounts to in exchange for the honor of his presence at the corner gas station. He'd also been in the same graduating class as a quiet, easily forgotten nerd named Kelly Gold.

Lola withdrew a knife from a drawer and sliced a tomato. Death's stomach growled. "Maybe it's good that you were fired, then," she said. "Why is it bad for people to be happy all of the time? Can you even imagine how different the world would be if no one was afraid? If everyone felt peaceful and happy?"

Death rolled his eyes. "Just because I got fired— er, laid off—doesn't mean people will be happy. It just means someone else will take my office and my job and probably ruin all of my current projects. I can't even imagine what they'll do about the San Francisco case... besides mess it up royally, that is." He shook his head. "Why did you steal those papers from me, anyway?"

"I was hired to take them from you, so I did."

Death imagined Lola as part of some scary mob movie, standing just beside Al Pacino, wearing an impressive gun in a thigh holster. "Hired by whom?"

"By my employer, Mr. Wellington."

"Why did you kiss me?"

Lola let out some quiet noise of displeasure and set aside the knife and tomato. She walked out of the kitchen and toward the bathroom. "Stay there," she said, and closed the door behind her. Death heard a fan switch on and sighed to himself.

Great. She was leaving, now? He was hungry and the tomato she'd sliced almost looked appetizing, even if he didn't really like vegetables.

Death moved closer and closer to the tomato, the shaky need of mortal hunger washing over him again. He'd forgotten about hunger. It was positively maddening to have to eat all of the time!

Mmmm but that tomato smelled really good, and it looked so juicy. Maybe he could just take one little slice of it…

One slice turned into two, and then three, and then a search for something to drink. Death found a clear bottle without any marking on it and stared at the liquid inside. It wasn't water, because water was not gold. But hey, it didn't have any skull and crossbones on it, or anything. He took a sip and realized that it was some sort of alcohol.

Death, being rather diminutive, had avoided alcohol for most of his life, even though his aura would have protected him from debilitating drunkenness or a raging hangover. It was times like this, though, when stress and the weirdness of everything were weighing on him, that a little alcohol didn't seem like such a bad idea.

And the taste was interesting. Hmmm, yes, very interesting. A little nasty…no, very nasty, and almost unpleasant. It tasted like something he would invent just to frighten someone. Death finished the bottle and put it back, coughing a few times. Alcohol was such a popular pastime, and yet it tasted revolting and he didn't feel any pleasant "buzz" like everyone always talked about. Even back in his mortal days, he'd stuck to beer or wine coolers, and only one at a time, at that.

The apartment was so small that it took only seconds for Death to wander it, poking and prodding and investigating. Lola didn't own many belongings, and the ones she did have looked as if no one ever used them. She must not spend a lot of time in her apartment. The only thing of interest in the whole place was a little drawer by the couch. That was only interesting because a whole stack of cartoon-y drawings had been shoved inside.

"I'm hungry!" he said, and his voice sounded a lot louder than he'd meant it to. "Wow, I'm so hungry." Was that his voice? It sounded like it was traveling through a tin can. "Soooooooooo hungry," he said, just to test. Yep, definitely sounded like it was coming through a can. How odd.

Lola reemerged from the bathroom then, and glanced over at him. "You don't have to yell about it."

"No. No, I'm not yelling."

"You're yelling."

"I'm not yelling!"

"You ate the tomato?"

"A little," Death said. "I'm hungry."

"You're yelling again." Lola placed what was left of the tomato on a plate and then produced cheese from seemingly nowhere. "Sit down and I'll feed you." She walked toward him, and every motion seemed as if someone had cut it up with scissors and removed a frame at random. Had she walked like that earlier? He didn't think so.

"You're suspicious," he said, and Lola laughed.

"Suspicious? I'm not the one who said he can see nightmares." Lola sat down on the couch and patted the spot next to her. "Sit down and eat before you pass out. You're sweating. When did you eat last?"

"Oh. A while ago. Except that tomato. I ate some of that tomato a few minutes ago."

Lola's eyes narrowed and she motioned for him. "Did you drink something?"

Why was she asking that? Was she going to murder him for drinking her bottle of gold liquid? He pictured her shoving him into a giant fountain and holding him under and then dragging him out and setting fire to him on a piano and it was probably the most hilarious thought he'd ever had. In fact, he started laughing and felt like he was floating up and down and up and down and soon he was sitting on the floor and couldn't remember why.

"I…I…see…there was a bottle of gold. Wait. My last name is Gold," he said, raising his head. Everything shifted around a bit, which was also suspicious. Things weren't supposed to move…unless they were humans. Or animals. Or…cars? "Hey now, don't kill me in the fountain!"

"Bottle of gold?" Lola repeated. She stared at him for a few seconds and then let out a startled gasp of surprise. "Not the tequila bottle?" She jumped up and ran away from him and he laughed again because it seemed like she was flying. Before he knew it, she was kneeling in front of him and holding an empty bottle in his face. "This? You drank ALL of this?"

"Ooops?"

"This bottle belonged to the old guy who used to live here. I'm pretty sure it's about ten years old," Lola said.

"Oh...then it should be starting school soon, right? In America they call that first grade."

"You drank the whole bottle?"

"I can't remember, but I think so. Unless it has a secret compartment where it hides and then reappears later when it's safe to come out."

"You...are going to be really sick."

"Nah, one time at the holiday dinner party. One time, one time Despair drank four bottles and said he didn't feel like he was walking on the moon yet."

Lola shook her head. "You're the size of a teenage girl. Do you understand that? Even a huge guy shouldn't drink this much."

"You're just jealous because I drank it all."

"Why would I be jealous? You're probably going to be sick for days." Lola groaned. "I'll get you some water."

Death stood up, though it felt like he teleported, and he snatched up a tomato slice from the plate on the couch. "I'm fine, see? I can eat."

"The tomato is not in your mouth."

He told his hand to connect with his mouth, and after a few seconds, was successful. "See?" he said. He ate another slice just to prove his point, and then walked toward the door. "I'm walking in a straight line!" he said. For some reason he was lying across a wooden table, though, with his head dangling over one side.

"Please don't break my furniture."

Once he was on his feet again, Death headed for the door. He reached it, but then felt like he was spinning around and around. Lola grabbed hold of his shoulder and he tried to figure out how she'd appeared beside him that quickly.

"You can't leave the apartment."

"I can walk fine!"

"You'll fall down the stairs," Lola said.

"Oh yeah, the stairs! Why would anyone live at the top of…of…four hundred flights of stairs? What about that? Why? Yeah. I'd rather fall down them than climb them, how do you like that?"

"If you want your skull fractured, that's a great idea."

"Naaaaah, did that already. The big game at school. Nurse said I should go back to class because it wasn't that bad and I just wanted to get out of class, but believe me if you saw that nurse you would know that no one would ever ever want to see her on purpose unless they had to because they were like, bleeding to death or something."

Lola grabbed his arm and tugged, and then he found himself sitting on the couch. "Stay right there," she said, in an incredibly stern tone. Death glowered after her but did as he'd been told. When she handed him a glass of water, he drank it. It was a tricky glass of water though, and spilled all over his shirt. "Did you want to die or something?"

"No."

"Then why would you drink that much tequila?"

"It's not so bad, Lola. It's just a little strange, but not that bad."

Lola shook her head. "It hasn't even begun to kick in yet. When it does, you're going to be very, very sorry that you ever even looked at that tequila bottle."

"I'm not like you, Lola Lane. I'm an agent." He stood up, but then he was on his belly on the floor and the entire world was tilting to the left. Death closed his eyes and cursed himself for getting on a boat. Especially a boat like this, a boat that tilted to the left and then the right and then the left.

"Are you going to be sick?"

Oh, he was going to be sick, all right. He was going to be sick forever and then he was probably going to die. Yes. Yes, he was going to die. Death was pretty sure he cried a little, but maybe he was laughing. It sounded like laughter.

"Alright, come on," Lola said, from far away. Death felt her take hold of him under the arms and then he was being dragged and then he was in the bathroom and then he was sick about six hundred times.

Eventually the room stopped spinning and he called for Lola in what he assumed to be a very in-control sort of tone. "Lola? Lola? Looolaaa."

"You sound like a drowning kitten."

"I'm never ever ever ever ever ever ever going to drink again. Not even water. Nothing. Ever. Nothing ever again. I think my kidneys came out. And maybe two gallbladders and a couple other things."

Lola laughed, and it sounded like thunder. "You don't have two gallbladders. Come on, I'll help you to the couch, but only if you're done throwing up."

"There's nothing left," he said, and laugh-cried a little more.

"Well, next time you won't drink an entire bottle of tequila."

"No, no, I'll never drink anything again."

"Just go to sleep. You're going to have a headache in the morning."

Death decided then and there that he would just stay asleep forever, and thus avoid the headache and hangover. He felt quite pleased with himself about this decision and drifted off into a black abyss of unconsciousness, all the while telling himself how clever he was.

CHAPTER TWELVE

"You look like death," Lola said, and tried not to laugh at the contorted position that her sickly pale, blue-haired little guest had worked himself into. A couch pillow was clutched against his chest with one skinny leg wrapped around it, his knee tucked up almost under his chin. Sweat had made his hair lose its spikiness and left it rather limp around his face and in his eyes. His glasses hung crooked at the end of his nose.

He groaned and clutched at his head with one hand. "I AM Death."

"Well, you certainly look like it right now." Lola poked at him. "Sit up and drink this water."

"I'm not sure I can sit up."

"You need to drink this water."

"Never drinking anything again ever ever." He moved a little and groaned again. "Something's in my mouth. Fabric or something. Like that time Francis shoved cotton balls into my mouth while I was asleep. Did you put cotton balls in my mouth?"

"You need to drink this water."

He sat up, very slowly, moaning and groaning all the way. He squinted at her, the little lines around his eyes deeper than ever. "You say things over and over, do you know that?" A tear rolled down his cheek and for a few seconds, Lola thought he might burst into tears again like he had the night before (repeatedly). Much to her relief, he just wiped it away and sniffled a little, staring at her as if seeing her for the first time. "All right, give me the water."

Lola handed over the water.

"It's so bright in here, owww." Death slurped noisily at the water and then shot Lola a somewhat sheepish look. "Thank you for taking care of me last night."

"I didn't do much," Lola said.

"You DID push me in a fountain and steal from me, so I guess we're even." Some glimmer of life came back into his eyes, and despite the moaning and groaning that continued over the next few moments, Death seemed more alert. "I'm really, really hungry."

Lola had to laugh at that. "I'll bet you are, after how much you threw up last night. I think you said you threw up your kidney and a couple gallbladders?" She pointed at his shirt. "You're going to need to take that off, because you definitely threw up on…well, you probably threw up on everything. And you'll need a shower." Lola sighed and motioned for him to hand over his shirt. "Come on, you smell awful."

Death grumbled something that sounded like curses and slurped at his water again.

"I'll give you some clothes until yours have been washed, but you need to clean up." Lola rummaged around in her belongings, found an old T-shirt and a pair of black jeans that might fit her strange little visitor. She coaxed him into the bathroom and after a long moment of him staring helplessly at the shower, she directed him in how to use it.

"It's been a while since I needed one of these," he said.

"What, you just always smell good, where you come from?"

"Usually. And if I don't, I just redesign myself."

Lola shook her head. "Yeah, okay, whatever. Clean yourself up and then we'll go get you some lunch or something. It's after 2 already."

"You gonna give me my papers back?"

Lola pulled the door closed on him and walked away.

Now, Lola had always been a girl of the primping variety, if only because she liked to experiment with colors and disguises. Her record time for "getting ready" was 35 minutes, and that had been because she had painted her entire face for an undercover gig at a carnival. She was proud of this record, because Mom used to take a long time putting on her lipstick and fake lashes and curling her hair, and it felt as if primping was in Lola's genes.

Death didn't emerge from the bathroom for 58 minutes.

"Did you find Narnia in there or something?" Lola asked as he patted at his skyward-facing hair. She shook her head and sighed. "The clothes fit you, at least." Well, sort of fit. The jeans were too long on him by about three inches, which he had attempted to remedy by rolling them up. The end result was comical, but she had a feeling that laughter would only serve to push him back into the bathroom for another hour and possibly an existential crisis.

"What does Green Day mean?" he asked, his voice smothered in suspicion. "What exactly do you know about the color of the sky, Lola Lane? Have you stolen top-secret information from other agents? Despair, maybe?"

"Did you seriously just ask me who Green Day is? Wow. Okay, I might have to shove you back in the fountain just for that." Lola was very tolerant about people being unfamiliar with most of her favorite bands. Juicy Bed, for instance, was a cult favorite, an underground love affair. And Fourth Squid Movement was something that only fans of a certain brand of weird indie music would know anything about. But Green Day? There was no excuse, barring coma or preschool age, for not knowing who Green Day was.

"Why? What do you know?"

"Green Day is a band, and only one of the most important bands in the history of music."

He faltered a little here, the narrowed eyes giving way to a confused sort of blinking/staring combo. After a while he said, "Well, I saw Duran Duran in concert once."

"Duran Duran? How old are you?"

"Errrr. Almost fifty."

Crazy, crazy, crazy. Or creepy. Or both. "Fifty, huh? You must use a really good face cream."

Death smiled then. "Ah, well, it's not *too* bad, I guess. It's not the priciest kind, but Mandy bought me a couple tubs, because it's made by monks. I didn't even know monks made face cream, but they're surprisingly good at it. The consistency is really smooth."

"All right, we'll get you some breakfast, and then you'll answer all of my questions."

"And then you'll give me my papers back!"

Eventually they reached the bottom floor and headed out into the street...though it took forever because Lola had to repeatedly stop and wait for Death to catch up. Not only was he unaccustomed to having to walk down stairs, but he was still hung over. If she forgot the latter fact, he reminded her by hissing, groaning, or making a mewing sound that was both pathetic and a little endearing. Only a little, though.

"I thought you couldn't keep up because you're wearing heels, but maybe I was wrong. Maybe it's just because you're old," Lola said, which earned her a scowl.

"Actually, I'm not old. I'm the youngest agent."

"Where, at an old folks' home?"

"Up *there*!" he said, raising a hand and pointing at the sky.

"You don't look fifty, I'll admit. Thirty, maybe, but not fifty."

"Tweeeenty-siiiix, thank you," he said, drawing out the words. "I was twenty-six when I was promoted." He hurried his pace so he could keep up with her, and lowered his voice. "I'm fifty in your years, though. Some of the agents really let themselves go when they're promoted, but I never wanted to be like that. Aging slowly is no excuse for laziness."

Lola spotted a gaggle of hipster guys leaned against the side of a building, smoking and wearing bow ties and oversized glasses and elbow patches on their cardigans as they took part in a loud conversation about Kerouac. One of them pointed at Death and called out, "Nice hair, bro."

"Why are they dressed like they live in the 60s or something?" Death whispered to Lola, staring at them in raw confusion.

"They're hipsters."

"Hipsters?"

"Yeah, you don't get much more hipster than the flannel bow-tie boys on Newbury Street," Lola said and rolled her eyes. "They like old things, but only ironically."

"Ironically?"

"Just forget it. So, if you're immortal or whatever, why don't more people want to get promoted?"

Death clicked his tongue. "I didn't say we're immortal, Lola. I said we age very slowly. Agents are different from…well, from the big guys. The big guys don't die, though some of them look pretty ancient." Death snickered to himself.

Lola ducked into her favorite café and grabbed hold of Death's shirtsleeve to steer him inside, too. "And how does someone get promoted?" When she received no answer, Lola placed the order for their lunch. "All right, I think you'll like—What?" she demanded, noting the rather dumbfounded expression on Death's face. "What?"

"I suppose I'll have to forgive you, since you clearly don't know anything about getting promoted. But still...you should be more careful next time, asking about something like that," he said in a quiet, flat voice.

Lola tried to laugh it off, but his face remained stony and his eyes serious. "Why, is it something bad?" she asked at last. She paid for their food and led the way to a table for two.

"Driving at night, ran off the road. They gave me a choice between this job or...whatever. I chose the job," Death said, peering right into her eyes.

"So you were in an accident."

"It made national news, because a couple of us died."

"Oh."

"Everyone talked about it for like, six days. Then, this library burned down a few towns over. That got a bunch of newspaper mentions and some guy from LA made a documentary about it. No one even died, but it took the attention off us!"

"Well...that's good, right?"

"It's stupid. People forget things. And I don't think my accident would have even made national news if the guy in the first car wasn't the mayor's stepson." Death seized half of the sandwich she'd bought. "I was one of the lucky ones in the accident, though. Ran off the road instead of ending up in the middle of Carmageddon. It was hard for them to pick the bodies out of that mess."

"Well, uh, *that's* good, right?" Lola said, though more hesitantly this time.

Death glanced up from his sandwich, fixing her with those weird blue eyes. "They mentioned my name in the report, but they didn't even spell my last name right. I don't know how much research it could possibly take to spell 'Gold' right, but I guess you don't get the same treatment when your car doesn't end up in a fireball with the mayor's stepson."

Lola still wasn't sure if anything he said was real, fake, or the product of a very disturbed mind, but laughing at someone else's tragedy wasn't on her list of favorite things. "I'm sorry I brought it up."

Death ate in silence, leaving Lola to do the same. As much as she was sorry to have caused him some kind of mental anguish, she had questions and he was going to have to answer them.

"What do you know about my parents?" she asked.

"Mother, actress. Father, performer."

"And how do you know that?"

"You told me."

Lola set her sandwich down. "I told you? And when exactly did I tell you about my parents? I don't tell people about them."

"Not out loud, of course. You told me in your nightmares. One time you dreamed that your mother was teaching you how to…what was it? Dye eggs. It was Easter. She was teaching you to dye eggs, and you were wearing bunny ears, and then she spelled out 'GOODBYE' on an egg. Then she was standing outside the window with your father and they said you were a bad kid. I think your father said he was never coming home again and then I was standing next to you and you told me to help you find them."

No...no, he was wrong. They'd been in a mirror, and Mom was the one who said they were never coming home. But the dream-voice of her mother still rang in her ears, "You're a bad little girl. You're a very bad little girl," she'd said. Lola had tried to break the mirror, but had been unable to even touch it.

"I wasn't a bad kid," she whispered at last, swiping her sleeve across her eyes to get rid of bothersome tears. "And you weren't in that dream."

"Yeah, I was. You just don't remember me because I'm good at erasing myself."

"And I told you about my parents? Don't think so. I would remember the blue hair."

"You said your mom was an actress and that your dad was a performer. You also said you hate puppets, so I constructed a pretty great nightmare involving that puppet with the eye patch." He shot her a smug look, and she had to resist reaching across the table to throttle him.

"So you made the nightmare about my parents?"

Death shook his head, the smug expression slipping. "No, that wasn't me. People have nightmares without my help, you know, and sometimes I drop in on the strong ones to watch. I make about half of people's nightmares, probably. The nightmare ratio went way up when I became Death." He paused. "See, the guy before me got into this rut. Everyone was having nightmares about a goblin sitting on their chest and then someone painted it and…well, it was so mainstream. He got stuck, creatively. Then he kinda lost his mind and started trying to eat himself or something. A couple fingers in, they fired him."

"Look, I don't know if you're…if you're crazy or you just work for someone who knows a lot of stuff," Lola said finally.

"I scored really high on the aggression scale, so I guess I'm a bit crazy, but I'm not lying. All of this is true."

"And you were in my nightmare. The one about my parents dying. Which, by the way, happened in real life."

His mouth turned down a little in the corners, and his eyebrows came together in some odd harmony of guilt, or maybe even sadness. "If a nightmare is drawing a lot of energy, sometimes I visit it. Yours drew a lot of energy."

"But you…"

Death vaulted out of his chair as if someone had kicked him, and ran outside without a single word.

Okay.

"Lola?" a familiar voice said, and Lola turned to find her employer standing just behind her. He was smiling. Uh oh.

CHAPTER THIRTEEN

Mr. Right had spent most of the last two hours attempting to actually locate Jason Wellington. The man wasn't an easy target by any means, but after some bad directions Mr. Right was able to track him down.

Mr. Right had always appreciated coffee, so he gave a lot of wiggle room to havens of the great bean. Wellington's shop, however, looked like it might cave in at any moment. A step inside revealed only a faint burning stench and an empty room. Maybe he'd gotten the wrong address again? But no, there was Jason Wellington, just behind the counter, looking a bit rougher and older than he had in the photograph in his file.

"What do you want?" Wellington demanded, in a very polite English accent.

"A mug of house blend. You don't need to bother with cream and sugar."

Wellington placed a mug of coffee in front of Mr. Right. "Wasn't going to. There's a table behind you if you want that kind of thing."

Mr. Right slowly turned and glanced at the table. It held a sad half-jug of milk and a salt shaker with a handwritten sign taped to it that said SUgaR. "How much do I owe you?" Mr. Right asked, turning back again.

"Two bucks. Three if you're going to stay and chatter. I'm not a bartender."

The file had mentioned, around line 10, that Jason Wellington was a bit irritable and sometimes difficult to reason with. Mr. Right had guessed this to be a misinterpretation on the part of someone who didn't understand basic human behavior. It would seem he might have been wrong, though.

Time to use a little celestial influence.

"You're a really nice man, Jason Wellington. You're very independent," Mr. Right said, just as his new client walked away. Wellington froze, mid-step, and then slowly walked back. His blue eyes took on the unfocused, teary glaze of one touched by celestial influence.

"I'm very independent, yes. Came to America alone. Started this place up alone. Run the place alone."

Mr. Right frowned. "I thought you had some bald guy named Phil who works here every weekend?"

"Well, except for Phil. I run it alone, except for Phil."

"Sounds very independent."

"She didn't think I could do it. But she's just a drunk tosser."

"Who?"

"Who do you think?" Wellington shot Mr. Right a rather acidic look. "My mum."

"Ah, all right. Back to the subject at hand. You're independent, and you're still young, of course…but aren't you missing out? When was the last time you went to a concert?"

"Don't have time for them."

"Wouldn't it be nice to go to concerts and keep up to date on things? To stay young and current?"

Wellington's eyes softened a little and he said, "I'm only 35."

"In five years, you'll be 40. Wouldn't it be wise to regenerate?"

This time Wellington blinked and cast a suspicious glance in Mr. Right's direction. "Regenerate?"

Mr. Right sighed. "Don't you know any nice girls? Young ones, maybe, who know a lot about concerts and music and current things?"

After what felt like an hour, Wellington nodded. "There's this saucy little thing down at Junky Monkey. I think her name is Erika."

"LOLA, OKAY!? LOLA. LOLA LANE."

The man finally gave that dazed expression that showed he'd either taken of a lot of drugs or gotten the idea. Thankfully, it was the latter. "Ah yes, Lola. She's rather young and current."

"Yes, good. And you like her, don't you?"

Wellington shrugged. "She's all right."

"Wouldn't it be nice if she was your girlfriend? Or, somewhere down the road, your wife? Imagine your mother's face when you bring home a beautiful, lively young woman. And think of all the money you two could make if you were truly in business *together*."

Mr. Right sent more persuasion and loving feelings in Wellington's direction, crowding his mind with images of jumping up and down on a bed with Lola, both of them throwing fistfuls of money into the air and laughing…wearing designer clothing, of course.

"You know…" Wellington said at last, "I think you're right. And after all I've done for her, giving her a job and helping her find an apartment, she must have some warm feelings of gratitude toward me."

"Of course, of course. And you love her, don't you?" Mr. Right asked, sending an even stronger wave of compulsion toward Wellington. He held his breath, waiting for the reaction.

"Love is such a strong word."

In all of his years, Mr. Right had only run into about eight people who were this stubborn. (Of the eight, he'd given up on one and hit one on the head with a tree branch after getting particularly frustrated). Thankfully, patience was one of Mr. Right's virtues.

"You love Lola Lane, don't you?"

Wellington's lips arched upwards into a slow, somewhat shark-like smile. It wasn't the most comforting smile of all time, but his eyes echoed the dull heaviness of compulsion. "I do love Lola Lane. I do."

Finally.

Then there was the issue of finding Lola. Mr. Right turned invisible and followed Wellington, not entirely trusting him to his own devices quite yet. The first flush of love could easily be lost by distractions or bad made-for-TV movies.

Besides, Mr. Right needed to steer Wellington in the general direction of Lola.

Lola was sitting inside a café when Mr. Right spotted her. He directed Wellington to Lola through a series of complicated and completely undetectable motions, stepping aside only when the Englishman spotted his future love and approached her.

Really, it was completely sewn up! After all, Wellington was Lola's employer of some sort—or so it said in the notes—which meant they already knew each other. From here it would just be the usual yadda yadda. I love you, I really love you, how did I never see this before? I love you, let's run away to Paris. Let's run away together, my love! You complete me! I love you, I love you!

"Lola, my pet. Lola, you complete me."

It was a little sad, this part, if only because Lola Lane would forever be connected to Death in Mr. Right's mind. She'd been the downfall of his friend, and it hadn't even been fully her fault. Sure, she'd tricked him and stolen from him and kissed him and—okay, well maybe it had been her fault. But still. It was also Mr. Right's fault.

Mr. Right sent vibes of adoration and love in Lola's direction. She would realize with a gasp that Wellington's presence was comforting, authoritative… like a professor…the older man she'd always needed and wanted in her life. She would melt into his embrace and they'd fade into the sunset of Mr. Right's assignment book.

"Have all the men on the planet been abducted by aliens?" Lola demanded.

Odd. That wasn't what Mr. Right had expected.

"Whatever do you mean, my pet?"

"First Death runs out the door like the mothership came back for him, and now you're staring at me all googly-eyed and saying I complete you. This is *not* normal."

Wellington shook his head, apparently as confused as Mr. Right was. "But you *do* complete me. I've just realized how much that statement is true… You've been there for me since I first caught you trying to steal my wallet. We have so much more than just a business relationship, Lola…we have something that could last the ages."

Mr. Right sent warm, loving feelings in Lola's direction.

"You've really lost your mind," Lola said to Wellington. She stood up and Wellington took hold of her arm, his face a maze of confused emotions. "What are you doing? Let me go."

As if the moment couldn't get any stranger, Death appeared from seemingly nowhere, one hand perched on his bony hip. His mouth was pulled into an exaggerated "O" as he all but collided with Wellington and Lola.

"We need to get out of here!" Death said, his voice reaching the pitch that it usually did before he started shrieking and throwing things out of self-defense. He smelled like blood. "Look, sir, Lola needs to come with me right now."

"I am in love with her."

"No, he's my boss," Lola said.

"Your boss is in love with you?"

"Since about two and a half minutes ago." Lola shook off Wellington's grip. "I don't know what's gotten into him."

"I'm in love with you, Lola, that's what!" Wellington fell on his knees, right there, clasping his big hands together. "Somehow, I never saw it before, but today my eyes were opened. Lola, I love you! Lola, you're my…my…the reason for my existence."

A few other patrons of the café snickered loudly. Lola seemed unmoved.

Death grabbed for Lola's hand. "We have to get out of here right now."

"You can't take her away from me, you little blue-haired *freak*. She is the love of my life. If you attempt to steal her away, I'll have to call Jerome and ask him to kill you," Wellington said, and somehow, Mr. Right didn't think he was kidding.

Neither did the other patrons of the café, it seemed, as all of them stopped snickering and a few of them made speedy exits.

"Wait a second," Death said, his eyes narrowing. "You suddenly decided you were in love with Lola?"

Wellington frowned.

"Just today?" Death said.

"Yes, today I realized how much I love her."

Death looked around, and Mr. Right realized with a start that his old friend was looking for him. They'd worked together a few times, on covert missions and one rather comical assignment in Australia. Death and Mr. Right knew each other's work, their patterns, their quirks and stamps.

"I know you're here," Death hissed, and Mr. Right felt incredibly guilty all over again. "Leave her alone. And tell *them* to leave her alone, too!"

With that, Death surprised everyone by slipping one arm around Lola's back and the other around the back of her knees, lifting her and carrying her out of the café.

CHAPTER FOURTEEN

Death dropped Lola the moment they were out of the café. He tried to shrug and act as if it had been planned, but he was pretty sure they both knew his arms had just given way.

"What's going on?" Lola demanded.

Death snatched her hand again. "We have to get out of here, come on."

"Why?"

"Because I saw a reaper." A reaper, and not even cloaked in invisibility. The Reaper and his little crony reapers were supposed to tread carefully on the face of the earth, blending in or staying out of sight entirely, as instructed in just about every ancient rulebook ever. The reapers were even forced to carry their auras inside of a bottle, somewhere on their person. It had something to do with keeping them from being too powerful. Mandy liked to talk about it while painting her nails, because "their little aura bottles look almost exactly like nail polish bottles. Odd, innit?"

Death had rarely seen reapers, even in Alantis, and when he had...well, he'd only seen them because he'd had his aura. Aura could see aura.

"You saw a reaper."

"Yes! At first I thought maybe I was wrong, or that it was some guy in a costume, but I chased him down and he turned around and tried to kill me."

Lola laughed nervously. "Tried to kill you?"

Death paused just long enough to turn his head to the side and motion at the fresh scratches on the side of his neck. "I was too fast for him, though. Good thing, or he would've taken my head off."

With a quiet gasp, Lola brushed her fingers against the wound on his neck. Death hissed and danced back from her. Reapers were well-known for the poison on their nails, the poison on their fangs, the deadly hypnotism of their eyes and the swift swing of their weapons. The wounds they left were always nasty...and painful.

"Look, you need to tell me right now if all of this is...if... Are you telling me the truth?" Lola demanded. Death might have given her a long and thoroughly satisfactory answer, but he spotted the reaper in the distance. Headed in their direction.

"Lola, Lola my pet, I love you!" the English boss guy yelled, bursting out of the café.

"Keep up with me," Death said, this time grasping Lola's hand too tight for her to let go. Boots or no boots, Death ran faster than he'd ever run. Along the way, they wound their way into a crowd of confused tourists and dodged and ducked wayward elbows, water bottles and fanny packs. On the other side of the crowd, Death threw himself into a hard right, down a street that seemed promising. At the end of a street, he glanced both ways and chose left, trusting nothing other than raw instinct.

Raw instinct led him to a dead end, where an elderly homeless man was talking to a dirt-covered sock puppet and an empty bottle of booze.

"Why don't you let me lead?" Lola said. "Unless you *wanted* to come here for some completely nonsensical reason."

Death fought to force air back into his burning lungs. "Uh, sure. You lead."

And so they ran, Death looking back over his shoulder every few moments. It seemed that, no matter how fast they moved or how many turns they took, the reaper was always within sight and closing in fast.

"In here!" Lola shouted, yanking Death into a dimly lit shop. She nodded to the little woman behind the desk and tore past ugly sweaters and scarves, dragging Death along with her. They burst out of another doorway and she slammed the door shut behind them. "Up here," she said, motioning at a rusty-looking ladder strapped to the side of the building like a bad afterthought.

Death sighed and scrambled up the ladder, hoping all the while that it would hold his slight weight. When he reached the top, he whirled around and offered his hand to Lola. "All right, what's the deal with this roof?" he asked.

Lola led him to the other side of the roof. "Do you see him? Or it? Or…whatever?"

If Death had his aura, he easily could have spotted the reaper from a hundred thousand paces, but he found himself squinting and searching the crowd for a large, cloaked figure. What if the reaper had gone invisible again? Death shuddered to even imagine, because they would be defenseless against it if that were true.

But no, there! The reaper pushed by tourists and locals, and frightened a man on a bike so badly that he crashed into a black-haired woman. It would seem that he hadn't noticed Lola and Death's detour into the shop, because he crashed onward right past them.

"Wow, that's...not something I've ever seen in Boston," Lola said in a quiet voice.

"No one's supposed to see them. They're supposed to stay invisible! Same with the Wings, same with the agents. We're not supposed to let anyone see us, because it creates questions and usually a lot of fear and rioting. And I mean, once photography was invented? Forget it. Bigfoot decided he wanted to show himself to some campers or something and we had to write him off."

Lola's worried expression slipped and gave way to a raised eyebrow. "Oh, so Bigfoot is real."

"Of course he is! Not officially. We had to deny his existence but...well, point is, it's one of the Sacred Laws!" He watched as the reaper continued on and on, finally disappearing into the distance. Death let out his breath in a rush, closing his eyes for a few seconds. "I think someone sent him for me."

"Why?" Lola whispered, and this time it sounded as if she believed him.

"I have no idea. But I've seen them close in on their targets, and when this one spotted me…" Death shuddered again, this time so hard that Lola grabbed his shoulders. "He recognized me, because he said my name."

"Well, I'm sure they say 'death' a lot, if they're reapers."

"No. He said…err, you know. My other name."

"Kelly?"

"Yeah."

Lola held him a little longer and then stepped away, peering down into the street again. "So, if he said your name and he's looking for you, he's likely going to keep looking for you."

Death nodded.

"Is he looking for me, too?"

"I don't know. Mr. Right was manipulating your boss, trying to make him fall in love with you, so maybe not. But I can't take any chances."

"Who's Mr. Right?"

"Uhhh, he makes people fall in love." Death hesitated. "When I met you, the big guys accused me of falling in love—which, by the way, I did not—and very soon after, Mr. Right used his little spell on me and…"

Wait, should he be telling her this? Death caught sight of Lola's curious expression, her big olive-colored eyes. She seemed innocent and sweet, but he knew from experience that she could dunk people in fountains and kiss them without meaning it.

"He made you fall in love with me?"

Oooops.

"Well, for a minute, maybe. But it was all fake! Just like what's happening to your boss right now. He made it happen for just long enough that they had a good excuse to fire me. Well, also because I lost the names of the damned but…mostly because of the Sacred Law thing."

Lola's eyes narrowed. "So there's a law against falling in love?"

"Well, yeah. It would be a horrible conflict of interest. The big guys can do what they want, but agents? Nah, we need to concentrate on our job. It's all part of the choice to be promoted."

He'd always thought it a fair enough requirement. After all, love could get really messy. Love caused accidents and tragedies. Love caused people to get in cars at 3AM, exhausted to the point of collapse, and drive two hours south while crying and listening to bad pop music.

"Do you still like me?" Lola asked, ripping Death from some deliciously graphic memories of his own demise.

"What? *No!* No, I want my job back. I mean, I won't let them kill you or anything but no, I don't love you!"

"I didn't say love."

"You're not as bad as I thought at first, but you're a thief and you stole my papers," he said, losing a lot of his bluster by the end of the sentence. "Anyway, though, Mr. Right is manipulating your boss into thinking he's in love with you. You're probably safer staying with me for now, because I know his tricks."

Lola cocked an eyebrow at him, crossing her arms over her chest. She opened her mouth to say something, but then her eyes widened and she let out something like a squeak.

"What?" Death asked, just before realizing that everyone always did this sort of thing just before getting stabbed in the back by some sort of six-armed alien monster. He turned around and danced backwards, barely missing the razor-sharp claws of the reaper that he'd encountered earlier. He would have known it anywhere, because its hood hung crooked, as if it had some sort of protruding horn on one side of its head.

Maybe it did. He'd never seen one of them without its hood.

"Kelly Gold," it said, and lunged at him.

Death threw himself out of the way and slammed his elbow as hard as possible into the reaper before it could turn on him again. His elbow certainly connected, because the shock curled clear to Death's feet, but it did little to unbalance or impair the reaper.

"Keeeelllllly."

"Stop calling me that!"

"Kellllly. Kellllly Gold," the reaper said, reaching one clawed hand toward Death.

A burning, fiery pain blossomed across Death's neck, where the claw wounds remained from earlier. He yelped and danced around from foot to foot before realizing that motion was certainly not going to stop the pain.

"Kelly," the reaper said, flicking its fingers again. The pain increased until Death thought his head might explode. "Come here, Kelly. Come here..." The voice changed, sounding eerily like the husky nasal-tone of his least-favorite peer in high school, Carter Reed.

"Stop it!" Death gasped out, taking a step backward.

The reaper's voice rang close, as if right in Death's ear. "You know you'll never be anything." The wound burned with a new vigor, unyielding. "Not in this town, not anywhere."

Death looked around for something he could hit the reaper with, gasping and cursing. Apparently looking away from his opponent was a bad idea, though, as the reaper used this opportunity to side-swipe Death and send him flying across the rooftop.

Okay, so that hurt, too.

Especially since Death had ended up landing in a circle of glass bottles, one of which decided to helpfully break into about a million pieces. Several of those pieces dug into Death's back.

The reaper strolled toward him, hissing all the way.

"You're not supposed to be visible," Death said, pointing at the reaper. "You hear me? You're supposed to be cloaked." He scrambled backwards, catching his palms on broken glass and wincing. "That's a Sacred Law. You're going to get demoted or—or you'll get executed! They execute for the big stuff, like walking around in Boston and scaring people! They'll take your aura bottle away!"

Oh great. His back was against the wall that lined the edge of the roof.

"Orders," the reaper breathed, bending down over Death. "Orders from the top, to execute Kelly Gold."

"I didn't do anything!"

"Of course not, Kelly." The reaper's voice took on that Carter Reed tone again, this time so unmistakably that a shudder ran clear to Death's toes. "You've never done much of anything except sit back there staring at the wall like a freak."

A memory. A memory of one of the most popular kids at school standing, menacing, over one of the quietest kids at school, while a crowd of a dozen students looked on in sick curiosity.

The reaper's laugh echoed Carter's as it leaned toward him. "And you have nothing to say. Not surprising."

Death snatched up a piece of broken glass, the biggest one his hand could find in its blind, frantic search. He waited until the very last moment, until the reaper had leaned down and taken hold of him, before he stabbed the creature with every remaining shred of strength that he had.

The reaper shrieked and jumped away from Death, the glass still wedged somewhere in the general area of its neck. And then it tumbled forward as if it had been hit. It overshot Death and tipped over, off the roof. The reaper's scream was cut short, likely from hitting the ground, and Death turned appreciative eyes upward to Lola.

"Thanks," he said.

"I didn't know what else to do, sorry."

"No, it's okay. It was after me, not you," Death said, but he couldn't do much to stop the wavering and shaking in his voice and hands. "You throwing it, uhhh, off the roof…that was good enough." He tried to stand up, but found that his legs were too shaky.

Lola knelt in front of him, taking his hands and wincing a little. She fished a piece of broken glass out, even as he hissed and whined. Lola turned her olive eyes up to meet his gaze. "We better get out of here," she said, and he nodded in agreement.

CHAPTER FIFTEEN

"OW!" Death said as Lola poked at his hand with a sewing needle. "That has to be all of it."

"I can't tell, so hold still."

They sat huddled together under her couch lamp as if warming themselves by a fire for the evening, except that Lola was digging tiny shards of glass from Death's hand with a needle instead of comforting him or telling stories.

"Why did that thing...why did it attack you?" Lola asked finally, as if she'd been holding the question in for a long time. She dug one last piece of glass out of his skin and then met his gaze. "I heard it talking to you."

Death had tried very hard to avoid thinking about the reaper's Carter Reed voice or any of the strange memories it had stirred up, but it all crowded back into his mind as soon as she mentioned it. "I don't know."

"He said 'execute.'"

During his years as an agent, Death had heard all sorts of whispers and rumors about agents who had really, really lost the plot, but only two of those had ended in execution…or at least, that's what Mandy had said. He had never been associated with any particularly fruity people and furthermore, during one rather ill-fated obsessive night in the Records Department, Death had only been able to uncover one report of an official execution.

"Why would it want to execute you?" Lola whispered, and Death realized he'd lost himself in thoughts.

"I have no idea. Even breaking a Sacred Law isn't usually punishable by…you know. Demotion is bad enough, because you become mortal again."

Lola nodded. "So, demotion is a long death sentence."

"Yeah, I guess you could say so. Longer for some than others." Death sighed, drawing his knees up against his chest. "Most don't last that long. I'm the youngest agent, so for me…well, things are different down here, of course, but I can usually figure it out. Imagine if you'd been an agent for 200 years, like most of them."

"Oh. Lame. The internet would probably be pretty hard to deal with."

A laugh escaped Death. "Yeah, that one would be pretty confusing."

"And you wouldn't know anyone. That would be kinda sad. Well, you could probably visit your great-grandkids or something, but they wouldn't know who you were." Lola shrugged. "Do you visit your family?"

"Family." The word bounced around without a strong sense of meaning, like a vocabulary test from last month. Vague images of Mom, Dad and Kirsten floated to the surface but then melted just as quickly. The only thing that replaced it was a dull sensation of loss and the smell of a dusty basement bedroom.

The last time Death had "visited" his family, he'd found his bedroom redecorated with a tennis table, Kirsten's broken television set and about six moldy boxes of KELLY'S STUFF.

"I did, a long time ago," he said and pulled his wounded hand out of her grip.

"Wow. Did you actually talk to them?"

"No!"

Lola sighed quietly. "We still don't know why that thing would want to kill you. If banishment is so bad, why bother? I mean, you said all you did was fall in love with me."

"I did not fall in love! He put his spell on me. It wasn't real love."

"Okay, okay. What could you have done that would make someone want to bump you off, though? Did you make some enemies up there?"

Death considered this question, running through all of the agents he'd had contact with. Mostly he'd stuck close to his friends, those being Fashion, Robby, Mandy, and, for a while, Dominic in Records.

Fashion was already a mainstay among agents when Death had first been promoted, and the two had hit it off over an impromptu laughing session centered entirely around Malcolm's three-week attempt at a mustache. Fashion had been awesome, and about 400 years old. Mandy had always been more than happy to talk to Death about her predictions and the latest office gossip. Dominic, before he'd gotten snobby and transferred to Ancient Records, had always been pretty cool, too. Most of the other agents had either been ambiguous in their feelings toward Death, or they were just background noise.

And then there was Mr. Right.

Death and Mr. Right had worked together a few times. An unlikely duo for sure, but a strangely productive one on account of their drastically different methods to achieve success. Mr. Right came off experienced (old) and somewhat of a stickler to rules, but he was a nice foil to Death, and at times even fun. None of it seemed to matter in the end, though, since Mr. Right followed orders and for some reason, those orders had been to get rid of Death.

Who else was there?

"Malcolm."

"Who?"

Death shrugged. "There's this guy named Malcolm, and he's kind of in charge of a lot of stuff because his dad's really old or whatever. Or, well, his dad *was* old. He's dead now. I guess it runs in their family to be in charge of things. He's sort of like the manager of HQ. He always wears suits to work and tries to seem important, but everyone knows that he's not really like…one of the big guys. You know? Not like *big* big."

"And he'd like to get rid of you?"

"He wants to get rid of a lot of people. But I've never heard of him executing anyone," Death said, shaking his head. "Demoting and banishing, yeah, but not executing. It's not really his style. His style is big ties and stupid-looking hair." Without thinking, Death reached up and patted at his uncharacteristically limp blue locks.

"Okay, well, who's above him?"

"Uh. I don't know."

Lola raised an eyebrow. "You don't know? How do you not know that? It's a pretty simple chain of command kind of thing. One guy works in the shop, one guy watches him work, one guy owns the shop."

"I...don't really pay attention to that stuff." "Don't really" was an understatement. The last time Death had truly paid attention to something office related was when Mandy had informed him that their next meeting was going to have an open bar and a feast table filled with goodies from one of Death's favorite bakeries. Strawberry scones were not a matter to be ignored. "I just do my job. I'm not interested in the office politics."

"It's not politics to know who's in charge."

Death scowled at her.

"So the Malcolm guy doesn't really like you, but you don't think he'd try to kill you." Lola grabbed his hand again, this time poking at it with her fingertips.

"Ow!"

"Sorry. I just wanted to see if you'd heal super-fast or something."

"No! I don't have my aura anymore." Death pulled his wounded hand against his chest, shielding it with his other hand. "That hurt."

"It didn't hurt as much as what that thing would have done to you," Lola said, standing up. She padded away from him on bare feet, walking into the kitchen and fishing around in the fridge. Death glanced in her direction to say something witty or cutting, but he noticed for the first time that she was wearing shorts. And those shorts left a lot of bare leg exposed.

Pretty nice legs, as it were. Long legs. Legs like that were—

"Are you staring at my legs?"

Death's gaze moved slowly upwards until it fixed on olive eyes and a raised eyebrow. He hadn't realized just how fixated he'd become. "Uh, no."

"You were."

"You asked if I am. I'm not. Not right this second."

Lola rolled her eyes and turned away just long enough to gather a few items of food onto a plate and then return to him with it. She motioned at the cheese, crackers and suspicious-looking meat-stuff on the plate.

"Who controls the reapers, anyway?"

Death shrugged. "Not people I know." He sat up bolt upright. "I bet it's the Sumner Organization!"

"Who's that?"

"They're these people, bad people. They do awful things to agents. I bet they're trying to kill me!" Death shook his head and fixed his eyes on Lola. "It all makes sense…they heard that I'd been fired and now they're trying to kill me. It said 'orders from the top' to execute me, you know? Because it came down from their leader! He hates agents. You know, if I could find Fashion, he'd know what to do."

"Who's Fashion?"

"He's my best friend. He taught me everything when I was first promoted. I tried to stop them from banishing him, but they did it anyway." Death rubbed at the painful wound on his neck. "I've looked for him, but no one has any idea where he went." The truth was, Death had searched for Fashion every time he journeyed to areas where his friend seemed likely to be hiding. He'd even paid some shady fellow named Phillip to look for Fashion, but to no avail. "For some reason, agents are always exiled to Boston."

Lola chewed thoughtfully on a piece of cheese for a while. "I bet I know someone who can help us find him."

CHAPTER SIXTEEN

Mr. Right returned to HQ after hours, partly out of raw embarrassment and partly out of necessity. He had taken care of three other assignments on his list, but he couldn't begin to remember what they were. His mind had been occupied the whole time, trailing over and over and over what had happened.

He'd never failed before.

As usual, Mandy was still at her desk. Mr. Right couldn't even be sure that the woman ever went home, which might have been part of why Death liked her so much. She was as much a part of HQ as the walls or the carpets or the bubblers.

"You saw him, didn't you?" she called, before Mr. Right had even stepped out of the elevator. "You saw Kelly? What was he doing?"

Mr. Right looked left and right, nerves fluttering in his belly, and then approached Mandy's desk. She bounced to her feet and leaned closer to him.

"Is it true he really did fall in love with that girl?" Mandy said. "Has he gone all mushy and started taking her places and winning her stuffed animals out of claw machines and kissing her in public?" Something about her voice said that a thread had come undone, that she might unravel from the fever of watching others live and do and be and say as she could only observe.

Mr. Right let out a heavy sigh and shook his head. "I'm not sure."

"He must be! Why else would they send a reaper to…" Mandy lowered her voice, motioning for Mr. Right to move closer. "You know. To execute him."

With a start, Mr. Right straightened again. "What are you talking about?"

"Well, Kim said she was on a mission for the Wings division, like she does every now and again, and she saw a reaper try to kill him. Kelly threw the thing off a building and it landed on a mortal, and Kim said a crowd of people saw it. They all went bananas." Mandy gave a self-satisfied nod. "You know what that means, of course. He's fallen in love and now he'll do anything to be with that girl, even if it means killing reapers and traveling the world and getting himself involved in secret societies or something."

Grace, one of the senior agents, emerged from his office down the hall and shuffled over to Mandy and Mr. Right. "You two talking about Kelly Gold?" he asked, eyes darting between them. "Kim said he threw a reaper off a building. I didn't know they could die. Did you know they can die…?"

Mandy huffed. "Of course I knew that. About 30 years ago it happened in London, during that big parade. Got crushed by a huge truck." She waved a hand. "I don't feel sorry for them, though, really. Nasty things. Oh, and they smell awful, too."

"Little Kelly, killing a reaper," Grace said. "Someone was talking at breakfast this morning, said Kelly's heard the Rattle four times now."

"Because of that girl, I bet. He's in love with that girl."

"The Rattle?" Mr. Right said, finally managing to speak again. "They've used the Rattle on him?"

The Rattle was a death knell, a warning that an agent had stepped out of bounds and was going to be eliminated within a relatively short period of time. Mr. Right had never heard the Rattle personally, but even the stories that circulated among clusters of whispering agents or Wings left him uneasy.

"It's because of that girl," Mandy said, shifting a few items on her desk and then jotting a note on a scrap of paper.

"I haven't seen her. What's she like? Is it true that she's incredibly beautiful?"

"She's just a pip of a thing, really, but he's gone mad in love with her, and what sense or objectivity does any man have when he's in love? And you know Kelly. Quite a single-minded boy when he wants to be."

"I can't believe they used the Rattle on him," Mr. Right whispered.

"Do you need a chair? You look pale."

"No, I just…Malcolm said he'd be looked after. No one's sent his things to him, though, and I wondered why. I never thought they were planning to…to…"

"To kill him? Oh, it's so awful. So, so awful." Mandy jotted more notes on her paper. "Of course they'll have to try again. They hate to fail. Do you think they'll send several reapers this time?"

"They haven't done anything like that in maybe a hundred years," Grace said. "If you want to know what I think, it's all due to Jessica taking over the Death position." Grace gave one of his wise nods, which were usually reserved for board meetings and predictions about sporting scores. "Jessica used to be all right, when she was still just a record keeper, but every time she gets promoted, things get worse around here for all of us."

"I think Kelly was drawn to that girl because her parents were agents." Mandy paused, leaning back in her chair and smiling smugly at Mr. Right and Grace. When neither of them said anything, her smile slipped. "Shocking, you know. I asked around a bit, looked into it myself. Her parents were exiles. They fell in love."

Mr. Right's attention finally caught at that. "Exiles? Who were they?"

"Drama and Muse," Mandy said, in a rush. "Exiled exactly 23 years ago. They had that little girl and then got themselves killed in an accident—"

The words trailed off into silence in Mr. Right's mind as he turned away from Mandy and searched his memory. Muse stood out as a tall, rail-thin rake who had charmed the collective pants off of a number of agents, but none more memorably, perhaps, than Jessica. Everyone had known how much Jessica fancied Muse. Inter-office romance was a particularly juicy subject for the gossip mill, because it was so forbidden, and as long as no one important found out, it provided hours and hours of mostly innocent entertainment for all involved.

Muse had moved on from Jessica, though, and taken up with flowery little Drama. Their romance had seemed destined by all of the laws of nature, but no one had been as surprised to discover it as Jessica.

To this day, Mr. Right was certain that Jessica had been responsible for Drama and Muse's exile. Their memory had been all but wiped out of Alantis, their pictures removed from the books and the framed photograph of Muse taken down from the Employee of the Year wall. Mr. Right had been as guilty as the next man when it came to forgetting about their existence, and he'd never checked in with them after their exile, even just in passing.

"You know what I find rather hilarious," Mandy went on, her voice fading back into Mr. Right's perception, "Remember that time Kelly got all brave and went up to Drama and asked her on a date at the holiday party? Now he's got her daughter. I wonder if he knows *that*?"

"Such a rebel," Grace said, with a sigh. "Throwing reapers off buildings and falling in love. Ah, I miss being young." He tapped his knuckles against Mandy's desk. "I should finish up my work and head out for the night. It's late. Good evening, Mandy. Good evening, Mr. Right. And good luck to you on all of your missions... you offer such an important service to the world, sir." Grace shuffled away, his steps hardly as graceful as they had once been. Mr. Right stared after him, wondering how much longer the old man would last.

"Oh, I know what you're thinking," Mandy whispered. "He's getting old. We're getting old too, you know. Who knows how long any of us will last around here, with Jessica changing everything." She let out another of her trademark huffs and pushed her chair back. "Kelly might be our little knight, in the end."

Mandy turned off the light at her desk, gathered her bag and walked away, leaving Mr. Right alone in the darkened lobby with only his thoughts and his guilt to keep him company.

CHAPTER SEVENTEEN

Death wasn't sure what he was wearing.

Lola had pawed through a dresser drawer, grabbed things (seemingly at random), and thrown them at him. Eventually, after more than a little coaxing, he'd agreed to put them on. But no amount of "we're going to a rave" explained why Death was wearing ugly track pants with a white stripe up the side and a V-neck T-shirt in fluorescent yellow. With light-up sneakers.

"How long ago did you wear these shoes?" he demanded for the third time that night. Lola had been leading him from street to street, crisscrossing and dodging into and out of shadows like a spy in an old movie. Well, if a spy wore a pink sleeveless shirt and tattered neon-yellow skirt.

"About ten years ago."

"Great, I'm wearing children's shoes."

"Your feet are small."

Death halted, dropping his gaze to his feet and the white light-up shoes that encased them. "My feet are not that small."

"Hey, I'm not accusing you of anything," Lola said over her shoulder, and then shot him a smile. "But you know what they say."

"Yeah, well, they're wrong."

"They say light-up shoes are for kids. But I think they work well for raves too." With that, Lola turned around again and pointed ahead. "That's where we're going."

"That," in this case, was a gross-looking building with a slimy exterior, somewhere along the waterfront. A line of freaks and weirdos snaked from the front of the building and wrapped around the side, out of sight. Death had never seen so many tacky color combinations. And that was saying something, considering that he'd lived through the 80s.

"What…is happening?" Death said, not sure if he dared keep staring at the fluorescent monsters. "Did you drug me? I think I'm hallucinating."

"No, but that reminds me. Don't put anything in your mouth unless I give it to you, understand? That's really important."

Death bristled. "Do I look like the type to go around putting strange things in my mouth?"

One of the fluorescent girls winked at him.

"Just don't do it," Lola said, grabbing his hand and tugging him toward the front of the line.

The bouncer gazed at them with a casual air before shrugging his skinny shoulders and pushing his glasses up on his nose. Uh, this guy did not look qualified to be a bouncer.

"Who's this?" the bouncer asked, motioning at Death.

"This is my friend, Kelly."

"Is she underage?"

Death propped his hands on his hips. "He."

The bouncer nodded. "We need more girls in there tonight, so in you go." The bouncer stepped aside, stirring up a lot of jeers and cursing from the line of freaks behind Death. "And Lola? You still owe me one from last week."

Lola smiled. "Thanks!" She tugged on Death's hand again and, before he could splutter any more complaints about being mistaken for a girl, they were inside the building.

So here's the thing about raves. The flashing lights stab you in the face like a murderer, the pounding, pulsing noises aren't quite slow enough to be considered music, and everything in the room is bouncing. EVERYTHING. Including the inanimate objects. Oh, and everyone is spackled in dizzying pinks, neon yellows and some sickening shade of emergency green.

This was much worse than Bill's German art-house vampires.

Death cringed a little as a man in a neon banana suit nearly fell into him. "What are we doing here?" he said, before discovering that his voice had been completely drowned out by the music. He leaned up and screamed his question into Lola's ear.

"Dance!" she said and then started bouncing like the neon banana and everything else in the room.

Death cast an uneasy glance around the spacious black room before half-heartedly bouncing a few times.

What was wrong with these kids? One boy bounced by, fell into a handspring and then bounced off toward the stage, waving his hands in the air. Another kid swung glowing whips, and a small gaggle of pacifier-girls jumped up and down as a unit, as if their bodies were fused together. Pacifiers. They actually had pacifiers in their mouths.

Lola took both of Death's hands and bounced even more frantically than before. Death bounced with her, but only with great reluctance. This music was ABSURD. The whole thing was absurd. Why would anyone do this? Why would they bounce like this?

Well, actually, it felt kinda good.

Huh, weird. It felt a little euphoric, actually.

Wow. Maybe it released a bunch of endorphins, kinda like normal dancing did. Death had never been very good at any kind of dancing that didn't involve him sitting in the corner and watching everyone else, but you know? This wasn't so bad. This was basically just bouncing. Anyone could bounce!

The banana guy bounced by again, this time waving two pink glow sticks over his head. It looked kinda cool, if you were bouncing too. And the pacifier girls had this weird trippy vibe to them.

Death bounced faster and discovered that, if he threw his body weight slightly to the left, he bounced to the left. And then back to the right. Which made the pulsing in his ears change, just a little. Ooooooh.

The music wasn't really that bad, once you got used to it. And if you bounced really high, you caught notes you hadn't heard before!

The banana guy bounced over to Death and Lola, and Death let go of Lola's hands so he could bounce with the banana guy. It seemed fitting. The three of them bounced together, and it was probably the most amazing feeling Death had ever experienced. His arms and legs felt lighter, his mind felt empty, the sweat that rolled into his eyes stung like acid and his glasses almost flew off his face. *So cool.*

The pacifier girls circled Death, Lola and the banana guy, creating a little insular world of color and awesome.

Oh, and then the tempo of the music picked up!

"Why didn't they have parties like this back in my day?" Death shouted. "This is AMAZING. I feel like I can bounce to the roof! I could do anything right now!"

The banana guy started peeling off some of his suit, which was a little weird. And one of the pacifier girls offered Death her pacifier, which was even weirder. But he just kept bouncing anyway. He bounced for what felt like a million years, and then all of the sudden the music stopped and Lola grabbed his arm and pointed toward the stage.

"Where's the music?" Death shouted, but he could barely hear his own voice over the sudden lack of deafening noise.

"We have to find her! Come on!" Lola said.

Personally, Death wouldn't have minded bouncing with the banana for a little longer, but Lola's grip on his hand was pretty aggressive. "Who are we looking for?"

Lola led him past a tabletop mountain of cups and water jugs and through a side door, into a dark room. The ringing in Death's ears lessened a little and his eyes adjusted enough to take in a tall, willowy woman angled toward a young couple.

"Lillian!" Lola said, approaching the tall woman and receiving a happy gasp in response.

"You made it, darling. What did you think, what did you think? Lord, I felt ridiculous up there, and so old, too. But I've always been curious, you know? Curiosities are medication for the depressed and ancient souls. And I don't think anyone knew me out there, except for you. They'll all run back to their rabbit trails and neon houses, forget about this." The tall woman pulled Lola into a hug and then glanced at Death. "Oh, what's this one? Is this your little list maker?"

Death tried to tear his eyes from this bewitching, statuesque woman's gaze, but found himself unable to move. He couldn't remember ever creating a nightmare for her, and couldn't get any sort of accurate reading on her fears. Usually, he was bombarded by dream-memories or phantom fears rising off of strangers like lazy ghosts, but here he only sensed quiet and earnest balance. "List maker?"

"Oh yes. Ooooh. You feel cold, like you're just warmin' back up from a long, long sleep." The woman's voice held a cadence of England and craziness, but the good kind. "Or maybe something else. You been dead a while?"

"He calls himself Death," Lola put in.

"But that's not your real name. You had a good name once, didn't you? A good name that you forgot about because everyone else forgot it first."

Death tried to laugh.

"What was your name before?" the tall woman asked, one ring-laden hand settling on his shoulder.

"Kelly Gold."

The woman nodded. "A good enough name. Stop putting it in your coffin box, little boy. Got that? And I'm Lillian Gale, it's lovely to meet you." She moved her hand then, tapping two fingers against the wound on his neck. "That looks a bit nasty. Like something I saw Leo with once. Doesn't it, Leo?"

The couple in the shadows laughed.

"But yours is no vampire bite. Something nastier." She let him go and turned her attention to Lola again. "And you, did you drink the tea I suggested for those nightmares, my dear?"

"I tried," Lola said, her voice so quiet that Death could barely hear her. He glanced at her, noting that her smile had disappeared and her shoulders had sagged.

"Nightmares?" Death said.

"Well, keep drinking it. They'll go away soon enough, I assure you. I have it on good authority from a boy who used to be haunted by the most awful visions." Lillian, even in the darkness, cut a striking figure with her orange hair and kohl-rimmed animal eyes. Death didn't think he'd ever seen someone who looked like her, in his mortal life or in his time as an agent. "What did you two chase me back here for? I know it's not the nightmares, and I bet it wasn't name-finding either."

"We need your help finding a person, a friend of Death's."

"Friend of Death's? I like the sound of that one. Proper ironic!" Lillian said, her mouth quirking into a smile. "All right, who am I looking for?"

Lola nudged Death. "Tell her. She knows everyone."

Knows everyone? Mortals were not supposed to know about agents, ever. Except maybe in extreme circumstances, like a reaper trying to kill said agent.

"It's okay," Lola said.

"You can't surprise me, boy. I've seen all kinds and they've seen me. Who are you looking for, some kind of exiled immortal, like yourself?"

Death's breath caught in his throat. "We're agents," he said finally. "His name is Fashion, or, well, that's what we called him. It was his title. His real name was Cornelius Matherson and he—he's from a long time ago. Like back when guys wore tights and had long hair or whatever. He's French."

All at once, as the words tumbled out, Death realized how stupid he sounded. There was no way that any mortal could help him, especially with a matter like this, and on top of everything else, he couldn't even give Lillian accurate information. All in all, he was once again the nerdy kid who had a hard time with his presentation because his brain and words didn't quite match up.

"Cornelius Matherson," Lillian said. "And you haven't heard from him, even though he's a very close friend?"

"Just never mind that. Listen, I need to get out of here."

Death propelled himself toward the door, burst back out onto the now-empty dance floor. Just before he could reach the building's exit, he heard Lola's voice behind him.

"Wait! Death, wait!"

He halted.

"Why are you running off? Lillian can probably find your friend. She used to be in my favorite band and she knows so many people. She's traveled the world." Lola shook her head. "Come on, what's wrong? You look really angry."

"This is stupid, and I need to leave."

Lola's face fell into a frown. "I'm trying to help you find your friend so we can figure out why that reaper thing tried to kill you."

"It was the Sumner Organization," he said, but his indignation melted into something like dull hopelessness. He'd been abandoned, forgotten, eliminated once again, and this time there was no promotion waiting on the other side.

"I- I need to go," he said.

Death stepped out into the cold night and walked and walked and walked until Lola took his hand and led him back to her apartment.

CHAPTER EIGHTEEN

Wellington woke up with the worst headache of his life. Or maybe it was a toothache; he couldn't be sure, but it was the sort of ache that made absolutely no sense in or out of context.

Images and sounds trickled into his mind then, one by one. Lola, his little punk partner-in-crime, some tall black-haired man with strange eyes and a stranger accent...a marriage proposal. Wait. A marriage proposal?

Lola. Wellington had fallen in love with Lola, hadn't he? For an afternoon, he'd been overcome with a sickening, passionate love for the scrawny young woman whom he'd trained and looked after since her unsuccessful attempt to steal his wallet.

He needed to switch to the old coffee beans. These new ones obviously caused hallucinations or something.

Wellington untangled himself from his uncomfortable position on the bed and stumbled into the bathroom. After splashing water on his face and trying to regain a more accurate memory of the previous day's events, he heard the distinct chirp of a missed call on his cell phone.

Not just a missed call, as it turned out, but also a voicemail. From Jessica.

The voicemail went something along the lines of *"Mr. Wellington, have your dear little pink-haired friend find the jar, will you? I'd like to have it within two days. You understand promptness, of course. Goodbye."*

"'Pink-haired friend?' It's as if fate itself is tangling with me," Wellington muttered, before realizing he sounded like something from a cheap vintage romance novel. He lowered his voice a few octaves and said "Hmmmph," in the manliest way possible, and then shaved his face.

Outside, rain fell in gloomy sheets and Wellington heard someone chattering into her phone that the weather was making her feel insane, insane, *insane*. Haloed above everyone's head, even Wellington's as he rushed into the rainy street to hail a taxi cab, were signs that proclaimed the answers to all such issues of depression and insanity.

Smiluset. Happinex. Grinposa. The names were garish and annoying if anyone ever really thought about them, but who took the time to think about the little pink and yellow and bright orange pills they took with breakfast? Depression, and all of her cures, was only water cooler conversation when something really abnormal happened...say, someone claimed to be happy without aid.

Wellington had never been one for medication, but he also couldn't be accused of being uncharacteristically happy. He liked to think he represented the Old Man, the man who could grit his teeth while a bullet was pried out of his leg in one of the war movies from the black and white days.

The expected opening for the coffee shop was 7AM, but Wellington locked the door when he got inside. He flung off his rain-drenched jacket and rooted around in the drawers in the back room of the shop. This mysterious jar that Jessica wanted could be anywhere.

And a chirp told him there was a new voicemail on his cellphone. *Wellington, this is Jessica. I need you to do me a favor regarding that blue-haired boy...*

CHAPTER NINETEEN

(1979)

Kelly shrugged into the room, throwing his slight body weight into his usual seat just behind Big Headed Idiot, as he'd once childishly called Carter Reed in a moment of blind anger. He pulled his books from his backpack and fanned them out across his desk top, eyeing each of them with increasing nervousness. They were reading *Jane Eyre* in class and, as much as Kelly appreciated some of the cool spooky aspects of the book (come on, there's a dead wife in the walls of the mansion or something), he didn't quite grasp the flowery aspect of the language.

Did the author really have to make every single sentence have 49 words in it? Big words, at that?

"Kelly?"

Nearly snapping his neck to look up, Kelly ripped his attention from his books and focused his eyes on the teacher. Everyone had rude names for the English teacher, because it was a cool thing to do in 11th grade, and Kelly had half-heartedly joined in. To everyone's faces, he referred to Mr. Jones as Book Balls (a term borrowed from one of the more popular boys, freckly faced Tanner) but in private, he just thought of Mr. Jones as being the husband of the eponymous Mrs. Jones from that really old song. It wasn't even derogatory, but it still amused him.

"Yes?" he asked, fully aware that every set of eyes in the room had fixed on him. He sank a bit lower in his chair when Carter Reed shot him one of those nasty smiles that only Carter Reed could shoot anyone.

"I'd like you to read for us," Mr. Jones said, and nothing in his tone hinted at punishment or cruelty. In fact, if Kelly was being honest, Mr. Jones seemed to like him. But that wasn't "cool" and it certainly wasn't of any benefit to Kelly, since his skills at reading aloud were on par with his bowling skills. "Can you start on page 250? Top of the page is fine."

He was going to have to stand up. Oh God, they were all looking at him. Oh *God*, Carter Reed was snickering and Kelly hadn't even started.

"Go on, Goldie," Carter said. "We know how much you love romance novels."

Actually, Kelly liked to sit in the back corner of the badly ventilated Room Number 1, the one with the faded graffiti on the door, and work out math problems in his head or read books about mutant frogs, diseases in South America, and other important things like that. Or science fiction novels. But Carter liked to push his buttons at every opportunity and then pretend he was just "joking."

Kelly stood up, his hands shaking a little as he found page 250. Such a nice number, 250. Half of 500, of course, and 1/4th of 1000. A good number all around. He could do a lot of things with that number, a lot of things that did *not* involve reading medieval language or, like, whatever it was.

He worked his way through a paragraph without a mistake, but his tongue betrayed him soon after. The words seemed to jump around the page and get bigger, longer, and more confusing. He heard a snicker from Carter's direction and shot him what he hoped was a menacing glare, but Carter just stared blankly back at him as if nothing had happened.

"Another page, please, Kelly," Mr. Jones said.

"I don't want to read any more."

Mr. Jones didn't look surprised. He just seemed sick of his job and probably his life, too. It was the same expression everyone over the age of 25 wore in this town. "One more page please, Kelly."

"Just pretend like you're acting in the school Christmas play again!" Carter said, loud enough for everyone else to hear. Snickers and outright laughs bubbled up from Kelly's classmates as shared memories of 6th grade's disastrous Christmas play filled their minds. "Except you won't have to worry about falling off the stage this time. That's a relief."

"Carter," Mr. Jones said, but even his voice held some trace of laughter in it. "Please continue, Kelly."

Kelly hurried his way through the page, skipping a few words because he couldn't wrap his mind or tongue around them. By the end, he slapped the book down on his desk and shot a petulant glare at his teacher.

Mr. Jones didn't notice, because he'd already launched into some speech about Jane Eyre's low self-esteem. Jane Eyre wouldn't know a *thing* about low self-esteem until she lived around Carter Reed for a few days.

When class was finally over, Kelly pushed his books back into his bag and tried to make a run for the door, but Carter stood beside his desk like a sentinel of all things smug and superior. "You don't mind that I brought up the Christmas thing, right? That can't still bother you. Come on, man, you have to admit that was FUNNY. Remember? I mean, even Mrs. Parsons was laughing."

Fat Jake was out sick for the day thanks to dental surgery, so Kelly couldn't even take solace in a friend. Instead, he had to stare up at the biggest jerk in town. Or, at least, the biggest jerk in Kelly's admittedly melodramatic opinion.

"It wasn't funny."

"You landed on your head. That's funny. And I was thinking about it the other day, actually, because Siri's mom taped it and we were watching the tape."

Kelly felt his face flame with embarrassment. "One of these days something will happen to you. You—you'll be so embarrassed that you'll…you won't talk to anyone for days. And everyone will talk about it all the time and you'll wish you could *die*," he said, raising his voice a bit more at the end than he'd intended to.

"But you won't be able to die. You'll have to just hate yourself and wish you could forget."

Carter shook his head. "Yeah, okay, sure. I'll take your word for it, Goldie. You *are* the expert, after all."

By this point, Carter's buddy (a slimy kid that Kelly avoided whenever possible) sidled up to Carter and gave him a manly punch in the arm. "Hey, whoa. Kelly's parents wanted a girl so bad they gave him a girl name. Fitting, since he's a fag."

The hearty laugh shared by the two of them was enough to convince Kelly that, in that moment of extreme embarrassment and anger, he would develop some sort of superpower and disintegrate both of them with his mind.

But nope, no such luck.

Carter and the slimy guy left with Siri and Jena, and Kelly realized that Mr. Jones had caught the whole exchange between his students. How kind of him to speak up.

In some fuzzy, just-before-Technicolor part of Kelly's brain, he knew that someday all of them would be sorry. He envisioned Carter getting injured in a world war and having to live in a ditch somewhere, smoking cheap cigarettes and begging for money because he lost an arm. And Mr. Jones...Mr. Jones...well, Mr. Jones would suffer too. But Kelly mostly just saw Mr. Jones getting old and bitter.

Which was kinda sad.

All of it was kinda sad.

CHAPTER TWENTY

Lola hadn't seen her roommate in so long that she picked up a baseball bat when she heard someone open the front door. She'd been awake for an hour and had consumed enough cheap coffee to put anyone on edge.

"Cara," she said, dropping the baseball bat back to its usual place in the corner. It hadn't left that spot since last Halloween, when a neighbor from the floor below had decided to play an elaborate prank on them that involved underwear, a jump rope, and a roll of two-sided tape. The prank hadn't worked out, but the baseball bat had become rather famous in their building.

"You're not going to believe what happened to me last night," Cara said, throwing her bags and jacket down and then gawping at the couch, where Death was quietly snoring and, occasionally, twitching his left foot. "What is that?"

"That is Kelly Gold." Lola tried to think of what might sound acceptable to a 27-year-old who wore Prada and worked 45 hours a week on the 32nd floor of an office building. "I met him in college."

"Wait, you went to college?"

"For a little while."

Cara blinked. "You never told me that. What classes did you take?"

Before Lola could come up with anything that even half made sense, though, Cara had crossed the room and leaned over Death.

"He's awfully scrawny. He's not homeless, is he? There's this homeless woman in our cafeteria and no one will get rid of her. It's not like they can't tell she's homeless. I mean, you walk close enough and you can smell the homeless on her."

"No, he's not homeless. He's a rock star."

Cara straightened, shooting Lola one of her trademark eyebrow raises. "Rock star."

"Yeah, he's pretty famous in the underground trip-hop world," Lola said, easing seamlessly into the lying mode she used for almost every job ever. "He goes by 'Death.' Honestly, I can't even believe he agreed to crash here last night, considering all of the little girls and boys that were trying to take him home. He's got such a rabid following."

"I don't even know what trip-hop is."

Lola tried to keep the triumphant smile from her face. "Oh, it's...not mainstream."

Shaking her head, Cara walked into the kitchen and tore through the cabinets. "Do we even have any food left in this place?"

"Not much. Work has been kinda slow," Lola admitted. "I think there's a tomato in the crisper. And a bag of chips in the cabinet with the broken knob. They're kinda old, though. I was saving them."

Every extra penny Lola earned went into the big purple jar behind the couch, but she didn't like to tempt fate by talking about that. Anyone who had seen Bjork's *Dancer in the Dark* movie knew better than to chance it.

Cara, with her great job, fabulous social life, enviably beautiful black skin, and inability to cook anything from scratch, spent most of her time living some magical life in clubs and restaurants that Lola had never been to. That meant the rent was always paid two months in advance, but Lola was responsible for keeping food in the house.

That also meant there wasn't food in the house. Ever.

"I'm going to have to buy some food," Cara said, in a barely audible mutter. "We're gonna have company tonight. I mean, I'd love to have you here when they visit." She cast a glance in Death's direction again. "Do you think…?"

"Yeah, he'll be fine. You said something earlier about having a crazy night last night?"

Cara shook her head. "Well, Brandon—do you remember Brandon? He's the one with the weird left eye—anyway, Brandon called me and said he was walking his dog and this guy in a costume falls on his head. Brandon fell under the weight of it, got all bruised up pretty bad, and a bunch of people saw this happen, and then the guy that fell on him just disappeared."

Costume. Fell.

Wait.

"So at first they thought it was a suicide case, but who knows? Maybe some kind of prank? Now Brandon won't leave his house and he keeps talking all of this nonsense about reapers or something. He's taking it real hard. And then my friend Georgia said she knows someone who saw a guy in a reaper costume running around last night too, and the two of us were just leaving St. Mingels, that new club, and some guy in a pink suit was yelling at everyone that 'storms are coming.' He had these weird little pamphlet things. It was creepy." Cara shuddered. "Just such a weird night."

"Uh, Cara...do me a favor and stay away from those people, okay? Just in case."

"The costume guys?"

Lola's cell phone chirped on the counter, in the obnoxious manner that told her that Wellington was looking for her. "Please tell me you're done trying to propose to me," she said, as soon as she'd flipped her phone open.

"Lola! Lola, my pet, I can't apologize enough for my behavior yesterday. I've no idea what came over me. I could never love you that way, good Lord. You're a child and besides that, you're way too skinny."

Wow.

"I have a job for you, top priority. Big pay. I need you to find something. Ah, hold on a moment. YOU CAN WAIT RIGHT THERE AND I WILL HELP YOU WHEN I'VE FINISHED THIS PHONE CALL." Wellington cleared his throat. "Excuse me, Lola. These idiots don't seem to understand patience.

But listen, I need you to find a jar. I will text you the information from my client."

"I'll do my best," Lola said at last.

"Lovely, pet. Now excuse me, I must help these monsters before they drive me to homicide."

Lola snapped her phone shut and sighed, looking at her roommate. "I have to leave."

"What this time?"

Lola shrugged. "I don't ask. The sooner I can get out of Boston, the better." Lola walked to the couch and gently poked at Death. He started, his eyes fluttering at her for a few seconds. He'd been so down the night before that he hadn't said a single word to her on the walk back to the apartment or after they'd gotten there. He'd gone to sleep with a rather despondent look on his face. "We have to go out."

"We?"

"Yeah, you need to get up." She grabbed hold of his shoulder as he sat up and leaned forward so she could whisper in his ear, "My roommate is here. Do not disagree with anything I tell her, all right?" She kissed the side of his head and smiled at him as she pulled away. "Death, this is Cara. I already told her about how you're a rock star and I told her all about your concert last night." Her eyes traveled down to the sleep shirt and shorts she'd given him to wear for the night. "And you need to get dressed in something other than my pajamas. I left some clothes in the bathroom for you."

Death put his glasses on and bounced up, approached Cara with a friendly smile and an extended hand. "It's really, really nice to meet you finally, Cara."

"Nice to meet you, too," Cara said, peering back at him with more than a little surprise. Her gaze fixed on Lola as soon as Death had installed himself in the bathroom to change his clothes. "He's kinda cute."

"Yeah."

"He's pretty nice, too. For a rock star."

Lola rolled her eyes and perched on the edge of the couch, praying Death wouldn't take an hour in the bathroom.

"I have a good feeling about that one. He has a good vibe," Cara said, and then disappeared into her room.

A few seconds later, Lola's phone chirped with a text.

It wasn't from Wellington.

CHAPTER
TWENTY-ONE

Oh no. Oh NO.

It wasn't something Death had really had to think about in a long time, but as he peered into the steam-drenched bathroom mirror, he realized that he'd gone back to aging. Sure, those were still only fine lines around his eyes, but they wouldn't stay that way. The cut on his neck from the reaper shone angry and scar-like. It wasn't going to heal up and disappear, not without his aura.

And his hair was a limp mess, with blonde roots threatening to break through his skull and take over the beautiful blue shade he'd maintained for years. In the past, he might have spent fifteen minutes drying his hair and carefully spiking it until it resembled a blue shark fin, but this time he couldn't bring himself to bother.

"They gave you three extra decades, Kelly," he muttered to his reflection and then grimaced. "And they're gonna take that away again, if they can."

He pulled on the jeans that Lola had lent him, and then the T-shirt and purple hoodie. The arms on the hoodie were a bit too long, but he'd just have to make do until he could get to a store and buy himself some clothes. And considering the events of the last few days, he'd have to adjust quickly or his life expectancy was going to shrink fast.

"All right, let's get going," Lola said the instant he opened the bathroom door. She looked irritatingly fresh-faced and energetic, especially in comparison to Death. His arms burned and his legs ached from all that bouncing the night before. And Lola's hair was a cheerful candy pink color, courtesy of a bobbed wig. Admittedly, it made her skin glow and her eyes seem even wider than ever, but that just added to his general irritation. Why couldn't she at least look a little hung-over or tired?

"You'll be back for my dinner, right?" Cara said, looking at Death. "I think everyone would really enjoy meeting you. They're a pretty fun group."

"We'll do our best. Come on, Death. The rain slowed down and we should make a run for it while we can." Lola grabbed Death's arm and dragged him toward the door. "Bye, Cara!"

Death did his best not to trip and fall down any of the zillion flights of stairs in Lola's apartment building, but doing so meant Lola powered ahead of him until she disappeared from sight entirely. When Death finally caught up to Lola, he found her pacing in the lobby.

"I need to talk to you about something," she said. They stepped out into the cold rain together and Lola reached over, pushing the hood on Death's sweatshirt up. "I'm guessing you haven't had to worry about getting sick for a long time, huh?"

"You want to talk to me about my immune system?"

"No, I just realized you're probably about as immune to our germs as a newborn baby, though, so you'll need to be careful," Lola said, shoving her hands into her pockets. They dodged a pack of umbrella-wielding girls wearing vintage dresses and then fell into step together again. "Cara was talking about reapers this morning. And I guess the one we threw off that roof landed on her friend Brandon."

"Whoa, is he okay?"

"Brandon? Yeah, I guess. He's scared, hiding out in his apartment, but this is also the kind of guy who hid in his apartment for two weeks one time because a rumor went around that people were going to get infected by the Mad Zebra Disease or something. He'll be okay."

Death shook his head. "I just don't understand. Reapers are supposed to remain invisible to mortals at all times."

"Well, I guess after it landed on Brandon, it disappeared. People saw it happen."

"I knew Sumner was evil, but I had no idea it was this bad. They've done other things, crazy things. There was this one agent, I can't remember his name, but the Sumner Organization found him and they took him into their weird underground lab or something and they sewed wings onto him. Like, giant feather wings. And they hung him up for everyone to see, because of the Wings Division."

"Wings Division?"

"They're the, uh, they're kinda our police force. They work *with* the agents, but not for them." Death started walking again, trying to calm the twitching fear that echoed through his body. "Those people, the Sumner people? They're dangerous."

"When did that happen, the guy getting wings sewed on him?"

"Sometime. A long time ago. I heard about it from Malcolm. He used to tell us to avoid the Sumner Organization, but I was smart and I got some talismans and stuff." Death shivered. "I wish I had them now."

"Well, there's something I need to tell you." Lola moved a little closer to him as they walked, and lowered her voice. "I got a small lead on your friend."

"What?" he halted, staring at her. "What do you mean? Did Lillian find something? Tell me!"

"It's nothing solid, but it's a lead." Lola raised one hand and rested it on Death's shoulder. "We'll find him. I'm gonna need your help to figure it out, though."

Death's first instinct was to charge ahead and find his friend, but he hesitated. "Why are you in a hurry to find him?"

Lola's hand fell away from his shoulder. "I thought it might make up for making you lose your job. At least if you find your friend, you might be able to figure out what's going on."

Cold rain splattered against Death's head, drumming louder and heavier through the hoodie fabric and drenching him with oppressive sadness, but he barely noticed. Something about Lola's face seemed open and vulnerable, and her eyes burned with the sweetness he'd only seen on the night he first met her.

"Thanks," he said, or he thought he said it, but he couldn't be sure because he recklessly leaned into her and stole a kiss. The pause that followed didn't last long, because they met halfway the second time. His free hand snaked around her waist and settled flat against her back, and her free hand pushed his hood back and knotted itself in his hair.

Now, Death had certainly been kissed before, and by Siri James of all people. Siri James, the most popular girl in White Meadow High, class of '78! Or maybe the most popular girl *ever* at White Meadow High.

But Siri had nothing on Lola.

Death felt a bit like someone had reimagined him, but without the reimagining station. And by the time he broke the kiss, he felt like he was going to pass out.

"Wow," he whispered. "That was good. That was really good."

Lola rolled her eyes. "It was all right," she said, but a smile quirked the side of her face. "And you have pink lipstick all over your mouth now." She pulled his hood back up, patted him on the head and walked away, leaving him to scrub antagonistically at his mouth with his sleeve, all the while chasing after her.

"The Sumner people are potentially really dangerous, Lola," Death said, falling into step with her again. "I mean, I don't think they'll hurt you since you're not an agent, but I can't be sure. And if they're going so far as to openly send reapers out into the world, they could be capable of anything."

"We'll be fine."

"I can't promise we'll be fine."

"You don't have to promise me anything. We're going to look for your friend, and then tonight we'll have dinner with Cara at the apartment. That's it," Lola said, ducking her head as another wave of cold rain flew at them.

Death fell into step with Lola, his eyes traveling skyward to take in the gray clouds. Just as he opened his mouth to say something to Lola, a sound filled the air, the same horrible screeching noise that Death had heard when he'd first been exiled to Boston. He clapped his hands over his ears, but the sound resonated behind his eyes and through his skin and bones.

He felt, somewhere in the middle of the anguish, that Lola had gripped him by the shoulders and shaken him, but the noise prevented him from doing anything but squeezing his eyes closed and praying for it to stop.

All at once, the noise faded and Death's knees almost gave away.

"What's happening to you?" Lola said. "Do you need me to call someone?"

He shook his head weakly. "No, no. No. It's nothing."

"That didn't look like nothing."

"It's a warning, I think. If I remember right, it's called the Rattle, and it's a, uh, a warning to agents when they're in danger."

"But you're not an agent anymore, so why would they look out for you?"

A shiver ran through Death. "I don't mean they're looking out for me. I mean they're telling me I don't have long left."

CHAPTER TWENTY-TWO

Even though the cold rain had only gotten heavier and more oppressive, Death felt intensely thankful when he emerged from the underground world of the Boston public transportation system. The train had been packed so tightly that Death had had to stand by one of the doors, clinging with both hands to one of the poles while four other bodies crowded around him and clung to the same pole. Even closing your eyes could only do so much to relieve claustrophobia in a situation like that, especially when one of the people crowding you had a cough that sounded phlegmy and incredibly contagious.

"You don't like trains much, huh?" Lola asked, moving closer to him and reaching for one of his hands. He tensed, but didn't pull his hand away. At least it would be harder for them to get separated this way, come crowd or sheets of murderous icy rain. "You'll get used to it eventually. You just have to pretend there's no one around you."

Death shook his head. "I'm from New Hampshire. You don't have to pretend there, because there *isn't* anyone around you there." The truth was, the screeching of the trains was at least as much to blame for his anxiety as the people were, but he wasn't sure if now was a good time for a detailed retelling of the sounds and sights of the car accident that had taken his life.

Especially when his ears still rang from the Rattle and his neck burned from the reapers' claws.

Lola snorted. "New Hampshire? Wow."

"What?"

"You seem too weird to be from somewhere small and forgettable like New Hampshire."

Despite the impending danger and slew of discomforts on Death's mind, he couldn't help the warm glow of pride that crept over his face. "I wasn't always like this."

"What, weird?"

"Unforgettable." They sidestepped a group of antagonistic-looking businessmen. "I used to be pretty forgettable."

"Even with a name like Kelly? I find that hard to believe."

"Let's just say, when I started 7th grade, my name was on the girls' sheet for sports sign-ups. And I'd lived in the same town since I started school."

Lola laughed and for some reason, Death didn't feel the usual rush of embarrassment. And after a few seconds he even found himself joining in, laughing until it hurt.

"I'm sorry, but that's just funny," Lola said. "Too bad they didn't make that mistake a couple years later. The locker room situation would have been a whole new world for you."

The laughter finally gave way to coughing and even after Death recovered, an occasional bubble of laughter fought to overtake him. "Yeah, true. Too bad I didn't have you around back then to help me see the potential upsides."

"Nah, I wasn't even born yet. Not for a couple decades." Lola cleared her throat. "Wow. Well, maybe you hit on my mom."

"Yeah, maybe."

"Maybe."

"She probably wouldn't have been my type, though. My type back then was the women on the covers of my favorite science fiction novels. You know. The fierce ones holding spears in one hand."

"Bikinis made from fur?"

"You got it."

"Oh God, that's so gross," Lola said, and laughed. "Here, follow me. We need to cross here." She led him in a mad dash across a street, barely dodging several drivers in their little rolling murder machines.

"You really know this city," Death said as they resumed their normal pace on the other side of the street.

"When you spend as much time wandering it as I do, you learn where things are."

Death didn't place her at much over 20 years old, tops. And she'd mentioned that her parents had died, so how long had she lived in this city alone?

"Do you have some, like, rich aunt or something?" he asked.

"What do you mean?"

"Well, I mean, how did you survive when you were younger? Did you have some rich old aunt who took you in and made you look after her fifteen cats in exchange for a small fortune?"

Lola laughed, but not a happy laugh like before. "No. I had to look after myself as much as possible. And I lived in the theater behind Wellington's coffee shop." Her steps took on a mechanical sense, feet falling too hard on the ground.

"Our theater?" Death asked. "Errr…I mean…the one where we…?"

"Yeah."

"You lived there?"

"For almost three years, yeah. No one noticed because I was very good at hiding. During the day I would walk around the city and steal money or make friends with people who would give me stuff for free."

"Oh. I guess I'm just seeing you as Oliver Twist right now, complete with tar on your face. Did you sell newspapers to survive?" Death asked, glancing sidelong at her.

"There was a guy at this one café, and he was probably 17. I told him I was 16 and I'd stop in to buy a coffee and he'd give me a muffin or a bagel, as long as his boss wasn't there. Sometimes he'd give me a couple donuts. And he'd tell me about how he always wanted to meet a nice girl and have a family. You'd be surprised how much you can learn about people when you have nothing."

Death thought back to his first meeting with Lola. Her face had been full of innocent curiosity and childlike admiration, as if he was the most exciting boy she'd ever met.

"You learn how to survive. And if you can use your looks or brains, you do," Lola said. She nudged him. "Don't get all quiet. You would do the same thing."

"No," he said, but then he thought about the stolen banana, how he'd tricked Bill into making him an ID and passport, how he'd slipped money from a number of people after first arriving in Boston. "Well, okay. Yeah, I guess."

"Anyone with any will to survive would. After a while, you learn your city and all of its customers. You know who to charm, who to steal from and who to avoid." She nodded to a cluster of hipsters under an assortment of checkered umbrellas. "Those guys? Easy to steal from. You just need to distract them and then you can take anything you want."

Death barely glanced at them. "And me? What was I?"

A long silence followed. "You're a charmer," she said at last.

"Because I'm so naïve?" he demanded, a wave of bitterness joining the churning nerves in his belly.

"No. Because people with more natural kindness are easier to win over with kindness." She shrugged.

Death let out a breath he hadn't known he was holding. "I bet Wellington is proud to have you as his little agent."

"Wellington? Wellington taught me who to avoid. See, I tried to pick his pocket one evening when I was really desperate. And he caught me." She pointed ahead. "See that place? I need to stop there for a minute."

The building in question was a bookstore called Mystery Ship's World Traveled Books, which had embarrassing window displays featuring headless dummies sitting in rocking chairs surrounded by stacks of books. Maybe this was supposed to convey that literacy was a safe and intelligent pastime, but Death thought it was a bit creepy. And that was saying something.

The inside of the shop smelled of dust, water-stained books, and lavender. Death sniffed at the air as he entered and tried to determine where the lavender radiated from. His internal question was answered relatively quickly by a pretty blonde girl who approached him with a smile and an armload of books.

"Can I help you?" she asked in a flat voice that rang of old money and years lost in the pages of books.

"Uh, actually, nah. She's the one who knows why we're here." He motioned to Lola, who was peering around the store as if she was waiting for someone wearing a furry spider suit to leap out at her. "Nice bookstore, though. Well, except the dummies in the window. They're kinda weird."

"Where's the owner?" Lola asked.

The blonde offered another smile. "I'm the owner. If you're looking for Nick, he's off for the day. Was there something I could help you with?"

Lola's surprise shone through, even if she hid it away quickly. "You're the owner?"

"I've been in Paris for the last two months, but yes, I'm the owner. Nick mostly works for me while I'm overseas or at events."

Death found himself pondering what would happen if the blonde girl took offense to Lola thinking she wasn't the owner and the two of them got in a fight and he had no choice but to stand by and watch them wrestle or bite each other's arms or even necks or something and then realized he should probably stop thinking such things just in case his mouth betrayed him and he said something dumb. "You guys should fight," he said. "I mean, shouldn't. Shouldn't fight." He pointed at a sign above a bookshelf in the back of the store. "Fantasy! I'm going to go look at fantasy books. It's been a couple decades. Errr."

Idiot.

As it turned out, Death didn't recognize the names of almost any of the authors. He traced a fingertip along the worn spines, cataloguing names and attempting to match them back to the fuzzy database in his memory. In school, he'd devoured fantasy and science fiction books almost as often as he devoured science books. And why not? They had cool battle scenes and dragons and castles and swords and creepy bad guys. And usually their covers featured hot buxom girls in less clothing than the girls around White Meadow High wore.

"Ah, Lovecraft," he whispered, moving to the horror section. Lovecraft, he knew. Lovecraft, he understood! That was horror and danger and fear and nightmare fodder right there.

Death pulled a collection of Lovecraft's stories down from the shelf and flipped through it, his eyes flicking over the words. He'd spent most of his 15th summer in the White Meadow Public Library, upstairs in the stifling reading room, curled up by the window with various Lovecraft stories. For a little while he'd dreamed in black and white, in monsters and mysteries.

After carefully replacing the book, Death searched out another very familiar title.

A Wrinkle in Time.

Back in his day, Death had taken *A Wrinkle in Time* quite seriously, relating to Meg's attic existence so viscerally that he had briefly considered asking his parents to let him move to the attic. It was, upon investigating, not such a good idea, mostly on account of a lot of spiders and the creaky boards that sounded as if they might cave in if anything heavier than a cat walked over them.

He flipped through the heavily loved copy of *A Wrinkle in Time* that this bookstore had to offer, noting that someone had written his name on the inside cover. Thomas Grop. Poor Thomas! What an unfortunate last name. Not as unfortunate as being named Kelly when you were a boy, though. "Why'd you give this book up, Thomas?" he muttered. "Bet it wasn't because you died in a car accident and your parents didn't want to keep all of your stuff."

"You ready to go?"

Death jumped at Lola's voice, turning to find her standing just behind him. "Yeah, I uh, want to buy something, though."

Lola's eyes fell to the book he had clutched in both hands. "You're buying a book?"

"Yeah, why?"

"I didn't know you liked to read."

"You don't know a lot of things about me."

Lola smirked and shrugged one shoulder. "Give me time and I bet that won't be true."

Death shook his head and pushed past her, carrying his book to the front counter. He dug around in his pocket until he located the bit of money that he had left and handed it over to the pretty blonde girl.

She inspected the book and then raised her eyes to Death. "Good choice. I like it when I give a customer just the right book. It's like playing cupid, but with literature."

"You don't want to be Mr. Right, believe me," Death said, before he could stop himself. "Or, a cupid, I mean. You don't want to be one of those."

The bell over the door chimed as Lola left the shop.

The pretty blonde girl just laughed, though, and pushed Death's money and book back at him. "Books are the breeding grounds of nightmares and daydreams. This one's on me. Enjoy."

"Thank you."

"No problem. I have a feeling you'll need it."

Death tucked the book into his hoodie pocket and ran to catch up with Lola.

CHAPTER TWENTY-THREE

The monthly donut and discussion meeting had never been dotted with so many empty seats. Mr. Right took his usual spot toward the front of the long conference table, only three chairs down from Malcolm's makeshift podium. Malcolm rustled papers with gusto, but Mr. Right knew for a fact that the papers were blank. Malcolm just liked to appear official.

"Everyone here?" Malcolm asked as the stragglers took their seats. Mr. Right glanced around without turning his head, noting that Grace and Balance were absent. "Listen, I only ordered two dozen donuts this time, so go easy on them. I mean, I think there'll be enough, but some people don't know when to stop." He laughed and rustled the papers some more, before clearing his throat and pinching his mouth into a straight line.

Jessica strolled into the room, clapping the door shut behind her. She angled her body into a chair with a certain cool finesse that only a very mischievous cat could manage. She turned her head to Malcolm. "I apologize for being late, but I had some projects that needed finishing. Please continue."

Malcolm scratched at his face, as if to call attention to his latest mustache attempt. If Death had been sitting in his usual spot, at the other end of the table, he'd surely be chomping on a donut and snickering behind his gloves about Malcolm and his string of adventures in unsuccessful facial hair.

Mr. Right pushed Death from his mind and withdrew a pen from inside his jacket, ready to take notes. Even if Malcolm had turned the meetings into fluff and meaningless chatter, a man was still obligated to learn what he could about his agency.

"So, by now you've probably met a few of our interns," Malcolm said. "I like them. I have to say, I really like them. They're new recruits and they're on fire for their job." He and Jessica exchanged a glance and then he rustled his papers even more aggressively than before. "We want that. We need people who're serious about their work and serious about the agency. I've seen a lot of interesting things since becoming manager, and I'd just like to take this moment to, uh, to congratulate those of you who have gone the extra mile."

Mr. Right heard whispering from the other end of the table, but didn't turn his head to see who it was.

"I think giving credit where it's due is good, so I'm going to just say this right now. Mr. Right, you've proven your devotion to your job, and to the agency. We all offer you a round of applause and our greatest uhhh..." Malcolm paused. "Our greatest appreciation."

Light applause sounded from around the table.

"Anyway, on to more important, uh, on to other things. It's been brought to my attention that someone has been leaving their—"

"Where's Grace?"

Mr. Right turned his head, matching the meek voice to the equally meek face of Gentleness. Mr. Right looked back at Malcolm, as surprised as anyone that Gentleness had spoken up during a meeting.

"Uh, what?" Malcolm asked.

"Grace. Where's Grace? He always sits with me."

Malcolm cleared his throat and tapped a pen against his podium. "I'm sorry, but that's...we're talking about something else right now. Someone has been leaving their assignments on the table beside the shredder. You all know that your assignments must be shredded when you've completed them. That's on almost every poster in the building. If we need more posters, I can make more of them, but I think it's pretty obvious by now that it's a priority kind of thing. And really, it's not too much to ask. A few minutes of your time, that's what I'm asking, a few minutes to walk to the shredder and shred your assignments when you're finished with them."

"Grace always sits here," Gentleness said, speaking up enough that her voice actually carried over top of Malcolm's. "He's my meeting buddy."

"That's nice that you have a meeting buddy."

"He's not here. Where is he? Is he sick?"

Malcolm pushed his hands into his pockets and leaned back on his heels. "I'm not really a police force over his immune system, Gentleness. Would you mind if I finished with what I was saying, though? If you're really feeling uncomfortable, you can ask, uh, you can ask Dan there to be your meeting buddy. I bet he'd be happy to hold your hand. Anyway, as I was saying—"

"Did he get exiled?" Gentleness demanded, standing up. Mr. Right, and everyone with him, turned their attention to the petite Gentleness as she shook and shivered and managed to raise one index finger to point at Malcolm. "You know, don't you? Where is he?"

"He's gone. That's all I'm allowed to say, Greta. Now, you can either sit back down and respect the privacy of your coworker, or you can disrupt this meeting and force me to call for security."

"It's just like what you did to Death," Gentleness said. "You got rid of him and told everyone he quit. Maybe Death would quit, since he was so young, but Grace wouldn't quit. Grace has been here longer than you!" She took a shuddering breath. "Someone told me Death killed a reaper. I hope he comes back here and—and—I hope he comes back and..."

Malcolm started to say something, but Jessica stood up and walked around the length of the table in a few long-legged, elegant strides. She took hold of Gentleness's arm and said, "Come on, Greta. You're very upset right now. Let's take a walk."

Gentleness's face crumpled, and she walked by Jessica's side as silently and obediently as a dog. They left the meeting room together and disappeared from sight down a hallway.

"Okay, to reiterate, we're all going to start doing better about this shredding thing, right?" Malcolm asked, a few seconds later.

No one asked questions for the rest of the meeting.

CHAPTER TWENTY-FOUR

Death couldn't help feeling relieved when he and Lola arrived back at her apartment, at least in part because of the drenching rain outside and the peculiar city smell that accompanied it. He worked his way slowly to the top of the zillion flights of stairs and sloshed into Lola's apartment. He was mid-kick in removing his boots when the clanging, familiar sound of dinner and conversation met his ears.

Oh, wait.

The dinner party.

Much to Death's horror, Lola's tiny apartment had been turned into a lounge area for the ten or twelve guests that leaned, sat and slouched around it, most of them clutching wine glasses or plates stacked high with the sort of edibles you buy off an expensive platter. And as if that wasn't bad enough, the first guest that Death's gaze settled on was none other than the crazy German art-house musician freak from Bill's apartment building.

Death ducked his head, but it was too late.

"Ah, bluebird! Little bluebird." The musician moved in a bit closer to Death, slipping a skinny arm around him without invitation and giving him the kind of hug that only three too many glasses of wine can produce. "How strange that fate has brought us together again."

"Alexander, you know him?" Cara asked, picking her way over lazy guests and casting a somewhat anxious look between Death and the German musician guy, whose name seemed to be Alexander.

"Know him? Not by name, of course, but by essence. Yes, I think, by essence. He fluttered through my apartment building not long ago and inspired me to write a new song." Alexander took a generous swill of his red wine. "Two songs, to be precise, but then I combined them into one. It may be my inspiration for the whole of my next album."

Cara's shoulders lowered with a relieved puff of breath and she smiled. "Well, this is my roommate's boyfriend. He's a trip-hop musician."

Alexander's brown eyes lit with intense interest. "Trip-hop?"

Now Cara's face was positively smug. "Oh yes. Trip-hop. Lola's into a lot of indie and underground music. And Death, here? Well, he's a trip-hop rock star."

Death felt his stomach plummet.

Trip-hop.

What was trip-hop?

"I'm sure Death can tell you all about it," Cara said, and Death realized she probably had no idea what trip-hop was, either. Judging by the effortless, understated makeup she'd applied to her face, the tiny stud earrings and the simple twist of her hair, she wouldn't be the type to read punk rock magazines and go to raves. "Right, Death?" She shot him a look that begged him not to expose her lack of music knowledge.

"Where's Lola?" Death said, trying to keep his voice from sounding too constricted. "She's really good with the technical stuff."

"Technical?" Alexander said.

"Well, you know. The labels. I don't really like to label myself with anything. I…" Death tried to think of what kinds of things he'd heard rock stars say on MTV back in the day. He decided to channel someone cool like David Bowie. "I try to remain true to my inner vision, no matter where that might lead me."

Alexander clicked his tongue. "Is that so? Fascinating."

Death gave a self-satisfied smile.

"Well, there hasn't been enough trip-hop in the last ten years, not at all! I think I did all sorts of awful things to trip-hop last decade." Alexander took another swill of wine, draining his glass. "I say *I think* because I can't remember and because I'm 34 now, and that's almost senior compared to most of the children in music these days. You talk about being born in the 70s and just watch their eyes glaze over."

"Try being born in the 60s," Death said before he could stop himself. "Well, hypothetically. That would be worse."

"And when were *you* born, little bluebird?"

The correct answer throbbed at Death's mind, trying to spill out, but he forced himself to attempt the math. Thankfully, Lola returned just then, dressed in dry clothes, and she sidled up next to him. "Lola! Lola, we were just telling Alexander here about how you told everyone I'm a rip-top musician."

"Trip-hop."

"Yeah. You really have to stop telling people that. You know I like to experiment as much as possible when it comes to genre and self-expression." Oooh, that sounded good. Very good! Very convincing too. "And you told them I'm your boyfriend."

Lola shot him a look, and he wasn't sure if she was threatening to kill him or if that was just her resting face.

And maybe it was the fact that Death currently felt like a drowned rat, or the fact that he'd been abandoned in Boston among a bunch of German art-house freaks and small-time thieves, but he decided that now was a better time than most to lean up and press a kiss to Lola's lips. When the first attempt didn't get him slapped or punched, he dared repeat the action, lingering a bit this time.

Surprisingly, Lola didn't respond strongly. She just stared back at him for a long few seconds and then looked away as if she hadn't noticed he existed at all.

"Well, anyway, why don't you go change?" Cara said, shooting an anxious look at the floor around Death, which had soaked up a bit of his excess accumulated rainwater. "Looks like Lola's all warm and comfy in dry clothes. Really, Death, it's okay for you to go change. You must be so uncomfortable. I mean, this rain is just oppressive."

"It's punishment," Alexander said, gleefully. "It must be. It just never stops raining and everyone's going to either get depressed or wash away."

One of the other art-house freaks launched into the conversation then, angling her small body toward Alexander. "Everyone's so depressed."

"So depressed!"

"I bet it's just crazy, if you looked at how many people are on those pills," the girl said, her words heavy and clumsy with alcohol. "My mom said that she's never met anyone, anyone, ANYONE not on the pills. Not one anyone. Not even one. I'm the only one, because they might take everything away from me, but they can *not* take my vodka!"

Death winced, remembering his own tequila experience. "All right, I think I'll go change," he said, just before realizing that he had no idea what he'd wear. Lola had taken his clothes after he'd been so sick from the alcohol, and he hadn't seen them since.

"Your clothes are in the bathroom," Lola said, without looking at him.

Death shuffled and sloshed and shivered his way to the bathroom, happy to peel off the wet clothes as soon as he'd shut the bathroom door. He felt as if the rain had soaked clear through to his insides, had settled merrily in his lungs and taken permanent residence in his bones. Even after he'd wrapped himself in the familiar warmth of his black work pants and well-worn black button-down, he found no relief from the rain.

On the other side of the bathroom door, laughter and conversation floated about, airy and cheerful.

Death stood just inside the bathroom, hand on the doorknob, listening. Those were people who knew how to mingle, how to chat with strangers and wear nice clothes effortlessly and, even if they were crazy and obsessed with art and bad movies made in basements, they could drift their way through life easily.

He'd never had that kind of experience with party settings.

Back when Death was still Kelly, he'd gotten a mysterious invitation for a Christmas party from a girl he didn't normally talk to at school. Jena. He'd found it in his locker and had weighed every single possibility for its existence, never mind the consequences of any action he might take in relation to it. After much internal debate, he'd asked his best friend, Fat Jake, if he had an invitation, too. Fat Jake hadn't, but they both had to agree that it wasn't so surprising. After all, no one really invited Fat Jake to anything except church dinners.

So, Kelly had asked his mom to drive him to Jena's house and had arrived at the door with a Yankee Swap gift in hand, as requested on the invitation. Jena had answered the door in her pajamas and stared at him in open-mouthed horror and confusion and asked him why he was at her house at 8PM, why was he at her house at all, what was he doing, how had he gotten there, what was going on.

He'd been so mortified that he had considered trudging the two miles home through the snow and back roads, if only it meant he could turn his back on her and leave her sight as soon as possible, but Jena's mom had come to the door and taken pity on him. She'd offered to let him come inside until his mom got home so he could call her and ask her to come get him.

In the end, he'd sat in the kitchen at Jena's house and endured her mom's sympathetic half-hearted questions about his school experience, parents, and older sister, all the while praying for his mom to hurry and pick him up so he could go die of embarrassment in his bedroom or somewhere private.

Word had gotten around about it at school, like a bad game of telephone, ending in the rumor that Kelly had a huge crush on Jena and had showed up at her house with gifts and flowers in hand. Somehow he knew Jena hadn't started the rumors, because she'd seemed genuinely mortified for anyone at school to know she'd done so much as speak to Kelly Gold.

One of the good things about being an agent was that your memories tended to trickle slowly downward into jars and cups and bowls in your mind, until they were nothing more than little puddles that went undisturbed if you wanted them to. If you left them alone, they didn't sneak attack you or jump out of shadows. And maybe, over the centuries that could stretch in front of some of the agents, all mortal memories would eventually become lost entirely.

But mortality had a way of reminding you of things you'd like to forget.

Death heard someone tap on the door, and took a deep breath. The old days were over. He wasn't Kelly Gold anymore; he was Death, the agent of nightmares, mischief-maker. He could bounce his way around a few drunk art-house freaks and, soon enough, Lola would help him find Fashion and he'd figure out what was going on, get his job back and return to his life.

Easy.

With that thought as comfort, he raised his chin and emerged from the bathroom.

CHAPTER TWENTY-FIVE

Two minutes ticked by and Death already wished he'd just stayed in the bathroom. Or maybe he should have climbed out of the bathroom window and taken his chances on scuttling along the side of the building until he found a handy fire escape.

Alexander had immediately insisted that Death sit next to him on the uncomfortable couch that had been Death's bed for the last couple nights, and the NO ONE CAN TAKE MY VODKA girl had installed herself on Death's other side. She used every opportunity possible to lean over Death toward Alexander, laughing at his words like they were expensive jokes and calling him a genius repeatedly, in a mostly English accent.

"Don't you want a drink?" Alexander asked suddenly, pausing mid-sentence in the middle of a story about an ill-fated concert he'd attended in the 90s.

"Uh, I don't need one."

Alexander frowned. "Of course you do. Here, have mine, and I'll get another."

"Alexander, you are SO funny!" the girl burst out. "What a genius idea. Genius!" She laughed and prodded at Death's knee. "Isn't he a genius?"

"I don't need a drink," Death said, but found a half-empty glass of wine in his hand anyway. He stared into it for a few seconds, contemplating life, death and hangovers. No use repeating his incident with the tequila.

"You don't drink?" Alexander asked, and the vodka girl gasped.

"Not since a few days ago." Death turned his head and looked at the vodka girl, who licked her lips and pointed one finger at Alexander's cast-off wineglass. "You want this?" he asked her, and she let out another gasp.

"You don't mind? Really?" she asked, but she'd already snatched it away from him and drained it. "Alexander, you're a genius. A genius."

Cara approached them just then, holding out a tray of pink and yellow cupcakes. "Anyone want one? These came from that new bakery down the street," she said.

"Darling, you tempt me with wine and now cupcakes? You know I'll say yes," Alexander said, reaching for one.

"Ah yes, genius!" Vodka Girl said, reaching for one too. "Which bakery is it now? I only…I only like…well, I only like to buy things from independent shops. You know. Not the ones that *they* are trying to get us to eat. Eat from. Eat at."

With a nervous smile, Cara said, "Temper. The shop's called Temper. Brandon told me about them."

Vodka Girl's eyes widened. "Brandon! Brandon, oh poor Brandon, poor, poor thing, poor baby. How is he doing?"

"He still hasn't left home."

"Did you go see him? I wanted to go see him, but you know how it is at work lately. Haven't had a minute to do anything, not a minute. But poor, poor, poor, poor, poor Brandon. He's already so afraid all the time, never mind when something falls on him from out of the sky. What was it? That fell on him, I mean. Poor, poor Brandon."

"It was some guy in a reaper costume."

"Just what was a man doing on a roof? Or falling off it, I guess. What was a man doing falling off a roof, in a costume? Unless he's on one of those shows where they watch you do things and play it on television."

Cara shook her head. "I wish I knew. Might have been an attempted suicide, but you know Brandon. He always thinks the worst."

Death avoided Cara's eyes, suddenly afraid she would figure out he was connected to the incident.

"Someone fell on your friend?" Alexander asked. "In a reaper costume? How do you know it was a costume? Ahhh! Ah, what if it was not a costume, but a true angel of death?"

"Genius!" Vodka Girl said, but in a miserable tone.

"Nah, I don't like that. Weird stuff is one thing, but I don't need any more nightmares than I already have," Cara said.

Alexander jostled around a bit, sitting up straighter. "More nightmares! I was just talking to your friend,

Lola, a few moments ago, and to Tom, as well. So many nightmares!"

"Me, too," said Vodka Girl. "But no pills. No."

"You know what I think? I think someone's pulling the strings down here, making us depressed and afraid and then feeding us pink and yellow and green pills. Here, look." Alexander fished into the pocket of his black jacket and withdrew a tiny bottle. He plucked the top from it and emptied the contents into one of his slender, pale hands. "There you are. One for every color."

"You have sooooo many of them," Vodka Girl said, in a raspy undertone.

Cara shrugged. "I dunno, I think it's the rain."

"But for the nightmares? Come now, Cara, my darling. There is an agent of nightmares, I say, and she is wily and powerful and she is slowly transforming our world into a playground of apocalyptic visions. It begins in our heads and carries to our hands."

She?

"Why would the agent of nightmares be a girl?" Death asked.

At that moment, it seemed everyone in the room had turned their attention to Death and was staring at him. He felt a blush creep up his neck and into his face, and it took all of his willpower to speak again.

"Maybe he's a guy with a girl name," he said finally. "Or with a boy's name. But maybe he's a guy."

Alexander considered this. "But a woman, Death. A woman's touch might be braver and more frightening, in the realm of nightmares."

"Well, I think the guy they have now is doing just fine," Death muttered.

"So you agree with me! We are all puppets in the grand carpet of time and heaven and history and the world."

"Genius, yes," Vodka Girl said, helping herself to a half-empty bottle of wine on the tiny coffee table. "Puppets, Alexander. You're brilliant. Oh. Am I a puppet?"

"We're all puppets. Me, you, Cara, and Death here. But what a job that would be! Creating nightmares. I would make the most awful storylines," Alexander said with a sigh.

Death shook his head. "No, the best kinds of nightmares aren't storylines. They need to be vague and have personal meaning. If there's a storyline attached, it's easier forgotten upon waking."

"Ah! Talk on, little bluebird. What makes the best sort of nightmare?"

Even though Cara looked rather horrified, and Vodka Girl had taken to leaning on Death's shoulder while slurping directly from her wine bottle, he continued.

"The most frightening dreams are based in reality. They turn a waking sense of reality into something that feels wrong, but without an obvious explanation. An otherwise unremarkable dream gets scary fast if the sun is tinged with red and no one else seems to notice. Or if your lover's eyes are the wrong color but everything else about him or her is the same. Or if your bedroom has an extra door in it."

Cara shuddered. "Oh, that's awful. Just thinking of an extra door in my room is creeping me out. How do you know all of this stuff?"

Death had forgotten about the possibility of that question coming up. "My mother studied dreams," he said, which wasn't a lie.

"Psychologist?" Cara asked, still balancing the cupcake tray.

"No. She just—she just wanted to know why I had so many nightmares as a kid." And that wasn't a lie, either.

Alexander pushed himself up from the couch, announcing in what equated to all-caps that he needed to use the bathroom, and then he was gone. Vodka Girl leaned back into the couch cushions and made out with her wine bottle.

The silence that followed was mercifully broken by Cara's little sigh. "Well, maybe you should talk to Lola, then. Poor girl's got some of the worst nightmares I've ever seen. Wakes up crying and the whole thing. I don't know how she's been lately, because I haven't been here much, but she must have tried a million different natural remedies and weird mind exercises to get a grip on it."

Death's eyes sought Lola around the tiny apartment, finally spotting her on the other side of the room, talking to some short girl.

"What are the dreams about?" he asked, but Cara had already walked away to offer cupcakes to other guests.

CHAPTER TWENTY-SIX

Lola woke with a start, just before her body could crash into a million bloody shards of bone and gristle at the bottom of whatever unexpected cliff she'd dreamed of. She struggled to calm her breathing and shuddered, shivered with the accelerated heart rate and burning memories. Why now? She'd been free of nightmares for several nights, free of dreams entirely.

Once her pulse had slowed a bit, Lola pushed herself up on shaking legs and glanced around the dark room. Death was sprawled across the couch as usual, sound asleep. A few empty wine glasses and stray plates remained here and there, left behind by Cara's guests. Lola forced her mind to the mundane so she could shake the dream.

When had the guests left?

Late, late. Very late.

That Alexander fellow had been so sloshed that he'd jokingly proposed to the half-asleep girl beside him on the couch, at which time they'd kissed and then progressed to actions that had caused Cara and Lola and Death to encourage them to call a cab and head elsewhere.

A flash of the falling sensation hit Lola again, combined with a powerful imprinted image of her father's face, just before he had gone away for the last time.

No!

Then what had happened? After the guests left. What had happened?

Well, Cara had said something about needing to be up early in the morning because the next day was Thursday and that was a busy day in the office. And Lola had wandered about, throwing away some of the trash that littered the apartment before finally saying her goodnights to Death.

Another flash of the dream washed over her, slicing into her mind. This time it was her mother's face, as clear as if she stood just in front of Lola.

No. No, no.

Lola ran a hand back through her hair, tugging on it to force her mind fully into the present. She needed light. If Death weren't asleep on the couch, she'd have turned on every light in the room, but it was still 5:30AM and waking him up after only 3 hours of sleep would be just cruel. Especially since he'd all but passed out the instant the guests were gone.

Finally, Lola fished her small, ancient, and incredibly beaten-up laptop out from its computer bag. She sat facing Death so the light from the computer screen wouldn't shine in his direction, and opened the lid a bit too aggressively. Blue light flooded into her eyes and chased away the after-images of the dream.

There, good.

Lola put "Paris" into a search engine and pulled up a few photographs of the city. She'd seen most of them many times before, in similar sleepless situations, but they always soothed her nerves anyway. And at the rate she was saving, she might be taking her own photographs of Paris in less than a year.

A noise from the couch sent a jolt through Lola. She peered over the top of her computer screen at the couch, finding that Death had rolled onto his side and draped one leg over the side of the couch.

Hmmm.

Lola typed "Kelly Gold" into a search engine and found advertisements for gold buyers and other things that were decidedly not the man currently sleeping on her couch. She put quotations around his name, and added the words "car accident," before searching again. The first link said something about White Meadow High, and sure enough, Kelly Gold's name appeared on the page preview. Lola clicked the link.

The photo that came up *was* Death. Well, sort of.

Mousy blond hair fell on either side of his face, ending just above his chin, and his eyes were framed by wire-rimmed glasses. His half-smile was hesitant and echoed with the peculiar sadness she'd glimpsed in his eyes many times. Even the tilt of his head betrayed a cautious fear, as if he knew he would be judged by anyone who glimpsed the photograph.

Under the picture was a short paragraph:

Kelly Calvin Gold, 1962-1988, class of '80. Kelly will be remembered as a good-natured young man who loved science and science fiction novels. Kelly was taken from us in a tragic car accident in the summer of 1988. His favorite book was A Wrinkle in Time*.*

"...there's very little difference in the size of the tiniest microbe and the greatest galaxy."*

-Anna Galliano, White Meadow Public Library Director

Library Director? His memorial had been written by a librarian? Lola looked up from the computer again, at her sleeping guest. What kind of life did someone have to have for his town's librarian to write his memorial?

Lola clicked BACK and returned to her search. Another link provided a second picture of Kelly Gold, this time with a beautiful girl who was credited as KIRSTEN GOLD, SISTER. Above his picture were half a dozen other pictures, all of them of a handsome, dark-haired young man named Joshua. Lola copied and pasted Joshua's name into a search engine and found countless hits about a "terrible tragedy," "horrific loss" and someone named Mayor Richardson feeling devastated over the loss of his stepson, Joshua.

The top hit in the search was a transcription of an article from 1988. Kelly's name was mentioned near the bottom as a victim in the accident. One of the articles referred to him as Killian Gold and another as Kelly Golde.

Near the end of the first page of search results was a link for a message board. Lola clicked on it and found a post, dated 2 years ago, from someone named Olive:

*it was so nice to see everyone at the reunion. I thought this
would be a nice way for us to keep in contact. Thanks, Sarah, for
helping me set this up!! I still can't believe it's been so long since
graduation. was hoping to see Carter there. Anyone know where
Carter is these days?*

Under that was another post, from a month after
Olive's post, from someone named Charlie:

*Not that surprising if you think about it. He probably still
thinks that Kelly's ghost is going to come get him. Lol. If anyone's
ever going to haunt us itll be Kelly Gold.*

So, he hadn't been lying. Somehow, even though it
made no sense, he'd been telling the truth about being
a teenager in the 70s and having a silly name and dying
in a car accident.

And if all of that was true, so was the nightmare
business. And she'd been responsible for him losing his
job, losing the only thing that halfway made up for the
unfairness of his very short, and apparently rather sad,
life.

A shifting noise and quiet groan from the couch
made Lola close the lid on her laptop, a hint of guilt
nagging at her. Just as she put her laptop on the floor,
Death sat up and stretched with another quiet groan.

"What time is it?" he whispered.

"It's—it's probably, like, 5:45. It's early. Are you
okay?" Lola stood up, walking toward him in the dark
and perching on the end of the couch. "Did something
wake you up?"

"Yeah, I just felt like…no. No, I dunno. Why are
you up?" Death asked.

"I don't know."

The last person she wanted to talk about nightmares with was someone who had spent the last few decades creating them. Lola shifted on the couch and her hand brushed a book. She glanced down, curling her fingers around the book and lifting it closer to her face in the darkness.

A Wrinkle in Time.

"Oh," he said, putting his glasses on. "That's what I got at the bookstore today, or yesterday, whenever it was now." He cleared his throat. "I think I still have three dollars to my name, though, because she didn't charge me for it. So that's all right." He blinked at her in the dim lighting, looking at the book as if she was holding it hostage.

Lola handed it back to him. "Only three dollars, huh? What were you planning? To wait tables or something?"

"I don't think I'd be very good at that."

"No, I don't think so, either." Lola sighed quietly and then stood up. "But you know, I think you'd be pretty good at other ways of acquiring money. Come on." She held her hand out to him. "Let's go shopping."

CHAPTER TWENTY-SEVEN

Death couldn't remember the last time he'd seen a dawn, and certainly not the last time he'd witnessed it from anywhere besides a sleepy perch somewhere with a pillow just behind his head. He'd never been a morning person, despite all of the celebrations of dawn that fantasy novels attempted to create.

But this dawn wasn't so bad, mostly because he and Lola greeted it with some cheap pastries and gigantic cups of cheap coffee in hand.

"Do they just give you money?" Lola asked suddenly, as if they'd been talking for hours already.

"Who?"

"Them. The people you worked for."

Death took another bite of the flaky, gooey bad-calorieness of his strawberry scone and considered the question. "We don't need it most of the time, because there's not really any currency up there. When we're earth-side, we take money with us. Or I do. When I first got to Boston, I had the amount I normally carry."

"Oh? You spend it on something?"

Images of the thief incident flashed through his mind. "Nah."

"Did someone steal it from you?" Lola asked then, a hint of teasing in her voice. "Let me guess…someone asked you for money, and when you reached for your wallet, they snatched it and ran away." She moved a bit closer, elbowing him. "Well? What was their sob story?"

Death had never liked to think of himself as naïve, but if he were honest, he'd been tricked and humiliated more than a few times in his life. While some of the incidents stood out as crushing, like Lola stealing his papers or that mysterious invitation to Jena's "Christmas party," plenty of others crowded for secondary places in his hall of embarrassing memories.

"I think he had a broken leg," Death muttered.

Lola cleared her throat, but it did little to shield her laughter. "But he beat a path with that wallet, right?"

"Whatever. Hell was built under Boston."

This time Lola laughed without restraint, her eyes full of a colorful mirth he hadn't seen before. "That's only a good joke because of how accurate it is."

"No, it's true. Hell used to be under Rome, but it was moved sometime in the 1800s. Fashion used to talk about it with Mandy all the time. I don't remember when they moved it, exactly, but it was this huge project and everyone decided it was just going to stay under Boston for a few centuries because moving it again would be too expensive and time consuming."

Lola stopped laughing and they walked in silence for a few seconds. "Well. That explains a lot," she said finally. "And they exile you here."

Death nodded, glancing upward. The sun had almost claimed the sky, but rain clouds hung heavy on the horizon, marching closer and closer at a slow but steady pace. "When I get back to work, I'll have to tell Mandy all about it." He'd tell her from the safety of HQ and the hallways and offices and messy desks and donut-and-discussion meetings and Reimagining Stations.

He'd be a returning crusader, a warrior who had braved the brutal world and returned to tell the story.

Lola wandered away from him to toss her empty coffee cup into a trash receptacle. "Yeah, I'm sure it'll be nice to get back to that." She returned to his side and smiled at him again, but this time without the laughter behind her eyes. "You're pretty good at losing things. How are you at acquiring them?"

"What, you mean like stealing?"

"Exactly."

He shrugged, finished his scone. "I'm not too bad at it," he said. "I mean, I've done it a few times. To pretty great success. But you know. I'm all right."

"Great success, huh? Well, I'm glad to hear that, because we're going to acquire some money and then we're going to buy you some clothes so you can stop wearing mine," Lola said, linking arms with him. "At least, until you go back to wherever you came from." She shot him a look, her gaze traveling downward and then back up to his face. "Not that you seem to mind wearing mine all that much."

"They're comfortable!" he blurted, but it sounded a bit too much like the time his mother had asked him why he was still reading *Jane Eyre* even though his school project was done, and he yelled that he wanted to see if Mr. Rochester's dead wife would kill someone.

"Yeah, yeah, sure. I would believe you, but I happen to know that my skinny jeans aren't that comfortable." She bumped hips with him. "I do think those pants look better on you than on me, though."

Death straightened at that, a little of his swagger returning.

"But that might be because I don't have enough hips for them." Lola snickered and pushed away from him, pointing ahead. "All right, you ready for our first rush of customers?"

Now, as stealing and all of that kind of thing went, Death had always gone with the easy method. He targeted money left in the open, on store countertops or park benches. Something about that felt less like stealing and more like collecting.

Lola's methods were a bit different.

"See this guy?" she asked, motioning at a skinny guy in a superhero T-shirt and baggy jeans. Morning commuters passed him on either side, some of them bumping into him in their rush to get to work on time. "What makes him a good target?"

"Bad taste in clothes?"

"While that's a very legitimate guess, it's not the answer I was looking for. Guess again."

Death eyed the guy again, noting only that he was loudly conversing with someone on his cell phone, something about having been up for three hours. "I can't see past the jeans, honestly."

"Well, that's good, because the jeans are what gives him away. He carries his wallet in his back pocket." Lola's hand collided with Death's butt, lingering there for a bit longer than needed. She stepped in front of him, grinning. "First things first, you identify your target. Distraction is useful but not necessary. Then you move in and move out."

"You're leaving out a few necessary steps," Death muttered.

"What? What part was confusing?"

"Well, we could talk about how you actually get the wallet without him noticing, for starters."

Lola took one of Death's hands and slapped his wallet into it. "Distraction is useful but not necessary," she said again.

Death's hand flew to his back pocket, unable to stop his mouth from falling open. "How did you…"

"You're pretty easy to distract." Lola winked at him and turned away. "Follow me and watch closely."

Death shoved his wallet back in place and patted his pockets a few more times just in case the wallet decided to spontaneously teleport back into Lola's hand. "Just so you know, I'm not grabbing that guy's butt."

"Oh, that's not necessary."

Lola reached into her small brown messenger bag and withdrew something that looked like a few pages from a magazine, folded into fourths. She approached their target from behind, leaning in at the last moment so that she brushed up against him. Death wasn't entirely sure if she'd succeeded in snatching his wallet but he ran to catch up with her.

"Well?" he whispered, falling into step with her as they moved a safe distance away from the target.

"Well, what?"

He glanced over his shoulder to find the man still talking on his cell phone and making wild gestures. "Did you get it?"

"Get what, his wallet?"

Death let out a huff of air. "Yes, his wallet! Did you get it?"

Lola bumped into him, leaning her head close. "Actually, you know what?" she whispered. "You better check your back pocket, because I think you might have it."

Sure enough, his wallet had been replaced with the stolen one. "All right, how did you do that? I didn't even see you take anything from him."

"You weren't watching close enough. And I'm a professional." Lola shrugged. "Here's your wallet back."

Death snatched his wallet back from her, a warm blush creeping up his neck and into his face. "Teach me how you do it."

"It's not that hard. You just slip the wallet out and replace it with something else. Most of the time, I replace it with paper of some kind, because it's flexible. And if it's folded up a few times, it's just sturdy enough that it'll slide right into place. Here, I'll show you what I mean." She grabbed hold of his arm, stopping him. "Just stand still for a minute."

With another loud sigh, Death crossed his arms over his chest. "Okay."

Lola retrieved more folded magazine pages from her bag and waved them in front of Death's face. "First I take your wallet," she said, snaking her arm around him. This time he felt the wallet slide out of his pocket. "Now I replace it with this," she said, very slowly and deliberately sliding the magazine pages into his pocket. "But, of course, I do it quickly. And with as little personal contact as possible. One little bump is usually plenty, and then an apology, and keep moving." She shrugged and handed his wallet back, along with the folded paper. "Cities are great because people bump into each other all the time and don't think twice about it."

"I don't think I'm fast enough for that."

"Only one way to find out. Here, test on me." She turned her back on him, then glanced over her shoulder with a teasing smile. "Go on, Kelly Gold. Steal from me."

Oh.

Well, that was probably the most flirtatious thing an attractive female had ever said to him.

Death approached her slowly, one hesitant hand reaching in the general direction of her butt. No, not butt. Pocket. Yes, just the pocket. This had nothing to do with her butt or her long legs or the smirk on her face or—no, none of that. Just the wallet. Just the wallet.

Just the wallet.

"You know, you're supposed to be stealing my wallet, not just groping for a long time and standing there like a creeper," Lola said.

Another blush crawled up Death's face. "I am," he muttered, slipping his fingers into her back pocket and attempting to free her of the wallet. "Stealing the wallet, I mean. Not being a creeper."

"Stop acting so shy about it. Be confident."

"This is kinda new to me."

"What is? Girls, or stealing things?"

"Stealing things!"

Lola smiled. "I can almost assure you that the wallets you steal for the rest of the day will come from old bald guys, so the distraction factor will be absent. Concentrate, Kelly."

"Stop calling me that."

"Then show me what you can do."

With a surprising measure of coordination, he slid the wallet out of her pocket and replaced it with the magazine pages. "There," he said, stepping away from her. "Now what?"

"Now I choose a new target; after we acquire whatever money they might have to offer, we go shopping." Lola adjusted the strap of her bag and her eyes roamed him up and down. "Maybe some new shoes?"

"Okay, whatever. Choose the target."

They walked together for a few minutes before Lola leaned in and whispered, "Right there. The guy with the blue polo shirt. His wallet's in his right back pocket. I'll meet you two blocks down." With that, she strolled away from him and Death found himself alone among a lot of morning-eyed strangers.

A prickly, nervous sensation danced its way up Death's insides and into his throat, squeezing at his breath. He approached the target slowly, speeding up only at the last instant. Wallet out, paper in, wallet out, paper in, wallet out, paper in.

Death slid the wallet free and replaced it with the magazine pages, muttering apologies and continuing on his way. His legs shook as hard as they had after the tequila, but he walked and walked until he caught up with Lola and they fell into step together.

A few streets down, they ducked into a T station and took a look through their stolen prizes.

"We've got about three hundred bucks here," Lola said at last. "Your guy carried a lot of cash on him." She laid a hand on his shoulder. "Not bad for a first try, Kelly Gold. Let's go shopping."

"Stop calling me that."

"Kelly, Kelly, Kelly. I like Kelly. It fits you better than 'Death,' too."

Lola walked away and Death followed, muttering all the while. Overhead, the skies opened and poured more oppressive rain on the streets of Boston, and Death was almost certain the horizon had taken on a dark purple tint.

CHAPTER TWENTY-EIGHT

Wellington stormed into Olivia's Vintage Treasures just moments after it opened for the day and proceeded to pound his fist on the countertop in what he hoped was a very commanding manner.

"Get her out here!"

The girl behind the desk stared back at him with her mouth hanging open.

"Olivia. Get Olivia out here," he said, enunciating each word carefully. "Who are you, exactly?"

"I'm the new assistant."

"Well, then, assist both of us by finding your boss!" Wellington said, pounding his fist again for emphasis. A small elephant figurine fell off the counter and landed on the floor with a spectacular crash. "I can assure you that won't be the last thing I break in this shop if she's not out here at the count of ten."

The assistant disappeared into the back room with a lot of spluttering and frantic mouth-gawping. Only seconds later, the comfortably round form of Olivia emerged, with the assistant at her heels. Both of them seemed to have been infected by the mouth-gawping syndrome.

"Mr. Wellington, I thought you agreed never to visit my shop."

"I thought you agreed to answer your phone. Have you even checked your messages today? I must have called you a hundred times!"

"I've been very busy, Mr. Wellington."

"With what?" Wellington demanded, pounding his fist into the countertop again. "With watching me? I know you've had people following me for months, like that fool with the ugly green hat."

Olivia's eyes widened to the point that they looked as if they might pop out of her head. "I-I have a right to know…to know what's…"

"Whatever, that's beside the point. The point is, *Olivia*, you can't just choose when to be professional. You don't choose that. Professionalism should be your priority at all times, especially in a business like this." He pounded his fist a bit harder this time.

Too hard. Pain shot clear from his wrist up to his elbow.

Wellington gritted his teeth against the pain and forced himself to keep eye contact with Olivia. "We've worked together many times over the last two years. I'd hate to see all of that thrown away because you're too busy sitting at your mirror applying another layer of lipstick."

"That was very offensive," the assistant said. "Don't you think so? That was very offensive."

"Of course it was offensive!" Olivia said, her eyes narrowing to slits. "What do you want?"

Wellington shook his head, glancing between the two women. They looked a bit like fairytale characters, painted eggs or something. Perhaps explaining himself would be a waste of time.

"I came to Boston with nothing," he said. "I've built myself from the ground up, as a man should, and I've made contact with a lot of very important people. My connections are famously extensive. I've thought of us as quite efficient work partners, considering your talent for finding old things that no one wants, and my talent for finding people to want them. But don't think for a minute that I can't go somewhere else if I need to."

For some reason, this didn't have the frightening effect he intended. In fact, Olivia just blinked back at him. "All right."

"I could go to Captain Asher," he said, lowering his voice just a bit to make it more threatening.

"You? Go to Asher?" Olivia said, laughing. "You're afraid of him. He told me how you won't even set foot in Salem anymore, for fear of him."

"This job will pay very, very well."

The antagonistic expression on her face slipped. "Well, what is it?"

If there was one thing that Wellington and Olivia had in common, it was a particular love for money.

Wellington opened his messenger bag and dug out his notes, as well as the papers he'd printed from the computer at the coffee shop. "We're looking for a jar. Here's a drawing of it. My associate and I have been researching the history of it, but can't seem to find any clues about its location." He pointed at another drawing. "Have you seen it?"

Olivia stared at it for a long time. "It doesn't look familiar. Who owned it?"

"I don't know. My client is very insistent on locating it immediately, though."

"How immediately?"

Jessica's words echoed through his head. "By tomorrow."

"Tomorrow!" Olivia said, pushing the drawing away. "I think before we continue this conversation, we should talk about just what 'pay very, very well' means."

Wellington pushed the drawing back. "It means four digits, if you help me find it by tomorrow morning."

Olivia pushed the drawing toward him again. "What kind of digit does that four start with?"

"Higher than 5." Wellington pushed the drawing back.

"And by higher than 5, do you mean 6?"

Wellington attempted to push the drawing back before realizing it was still where he'd last left it. "Perhaps. Perhaps I mean 7. What do you say?"

"By perhaps you mean 7, you mean 6."

"Do you want it or not?"

"He's very offensive," the assistant said, startling Wellington. He'd almost forgotten she was there. "And we do have a lot of boxes to go through this evening for that guy with the nice hair."

Olivia sighed. "Shut up," she said, squeezing her eyes closed. She rubbed at her temples. "Alright," she said at last. "I'll help you find it. But even if I don't find it, you owe me something in the triple digits that starts with at least a 4. Got it?"

"Fine, fine."

Olivia gathered up the papers Wellington had brought and disappeared into the back room, leaving her scowling assistant at the desk.

"I'll be back in a few hours," he said. "Tell your boss to call me immediately if she finds out any helpful information. My associate is ready to travel the moment we know anything. She's been doing her own research, since yesterday." He smirked. "She's very professional."

CHAPTER
TWENTY-NINE

Lola picked up a bottle of blue hair dye. "No, if you're going to use anything, this is what you'd need," she said, as Death prodded and poked at a shelf full of goth makeup and neon hair dyes. "This one."

Death peered at it, his mouth twitching to one side of his face, and then snatched the bottle away. "It's too dark. It's almost black!"

"Yeah, but it won't look like that on your hair." Lola pinched a few strands of his hair between her fingers, leaning close to get a better look at the roots. "You're very blonde."

"Yeah."

"No. I mean *very* blonde."

He pulled away from her grip and squinted at the bottle. "I can't read any of this. And it's not even because the print is small, it's...I don't think this is English. Or maybe a human language at all."

"Those are the ingredients, so no, it's not a human language."

Death let out an unhappy huff and continued holding the bottle about an inch from his glasses, leaving Lola to roll her eyes and wander away. They'd barely spent five seconds in Lola's favorite little alternative shop, Zephyr's, before Death had zeroed in on the hair dyes and become absolutely obsessed with the idea that he could "fix" his hair.

Lola perused the new vinyl selection in the back corner of the store, flipping through the titles and pausing when she spotted a special edition, remastered Juicy Bed album. Lillian's witchy, pretty face adorned the cover, smattered over with dirt and glitter. Lola felt a subtle tug of guilt and continued glancing through the records.

"What about this one?" Death asked, approaching her with several bottles of hair dye. "It's got a skull and crossbones on it."

"That doesn't make it better."

"But is it stronger? Since it has the…"

"No, I don't think there's any correlation between the picture on the front and the strength of the dye. Just get the one I told you about. Then we can actually leave and continue with our mission to find you some more clothes."

Death's face fell a little. "Okay," he said, shoulders slumping. He returned the bottles of dye to their shelves and retrieved the one Lola had chosen for him. "So you know how to use this?" he asked as they approached the counter.

"It can't be too difficult."

The girl behind the desk took one long look at Death as she rang up the dye. "Do I know you from something?" she asked. Lola had been fairly unsure before this point if the girl even knew how to talk, because she'd never said anything in the two years Lola had been frequenting the store. "You have a really cool look."

Death smiled, stood up a bit taller and tapped his fingertips together. "Thank you."

"I feel like I've seen you somewhere."

"Maybe you have, Holly."

The girl dropped the bottle of dye. "How do you know my name?"

"Your name tag," Death said, pointing at the brightly colored lanyard the girl wore around her neck.

"It says H."

"I'm a good guesser."

A long pause followed, and then the girl's eyes darted around the room, back to Death, at Lola, back to Death. "Where have I seen you? Are you in a band or something?"

"I dunno," Death said, placing some of the stolen money on the countertop. "Uh. So, do you think this color will match what I have now?"

The girl muttered a "yes" and accepted the money, bagged the hair dye and handed it over. She turned away from them and tapped at her cell phone as if they'd never existed.

Outside, Death shivered and tugged the hood of his hoodie over his head. "Where to next?" he asked, unzipping Lola's bag and putting his hair dye inside for safekeeping, right next to the pants they'd bought for him earlier.

"Why did that girl know you?"

He shrugged in response, avoiding her gaze, but something like a smile quirked at the corner of his mouth.

"Have you been in her nightmares?"

"Yeah, once or twice. Her boyfriend planted some pretty scary stuff in her head at one point, and she really ran with it in her dreams. She collected a lot of nightmare energy." He turned his face up toward the rain and then back to Lola. "I didn't recognize her at first."

"But she remembered you."

He swayed back and forth on his heels a couple times. "I guess."

"Why? Did you scare her or something?" Lola demanded, her throat constricting.

"No!" He walked away from her, leaving her to follow or give up entirely on this strange peace mission she'd chosen for the day.

After a too-long internal debate, Lola caught up with him. "What happened, then? Why did she remember you?"

"Some people just do."

"Why, though?"

His jaw tightened. "Because some people remember when they stop feeling afraid."

"*Stop* feeling afraid?"

He shrugged. "I said a few things to her in a dream, and it helped her out."

"Well…" Lola said, raising her chin. "It seems a little counterintuitive for the agent of nightmares to make people feel better about their dreams. But hey, right here. This is the place where you should look for clothes."

Just before they stepped into the shop, Death glanced at the sky again.

"You expecting something?" Lola asked.

He twitched. "What?"

"You keep looking at the sky like you think it's going to change color."

"Yeah, well, it could." He stalked away from her, toward the boots along the back wall of the shop. The first ones he snatched up were unmistakably women's boots, but he went about trying them on without hesitation. "What do you think?" he asked finally, parading back and forth in front of her.

"Those are women's shoes."

"They fit."

"Do you like them?"

"They feel good."

"The heel's better."

"Yeah, feels good."

"Can you run in them?"

He stopped pacing, a slow, unearthly smirk crossing his face. "Should I test them?"

"I guess it depends on what exactly that would entail," she said. She'd left stores with all sorts of items that didn't belong to her, but she'd never done so with a partner in tow. Working with a companion was risky.

Death cast one last glance at the beaten-up boots he'd worn into the store and then saluted Lola. "All right. Test time."

He tore out of the store so fast that Lola actually had to put some effort into chasing him down. When she did catch up to him, however, he was out of breath and battling laughter.

"I guess I can run in them."

"I guess."

"Hopefully, these weren't a mistake."

Lola eyed them. "They seem like a good choice. And I think the heel on these is a bit more sensible, too."

"Well, that's a plus. You know, since your thievery is rubbing off on me."

"We should probably put a little more distance between us and the shop, though, before we celebrate your conversion to the life of a thief," Lola said. "And I'll have to remember not to go back there for a while. As big as this city is, word can get around pretty fast when a guy with blue hair steals a pair of second-hand women's boots in a dramatic manner."

"Dramatic? Was I dramatic?"

"Everything you do is a little dramatic," she said, which only brought a smile of pleasure to his face.

"Mr. Right said something like that to me. He said I was the prince of showing off." Death sighed. "Of course, that was just before he betrayed me and got me exiled."

Their conversation came to an abrupt stop after that.

CHAPTER THIRTY

If Mr. Right were being honest, the last thing he wanted to do was sit down with Malcolm for a meeting over a meal. There was the issue of fraternizing, of course, but for once, his conflict ran deeper than unprofessionalism.

"Oh, here, here," Malcolm said, leading the way to a restaurant with glass doors and gold accents. "This place is incredible. Walking Turtle. I was here last week with Jessica and we were blown away. They're getting better these days, you know? They're getting a lot better." Malcolm waved to the hostess. "Hey, babe. Dinner for two."

The girl shot him a murderous look, but Malcolm didn't seem to notice.

"Have you ever been here?" Malcolm asked as they were led through the restaurant. "You don't get out nearly enough, do you? I mean, it's nice that you're so dedicated, but it's not really something you'll want to tell the grandkids, right?" Malcolm laughed. "Not that you'll have grandkids. But you know what I mean. Hey, look! Same table as last time!"

Malcolm slid into his chair and motioned for Mr. Right to sit down.

"I'll get your waitress," the hostess said, placing menus in front of them.

"Aw, you're not gonna help us? That's too bad. But I guess they need you at the door to draw people in, huh?" Malcolm winked at her and laughed to himself, opening his menu. "Gotta get 'em in here. Like fish. You've gotta reel 'em in like fish."

The girl walked away.

"Pretty nice, huh?" Malcolm said, spreading his arms wide. "The girl's not bad either, ha."

Mr. Right opened his menu and stared at it for a long time before he even recognized any of the words. His mind buzzed with worries and concerns, all of them fighting to push their way to his tongue.

"You're so quiet, you know that? I can't figure out if I like or hate that about you," Malcolm said and chuckled. "We'll just say I love it. Hey, they have a different soup of the day than last time. That's too bad."

"The sky," Mr. Right said. "It's purple."

"Oh, you like it? I think it gives a nice vibe." Malcolm glanced up from his menu and let out a long suffering sigh. "There's still a few glitches, though. I've been on the phone with Jonah every hour on the hour since three days ago. I think we're gonna have to replace him."

"Glitches?"

"Well, yeah. Uh. A bunch of the kids noticed the color changing."

In all of Mr. Right's years with the agency, he'd only heard of four children noticing the change in the color of the sky. A good deal of them inquired about the color, sure. And there was that incident a few thousand years ago, where the color change took place too quickly, and a rumor had spread like wildfire that the sky was falling.

But this was a new and troublesome development.

"What have you done about it?" Mr. Right asked, which earned him a surprised look from Malcolm.

"Wow. Well, that's new."

"I mean no disrespect. But I am curious how you intend to handle this. Your father…"

"Yeah, I get that. My father was great with this stuff, but he also ate something he'd been allergic to for years. No one's great at everything, Right." Malcolm stuck his nose back into his menu and grunted. "Jessica and I wanted to talk with you about a few things."

Their waitress approached, pitcher of water and glasses in hand. She cheerfully inquired if they were ready to order and Malcolm shot her a petulant smile.

"I'm gonna get the chicken Parmesan. Wow, you're even prettier than the other girl. They must only hire models here," he mumbled.

"And you, sir?" the waitress asked Mr. Right.

"I'll take the same."

Malcolm watched as their waitress walked away and then sighed, flicking his eyes back to Mr. Right. "Jessica and I have talked at length about our new policies.

She felt that, considering your long standing with us, perhaps you should be in on them." He removed his silverware from the confines of its napkin.

"But you don't agree."

"No, no, I think that's fine. I mean, you *have* been with us for a long time. But that's beside the point." Malcolm twirled a knife between his fingers. It might have been menacing if it hadn't been a butter knife. "I just need to know you're on the same page as us. We don't have time right now for anyone who wants to dance to their own, uhh…to their own music. Song."

A chill ran through Mr. Right. "I'll need to know what that means before I decide how I feel about it," he said, and Malcolm laughed.

"See, that's the problem with you. You never talk and then, when you do, it's stuff like that. You're an oldie, Mr. Right, but that doesn't mean that you know the best way to operate a business. Now I like you, but right now, I have to make decisions for the agency above all else. You can understand that, right? In some reptile-brain way?"

Mr. Right stared evenly back at Malcolm.

"In a week, we're sending reapers into 20 major cities around the world, uncloaked," Malcolm said, a smile lifting half of his face into the gummy, disturbing expression he usually saved for people like Death or Fashion or Mandy.

A long time ago, Death had talked Mr. Right into joining him in a crowded movie theater in London for a late-night showing of some stupid "action adventure" movie. While Death had fidgeted, snickered, and cheered throughout the movie, Mr. Right had felt mostly confused, dizzy, and uncomfortable. The plot had revolved around a government turning on its citizens and unleashing destructive weapons on innocent civilians.

Images of panic and disaster swam behind Mr. Right's eyes. "You understand that…"

"What?"

"There will be a level of alarm we haven't seen in a very long time." Mr. Right shook his head. "It could leave a devastating thumbprint on the history of the world."

"Aren't *we* the history of the world? It's hard for you to understand all of this, of course, because you're just an agent, but we have a responsibility to steer the events of the future. There's this overwhelming sort of apathy among mortals. Do you know what happens when you leave mortals to their apathy?" Malcolm paused. "Eventually, we have no power over them and they all blow each other up anyway."

Mr. Right glanced around the restaurant, his eyes landing on couples and businesspeople and a group of young women in short dresses. "While I agree that apathy is a problem, and while I've become rather frustrated with the state of love and marriage and romance these days, I can't agree with you on the solution to such a problem. If we reveal ourselves to the mortals, we'll destroy everything they've managed to create in the last few centuries."

"What, talking robots and booster shots? Come on, Right. They haven't created anything of any worth."

Malcolm shrugged. "Except maybe that peanut butter and chocolate spread stuff." He laughed to himself, laughed so hard that he pressed his palm against his mouth and leaned back in his chair.

"This is a grave decision, Malcolm."

"It is, it is." Malcolm cleared his throat and dabbed at the corners of his eyes with his napkin. "Look, I had a feeling you wouldn't really like the new direction we're heading in. Maybe it's just my excellent judgment where people are involved or maybe it's just my, uhh…what's it called when you know what's going to happen before it happens?"

"What exactly are the reapers going to do? Frighten everyone?"

"Psychic, right? That's the word?"

"You're going to frighten everyone, but then what?"

Malcolm snapped his fingers. "Yeah, psychic! That's it. I think I'm a little psychic about these things. I told Jessica you wouldn't like the idea of sending reapers out, changing the sky again, increasing the nightmares, stirring up a bit of excitement. You're too old-fashioned."

"It has nothing to do with being old-fashioned. You're asking for chaos. Even Death used to say that we had to keep some manner of balance in the nightmares, otherwise people will begin to feel so discouraged—"

"You're speaking of Kelly Gold, I'd assume."

"Yes."

"I'm starting to think, well, do you have some kind of weird infatuation with him or something? You talk about him a lot. An unusual amount. Especially considering that this is a guy who was exiled for breaking rules, stealing materials, selling information, and cavorting with the Sumner people."

For the first time in maybe 50 years, Mr. Right was at a complete loss for words.

Their dinner arrived just then, and Malcolm smiled at the waitress, thanking her profusely before digging into his meal.

"Well, I have a fun fact for you regarding Kelly," Malcolm said. "Someone reminded me the other day that his stuff was still taking up a locker."

Mr. Right shook his head. No one had taken Kelly his things?

You just don't do that to a man.

Malcolm shoved a huge bite of food into his mouth. "Yeah, so anyway. I had them send his stuff to the incinerator."

CHAPTER THIRTY-ONE

Death and Lola cut across a few streets, zigzagging until Lola was certain that they weren't being followed. They stopped into a few secondhand clothing shops and Death found another pair of pants and a long-sleeved striped shirt that fit him perfectly. They stowed their newfound treasures in Lola's messenger bag, playfully bantering all the while about whether or not Death's new shirt was meant for girls.

"So, how many people do you remember from dreams?" Lola asked, as they walked away from the quiet little restaurant where they had enjoyed dinner together.

"Eh. Not everyone. Maybe one in fifty, one in a hundred, three in a row. It just depends. Usually they remember me first," Death said. "They'll just stare and you can tell they're trying to place it. Seeing someone in a dream is an unexpected first meeting, though."

"It seems intrusive."

"For who?"

Lola tried to picture the inside of someone else's head, tried to imagine listening to thoughts other than her own as they bounced about and built castles from images, holes from memories. The idea of dropping into a mind other than her own was jarring and vague and intimidatingly odd.

"For them. Having someone in your mind, moving things around, influencing you. I wouldn't want someone doing that to me."

Death shrugged, glancing around. "See that short guy with the black hair? He's had nightmares for years and years. They're always about suffocating." Death stared at the guy for a few seconds before his blue eyes flicked back to Lola. "I thought the dreams and the people would blur together after a while, but you'd be surprised."

The buzz and energy of a weekday evening in the city was a common friend for Lola after so many years in Boston, but now her eyes snagged on more faces. Most of the faces were twisted into frowns or were dulled by the sleepy-coated pills that everyone took for depression. Lola accidentally met the eyes of an old woman, and then dropped her gaze to the comfort of some undetermined place that hovered always three paces in front of her.

"That man dreams about the end of the world. Every night," Death said. A few seconds later, "That one has a lot of nightmares about the ocean." Two blocks later, "That woman has a recurring nightmare about her doctor. I think she's attracted to him and that scares her."

"Oh."

"And that one, the old guy with the red-gray hair? He dreams about natural disasters." Death pushed his hands deep into his pockets. "Dreams are rarely about what they seem to be about. They're more of a reflection of personality and fear." He shrugged. "That guy up there, the one talking on his phone? He has nightmares about his father."

"Just stop."

"Stop what?"

"I don't want to know, I don't want to...that would be horrible, to...to have to see that. To know that," Lola said, cringing.

"Yeah. I can erase myself from their memories. I just can't erase them from my own."

Lola heard some note of tenacious confusion between worlds in his voice, as if he had been carrying around a hundred realities for a lifetime. She swept the sensation into the back of her mind and continued on, all the while avoiding faces and voices.

They crossed the street, cut through an alleyway, and continued in the general direction of Lola's other favorite secondhand shop.

"You know, speaking of, uh, of dreams," Death said, hurrying his pace a bit to keep up with Lola's long-legged, determined strides. "I wanted to talk to you about something."

Oh no. Here it came, all of the questions about her past and the brief flashes she had managed to hold onto of her parents. More often than not, Lola lied about her history. Stories about a rich father and a mother who worked for the government were perfectly acceptable substitutes for the truth, fake boarding schools and all.

Anything was easier than the fragile pieces that existed.

They walked past a group of several protestors waving signs and handing out pamphlets. Lola waved away the pamphlet that one of them offered her. "Are you going to color your hair yourself?" Lola asked, knowing it would distract Death enough that he'd forget his intended line of questioning. Sure enough, Death straightened and tapped his fingertips together, the serious expression fleeing his face.

"Well, actually…"

Lola waited a few seconds and then realized that not only had he stopped speaking, he'd stopped walking. "What's wrong?"

Death turned around, staring at the protestors. "What did that guy say?"

"I don't know. You stop paying attention after about 24 hours in this city."

One of the protestors rushed toward them, hand outstretched with pamphlets. "Do you know what's happening, young man? The sky is falling, it's changing. They're changing it, and they're among us."

Death's eyes narrowed behind his glasses. "What do you know about the sky?"

"Oh, young man, there's so much I can tell you about the frightening changes you've sensed. You've felt them, haven't you? The static in the air, the unease. The darkness." The protestor reached out and laid a hand on Death's arm. "Have you noticed that the sky is purple now?"

Lola laughed, moving closer to Death. "The sky is always purple."

The protestor and Death both turned their eyes toward Lola.

"Is it?" the protestor asked finally, in a gentle, soothing tone. "Is it really, or do you remember it being something else? Think hard before you answer. Wasn't it blue? They made you forget that it was blue."

What a weirdo.

"Let's get out of here," Lola said to Death.

"But you know, don't you, young man? You remember when it was blue. And you saw it turn red once, didn't you? Not long ago."

Death shook free of the man's hold, stepping away from him. "Who are you?"

"My name is Timothy. Don't be alarmed, friend. We mean only to open the eyes of all those who have been fooled by the agents of evil. They walk among us now, some of them in the guise of reapers of old, some wearing wings like demented angels fallen from the heavens. Some of them may even exist in the disguise of normal men or women like you. Like me." He glanced at Lola. "Like you."

"You're from the Sumner Organization, aren't you?" Death demanded, jumping back another step.

"You've heard of us! That's wonderful news. Has someone spoken to you already? Maybe at one of the other—"

Death blindly reached for Lola's hand, finding it after a few fumbled attempts. "Stay away," he said. "Stay away from us."

"What's your name?"

"Stay away from me, and call your reaper friends off. I already threw one of them off a roof and I'm not afraid to do it again," Death ground out between clenched teeth. He squeezed Lola's hand too tight, taking another step backward.

"Reaper friends...? You've seen a reaper?"

"Tell them to leave me alone. I'm dangerous. I- I had a 5.0 rating on the aggression scale," Death said, waving his free hand in what he must have thought a very menacing manner.

"We have no affiliation with those workers of evil," the protestor said, though with considerably less bluster and confidence than before. "Where did you see the reaper?"

"You see this?" Death demanded, slipping his fingers under his collar and yanking the fabric away from his skin. "That's what your reaper friend did to me!"

"He's been marked," the man said. "He's been marked. He's been MARKED! HE'S BEEN MARKED. He's one of them!"

Death looked at Lola and simply said, "Run."

This time, as they ran, Lola felt they *were* being chased.

CHAPTER THIRTY-TWO

Wellington's father had gone prematurely bald, so he'd always had a nervous fear that he might suffer a similar fate, and had decided at age 15 to take necessary precautions against following in his father's footsteps. One of the most obvious of these precautions was avoiding pulling his hair out.

Not receiving any news from Olivia about the whereabouts of the jar for 6 hours was enough to make Wellington undo about 15 years of hair upkeep.

"She's still looking," the assistant said, when Wellington called for the 15th time. He idly contemplated how long he would go to prison if someone found out he'd burned down the shop with both girls trapped inside.

"Tell her to call me *immediately* when she finds information. Any information," Wellington said, drumming his fingers on the countertop in front of him.

"I told her that when you called fifteen minutes ago."

"It was twenty minutes ago."

"Well, I already told her. I have to go now, we have a customer."

"This is important!"

"Don't you own a coffee shop or something?" the assistant asked, after a long pause.

"I don't see the relevance of that question."

"Perhaps you should look after your customers and let me look after mine. Olivia will call you when she finds your vase." The girl hung up before Wellington could tell her that it was a *jar*, thank you, and a very *important jar* at that.

Ugh, these people.

A voice cut into Wellington's angst-ridden thoughts and contemplations of arson. "Can I have a cup of coffee now?"

Oh, right. The customers. They always had a habit of arriving at the worst possible moment and mucking about with their questions and requests.

"Yeah, yeah, here," Wellington said and poured coffee into a chipped mug. "Now move out of the way so the next bloke can make his order."

As it turned out, the next bloke looked incredibly familiar, in a murky, troubling sort of way. He was about six feet tall and broad-shouldered, with a face that could easily become lost in a crowd, except for the exotic slope of his nose and eerie darkness of his eyes.

"Hello, Wellington," the customer said, his voice a hypnotic mix of accents and comforting oddness. "Do you remember me?"

Wellington nodded. "Yeah," he said. "From uhh… from…" He frowned, sorting through his memories. How did he know this bloke again? Not from poker nights over at Jimmy's. Not from the old days. Not from Lola. "From uhh…" He struggled, picking up an empty mug and waving it around a bit as if it might aid his memory. "I know you from somewhere. It's just not coming back to me right now, though, mate."

The man smiled, his teeth white and too straight. "It's not important that you remember, Wellington. What's important is that you tell me where I can find Death."

Wellington let out a nervous chuckle. "Well, that's a bit gothic of you, isn't it? Or emu? Is that what they call it? Those kids running around in their oversized black pants, showing off their arses and talking about how they're going to cut their wrists." He clunked the mug down on the counter. "Can I get you a cup of coffee, or are you just here to creep everyone out?"

"I'm looking for the man with blue hair."

"Oh, that little man Lola's been running around with? The one that looks like a girl from behind?"

"Yes, that's the one. Where is he?"

Wellington had the strangest sensation, as if he was remembering a dream from several weeks ago. Didn't this bloke already have something to do with the little blue-haired man?

"Why do you want to know?" Wellington asked, narrowing his eyes.

"I need to speak with him."

"Do you know Jessica or something?"

At this, the stranger's smile widened. "How do you know Jessica?"

"I asked a question first."

"Yes," the stranger said. "I do know Jessica. I work for Jessica. How do you know her?"

Now, Wellington had become one of the most influential thieves and businessmen in Boston by way of a few important things—patience, intelligence, and the ability to work with those others might scorn. All of those were key to becoming a somebody in crime. But Wellington was also a man of caution when it came to situations like this.

"She's hired my assistance, and it's not the sort of assistance that you share with the general public, if you understand my meaning," Wellington said.

"And it has to do with the little blue-haired man?"

Wellington crossed his arms over his chest. "That information is confidential. I'm a professional."

"Of course, of course," the man said. "I suppose Lola is assisting you in this confidential situation?"

And then, all at once, Wellington realized this was exactly the sort of bloke that you *could* trust. It was his dark eyes, maybe. Yes, that's what it was. The dark eyes. Only a trustworthy sort had eyes like that.

Honestly, Wellington felt rather drawn to the stranger in a way he hadn't felt since that bizarre afternoon when he'd fallen completely mad in love with Lola.

Wellington leaned across the counter, lowering his voice. "She's out keeping an eye on the blue-haired kid.

I'm waiting for a phone call from one of my associates so we can find out where the jar is."

"Jar?"

"Some jar that Jessica wants. As soon as I find it, she wants the paperwork and the jar. It's gonna be a big payday, and probably one of my most important jobs yet." Wellington nodded as he said it, feeling rather proud.

"Paperwork?"

"Lola snatched some paperwork and Jessica told me to hold onto it."

"Ah." The man smiled again, then, a toothy smile that felt both friendly and intimidating. "Thank you, Wellington."

"Do you want some coffee?"

"I'd love coffee, thank you. In one of those cups that I can take on the run, if you please," the stranger said. "Cream and sugar."

Wellington bustled about, preparing a cup of coffee. Just as he handed it to his strange customer, Wellington's phone rang from within his pocket. He fished it out, flipped it open. "Hello?"

Olivia's breathless voice echoed in his ear. "I found it!"

"You have it in hand? It's right there?"

"No, no, no, don't be an idiot. I mean I found out approximately where it is, and you can go search for it at your leisure."

"Where! Where is it?"

"You'll need to pay me before I share that information, Mr. Wellington."

Fog lifted from Wellington's mind, freeing his thoughts and allowing him to once again vividly imagine himself burning down Olivia's business. "At least tell me the name of the town it's in, so I know you're not lying."

Olivia spluttered.

"I'm sorry? What was that?"

"It's in Salem!"

"Salem, Massachusetts? The witchy place?"

"Yes, the *witchy place*, you moron. Now, when are you going to pay me?"

Wellington clapped his phone shut and then realized his customer had vanished. Hmmm, curious. Wellington couldn't remember what the customer had wanted, but for some reason, it felt important. Something to do with Lola and the blue-haired man, maybe.

Ah well, whatever.

Wellington called Lola.

CHAPTER THIRTY-THREE

Mr. Right cloaked himself long before he left Wellington's coffee shop. As he walked, his mind spun with new information. It was one thing to find out that Wellington was tied to Jessica, Mr. Right had expected that. But it was something entirely different to find out that Jessica wanted the names of the damned badly enough to steal them.

What could she want with the names of the damned, anyway?

And why did she want Lola to keep an eye on Death? What was it about Death that had gotten everyone's hackles up? Malcolm's snickering admission of plans to burn Death's belongings seemed to be just another small piece in a confusing puzzle.

And what jar was Jessica after?

Mr. Right created a portal for himself and traveled to HQ without paying much attention to his actions. Ever since the lunch with Malcolm, he'd felt as if his time there might be winding down.

Such a realization made any man appreciate the small things, like a cup of coffee. And it made a man ignore the big things, like an aura or the ability to travel instantaneously. Who cared about any of that when you were three hours from the noose?

HQ buzzed with a nervous energy and the crushing, black-hole sensation of the reapers that stood guard in corners and hallways. Mr. Right had never seen so many stressed sideways glances from his coworkers, and he'd certainly never seen Mandy away from her desk.

"Where's Mandy?" Mr. Right asked the first person to cross his path.

"Oh. She'll be back."

"Where is she? She always takes her breaks at her desk."

The woman shot a glance over her shoulder. "She's talking to Malcolm. He called her into his office," the woman said, and then scurried away with her head down.

Mr. Right took note of a reaper headed in his direction and ducked into the elevator.

The incinerator was at the very bottom of HQ and required a special password to enter. Rumors generously circulated around HQ that a melodramatic young agent had once decided to off another agent by pushing him into the incinerator, thus forcing those in the upper management to make it more difficult for such events to take place.

Mr. Right had no idea if the story was true, but he was well aware of the security precautions that people like Malcolm had taken over the last few decades.

Senior agents like Mr. Right had access to almost every part of HQ, though, so he typed his password into the keypad on the wall and entered the famous bottom level.

"You," he said to the white-uniformed incinerator operator on duty. "Is it true that you hold everything down here for two days before burning it?"

The operator removed his goggles and peered at Mr. Right for a few seconds before answering. "What're you doing down here? Aren't you the valentine love buggy one?"

"Where's yesterday and today's burn queue?"

"Malcolm doesn't like anyone coming down here."

"The Wings division sent me," Mr. Right said, which sent a visible shudder through the other man. If anyone was afraid of the reapers, they were doubly afraid of the Wings. "Now, show me to the burn queue."

The operator twitched and grumbled to himself but did as he'd been instructed. He took a box down from a shelf and opened it. "Now, hurry up," he said. "People are getting fired around here, and I don't want to be one of them."

Mr. Right pushed the operator out of the way and reached into the box. Most of the contents were ordinary things you might find in any office... documents, pamphlets with typos, old pens. But in one corner of the box, Mr. Right found a belt, a few talismans, a scarf, a plastic snow-globe with a goblin head inside it, a bottle of black nail polish, several keys on a ring, a notebook that said DEATH on the cover, three paperback books and a Depeche Mode CD.

"What do you want with it, anyway?" the operator asked. "It's trash."

Mr. Right sighed, turning his head to look at the man. "The Wings are investigating something. I'd hate to tell them that you're preventing me from finding out what I need to know."

"Not preventing. We don't get visitors down here. Not often, you know. Not for a long time. Malcolm doesn't want them down here."

"Of course he doesn't."

Mr. Right scooped the talismans out of the box and shoved them in his pocket. At least he'd take a few of Death's belongings to him. No one should have all of their personal effects destroyed like so much refuse. And if Death was still with Lola, it would be easy enough to find him. Mr. Right had taken note of Lola's address and favorite haunts during his failed attempt at making her fall in love with Jason Wellington.

"You taking something?"

"Excuse me," Mr. Right said, pushing by the operator and heading for the door. "Good day."

The twitchy little man called after him, "Be careful, Cupid. No one's safe around here."

Mr. Right shared the elevator ride up with two jittery women, both of whom barely shot him one glance before returning their gazes to the floor. One of them tripped over the other as the doors opened and they rushed past Mandy's empty desk.

Where was Mandy, anyway? Still in Malcolm's office? Poor girl.

But perhaps she would keep Malcolm occupied just long enough for Mr. Right to be able to slip away and deliver Death's things to him. He walked behind Mandy's desk, hunching down as he searched for a pen and paper. He would leave a note—

"Mr. Right?"

Mr. Right froze. The voice belonged to Malcolm, unmistakably.

"Yes, sir?" Mr. Right said, straightening.

"Someone mentioned to me that you were rummaging around the trash today. That seemed a bit odd, so I laughed it off but, uhh, well. It seems you really were."

Several agents craned their necks or inched closer to Mr. Right, eyes wide with the frenzied excitement of a potentially embarrassing or disruptive scene.

Mr. Right cleared his throat. "I'm afraid I don't know what you mean, sir."

"Oh come on, Right. What did you think you were going to do? Steal more supplies and squirrel them away to your little friend Kelly Gold? Then what? Were you two going to toast how stupid we all are? I'm sure the Sumner Organization can't wait to acquire whatever you just stole for them." Malcolm scratched at his bad mustache, and his eyes darted around to the other agents. "Funny, too, since I thought you were a pretty cool old guy. Guess you fooled me."

This was just entirely too much.

"I have nothing to do with the Sumner Organization."

"Is that right? You know, Kelly was seen at a protest today with a bunch of Sumner Organization yippety-yahoos. I suppose you knew nothing about that, either, huh?"

"I've never had any dealings with them."

"But Kelly has, and, uh, it seems pretty obvious that the two of you are just peas in a pod. Best friends. Maybe more than friends." Malcolm snickered. "You have something of his in your pocket, in fact."

Mr. Right felt as if all of the eyes of the world were concentrated on him.

"Anyway, theft is a serious matter. You've broken a Sacred Law, Mr. Right. And that means you're exiled. Enjoy Boston." Malcolm waved one hand. "Well, enjoy it while you can. It won't look the same for very long."

Five reapers closed in on Mr. Right, hissing and chattering and pushing him toward the elevator. One of them said something in a voice that sounded remarkably like Jessica's, but Mr. Right couldn't quite understand the words.

A weight lifted from Mr. Right, sucking the color and energy from him, yanking at his thoughts and senses until nothing was left but a dull emptiness.

Ah.

So this was what it felt like to be mortal.

CHAPTER THIRTY-FOUR

Death's breathing didn't return to normal until he and Lola fell back inside her apartment and closed the door. They'd run for what felt like hours, ducked into the train station and had barely spoken a word to each other on the journey back.

Lola stalked away from him, tossing her bag on the couch. "Those people were the Sumner people? The people who rip wings off of agents or something?"

"No, they—they sewed wings onto someone."

"Exactly how dangerous would you say they are?" Lola asked, her voice harder than usual. "Be brutal. Are they going to track us here?"

"I don't think so." Death took his glasses off and rubbed his eyes. A headache threatened to erupt, and his legs had taken on the approximate consistency of rubber. "But they're very dangerous. Dangerous enough to send a reaper to kill me."

"And you're sure it was them that sent the reaper?"

"Yes!" Death snapped, before he could stop himself.

"All right."

"Why?"

Lola shook her head. "I need to know something about my enemies, Death, and my exit strategies. It's just good business." She turned away from him, tugging off her hoodie and kicking off her shoes. She pulled off her long-sleeved shirt, revealing a thin sleeveless shirt underneath, which clung to her from the rain. "Stop staring," she called.

He cleared his throat and peeled off his own damp hoodie.

"Looks like Cara left us a note. 'Don't move, I'll be back in a minute.' The first part is in all-caps. Which means it's serious." Lola opened the little dresser by the couch and rummaged around before producing a pair of pajama pants. "Here, you can borrow these tonight. I hope you don't mind teddy bears."

Death snatched up the offered pants, rolling his eyes even as he tugged off his jeans and slipped into the soft pajama bottoms. He climbed onto the couch without another word, listening as his pulse pushed the headache full-force from ear to ear.

The door burst open just then and Cara rushed in, breathing hard. "You two. What were you doing…this evening…on the…what were you DOING?"

Lola turned and stared at her roommate. "We went shopping."

"No, I don't mean that. Why were you on television?"

"Television?" Death said. "What do you mean?"

"It must have been on four or five times, they just kept playing it. Here, I recorded it," Cara said, crossing the apartment in a few long strides. She opened the door to her bedroom and motioned for them to follow. "What were you even doing?"

"We weren't on TV," Lola said.

"Oh really? So I'm just imagining things now? You weren't yelling at a bunch of protestors and running away like the devil was chasing you? None of that happened?" Cara said, huffing and puffing as she turned her TV on and pushed buttons on a remote control. "I guess we're all hallucinating then, huh? Group hallucinating?"

The image on the TV changed from a woman in an apron talking about her favorite wasabi sauce to a wide shot of the Sumner Organization protesters. A reporter smiled from the foreground and shook her head. "First pranksters in reaper costumes terrorizing us and now this," she said, a bit too chipper for the subject matter, in Death's opinion.

"You know how that thing fell on Brandon?" Cara said. "They've been talking about it on the news. And I've tried to keep up to date with what they're saying. By the way, he still hasn't left his apartment." She paused, pointing at the television screen. "LOOK!"

Death and Lola appeared on the screen, Death grabbing hold of Lola's hand and saying "Stay away from us!"

Cara sighed heavily. "Did you know someone was filming you?"

Death didn't quite hear Lola's answer, because his entire existence had been sucked into the screen. His image looked smaller than he'd envisioned it, his movements less graceful, and his expression more fearful.

Did his voice really sound like that?

As the tiny television Death and Lola ran away from the protestors, the cheerful reporter returned to the screen. "Now, we've heard reports of these reaper pranks taking place all over the city, but this is the first report we've had of any form of violence. It would appear that the mysterious man with blue hair was either cut or possibly *bitten* by one of the pranksters." She paused, flashing painfully white teeth. "You know, George, something about this guy looks really familiar, but I just can't place it."

A similarly smiling man appeared on the screen. "With hair like that, you'd think you wouldn't forget. And he's got a...what was it? '5.0 on the aggression scale'?"

The reporter laughed. "No information has been found on this mysterious young man, but one thing's for sure. None of us are going to forget him anytime soon."

"Thank you, Julie. Our next story revolves around a little girl named Mary Gracie, who claims that the *sky* used to be *blue*..."

Cara switched the television off and shot a glance between Death and Lola. "You're all over the news. Even TMZ is playing that clip," she said. "And you know what I find really strange?"

Death sat down on the edge of Cara's bed, pushed his glasses back up his nose and took a deep breath. "What? What's really strange? Reapers trying to kill me or...?"

"No." Cara raised an eyebrow. "No, what's strange is that no one seems to have any idea of how they know you. You're either the most obscure trip-hop rock star of all time or someone hasn't been very honest with me about your occupation." She crossed her arms and looked at Lola. "Well?"

Lola shrugged. "Do you really want to know?"

"Want to know what? Is he homeless?"

"Not in the way you think."

"There's only one version of homeless, Lola. And I thought you wanted to avoid things like televisions and cameras and anything else that might lead people back here."

The girls shared a look that made Death feel as if he'd been forgotten entirely.

"It's okay," Lola said at last. "No one knows anything about me."

"You wanna bet? TMZ, Lola. You know I don't poke my nose too much into whatever crazy stuff you're doing, but this is bad. I don't mean bad for me, either. Bad for you." Cara sighed and uncrossed her arms. "You already stand out in a crowd, never mind dragging that around with you."

Death cleared his throat. "'That?' Did you just motion at me?"

"Just be careful, okay?" Cara said, stepping forward and pulling Lola into a quick hug. For a few seconds, the room echoed with silence, and then Cara let go of Lola. "All right, get out of my room, both of you." She pointed at Death. "You be careful, you hear me? I don't know who or what you are, but you better not get her in trouble."

Death nodded and then left the room as quickly as his legs would carry him. He and Lola reconvened in the kitchen, and while Death let out a breath of relief, Lola straightened to her full height and curled her fingers into fists at her sides.

"I don't think I've ever actually been on television," Death said. "They talked about me, after the accident, but that doesn't count because they didn't—"

"Wellington isn't going to be happy when he sees me all over the TV."

The interruption caused Death to lose track of not only what he'd been saying, but also all of the rather dim memories of grainy television reports. "Wellington…?"

"Yeah, you know what I do for a living. It's not really safe for me to end up on television. I'm easier to spot now, and a lot easier for people to remember. That's dangerous for me, and for Wellington, never mind detrimental to my work."

"It's dangerous for me, too," Death said, leaning against the kitchen counter. "But I'm going to do everything I can to keep them away from you. And once I get my job back, I'll pull some strings. Maybe we can use memory remedies."

Lola eyed him. "Memory remedies."

"Yeah, it's not that hard. We just make people forget things."

"Is that what that guy was talking about? When he said the sky used to be blue and they made us forget?"

Death hesitated and then nodded. "It's not something anyone is supposed to remember. They must be taking a lot of shortcuts if people are noticing. Either that, or they're doing it on purpose to freak people out."

"Your 'agency?'"

Again, he hesitated. "I don't think they'd do that. But I don't know." He pushed away from the counter. "Where's that hair dye?"

"Wow."

"What?"

"Nothing." Lola walked to the couch, rummaged in her bag and withdrew the bottle of dye. "Here. Good luck," she said, and tossed it to him.

"What?"

"Well, I know that's probably a priority item right now, considering everything that's happened. I mean, someone's telling me the sky wasn't always purple, but that's not a big deal. There's a hair crisis in process! Go for it."

Death opened his mouth to say something, but found he had no argument. Finally, his shoulders slumped and he trudged to the bathroom with his head down. Without the power of his aura, the blue in Death's hair had almost entirely disappeared and in its place were nothing but sad blond-blue strands.

"You know, everything has been taken away from me," he said, standing in the doorway. "Everything. I'd kind of just like to hold onto this one last thing."

Lola stared back at him for what felt like an eternity, and then sighed quietly and walked to him. "Look," she said, pushing past him and opening the cabinet under the sink. "Here's some bleach. Do you know what you're doing?"

Bleach. He'd never bleached his hair. "Uh, sure."

"Don't make a huge mess."

"I won't make a mess!"

"Okay, whatever, don't yell," Lola said. She stepped out of the bathroom again. "Good luck. If you need me, just come wake me up. I'm going to sleep. Tomorrow, we need to go to Salem."

Death frowned. "Salem? Salem, Massachusetts? Why?"

"It has to do with your friend."

At that, Death felt a deep breath of hope enter his lungs again. He'd wondered if maybe Lola had already given up on her mission to help him find Fashion. "Thank you," he said. "Thank you for helping me and for letting me stay here."

Lola shrugged and turned away. "Fix your hair and then get some sleep. We have a long day ahead of us tomorrow."

Death closed the bathroom door, grinning to himself. They were going to find Fashion. Death could get his job back, talk to some of the higher-ups and get things set pretty nicely for Lola as a thank you for her hospitality. Sure, she'd gotten him into this mess in the first place, but she wasn't so bad once you got to know her.

And Death was going to fix his hair. He wouldn't let bad circumstances steal the identity that he'd worked so hard to build over the last quarter of a century.

Bleach and hair color. Easy!

CHAPTER
THIRTY-FIVE

Death didn't dare emerge from the bathroom until long after he was certain that Lola was asleep, and even when he did he tiptoed to the couch and pulled the blanket over his head.

By morning, though, Lola was poking and prodding at him, whispering that he needed to get up so they could take the commuter rail to Salem.

"Uhhhh," Death said, though he'd intended to say something witty or at least semi-intelligent. He closed his mouth, still hiding under the blanket, and then tried again. "I can't."

"Can't? Why?"

"Can't."

A sigh issued from beside the couch, in the general vicinity of where he guessed Lola to be. "Did you catch cold? I told you about the germs."

"Uh, yes," he said, after a little consideration. "I'm very sick and I can't go." He coughed as realistically as he could manage.

"That wasn't very convincing."

"I'm too sick to cough," he said, but it was too late.

Lola tugged on the blanket and then gasped out loud. A few seconds later, she giggled. "What did you do?" she said, sitting down beside him on the couch.

Death attempted to cover his hair with his hands. "It's fine."

"I would have to tell the biggest lie of my career if I said it was 'fine.' What happened in there?" she asked, reaching over and tugging on a few strands of his hair. "Looks like you bleached this part successfully, and this part is…well, almost blue. And this part? I'm not sure what this is." She giggled again, brushing her fingers back through his hair. "It's interesting, that's for sure. And some of it is blue. In fact, maybe half of it is blue."

"It's awful."

"Yes, it's pretty awful. But you succeeded in giving yourself an unforgettable hairstyle, that's for sure." Lola patted his head and Death swatted her hand away. "You shouldn't try dyeing it again for a while." She paused. "And you probably shouldn't bleach it again. Maybe ever."

"Did I ruin it?" he asked, sitting up on the couch.

"Well, none of it fell out, from what I can tell. So, that's good. And some of it IS bluer now than before." She shook her head. "How did you get it so blue before? Did you have hairdressers waiting on you hand and foot or something?"

He looked at her as if she was a very young child who needed to have something explained to her in small, easily digestible words. "No, we used the Reimagining stations. I don't have my aura anymore, though, so the color faded away."

"Huh. Okay," she said. "I have no idea what any of that means, but okay. You'd better get up and throw some clothes on. We need to head to Salem." She rummaged around in the dresser by the couch and pulled out a little red hat. "Here, you can put this over your hair, if you want."

Death stared at the hat for a few seconds and then back at Lola. "This looks like something a grandmother knitted."

"Wow. Do you want it or not?"

Begrudgingly, and with a few grumbles and mutters that were imperceptible even to himself, Death tugged the hat over his hair.

Within maybe fifteen minutes, they were out the door and on their way to board the commuter rail. Lola kept to herself on the train ride, listening to headphones and focusing on some invisible figure just in front of her. Death stared out the window in what he felt was a quite gloomy manner, thinking gloomy thoughts and contemplating the gloomy purple of the sky, all the while wishing gloomy music was playing like some gloomy movie's hit soundtrack.

After what felt like forever, someone tapped Death's shoulder and he turned his head. Lola had taken out her headphones and stopped peering into space. "Your aura thing. Will you get that back if you get your job back?"

"I think so. Yeah. I mean, they kinda have to give it back to me, I guess."

"What are you right now, then?"

He frowned. "I'm a bit confused about this question."

Lola eyed him, shrugged and then reached over, slowly, tracing one fingertip over the fading marks on his neck from the reaper. "If you were in that car accident, well, what am I looking at now? You don't have your aura or your little reimagining station things, so what are you? You're not a robot or something, are you? Because I saw this movie when I was a kid and this guy took his head off and put it on a desk and it was really disturbing. To be honest, I think that freaked me out more than the puppet with the eye patch."

"A robot?" he asked, noting her genuinely concerned expression. He placed his hands on either side of his neck and twisted, as if to unscrew his head, and then laughed as she flinched. "Kidding, kidding. No, I'm not a robot, so you can scratch that off your list of things to worry about."

"What are you, then?"

Death considered the question, looking away from her again. "When you're promoted, you're given a one-time-only exact replica of your body. And when you have your aura, you're mostly preserved from aging. You age, but very slowly. Without it, you go back to aging. And even with it, things can kill you. You don't get a third time around."

"Oh." A long silence fell between them, and then finally Lola nodded and said, "And were your eyes that color before? Or was that your aura thing?"

"Nah, I guess they were always like this. I didn't spend a lot of time staring at myself in the mirror, though."

"Because you were kinda goofy-looking, with the chin-length bob?"

Death twisted in his chair. "What?"

Lola stood up. "This is our stop, come on." She straightened her backpack strap as the train shuddered to a stop, and then she walked away, forcing Death to get up and scramble after her.

"How do you know what my hair looked like?"

"The internet is good for a lot of things."

"You saw me? You saw me back then?"

Lola fished her cell phone from her pocket and tapped away at it, peering intently at her screen for a few seconds before raising her head. "Come on, this way."

Death had never been to Salem, though he had heard a great deal about it in school. And as luck would have it, when his tenth-grade class had taken a field trip to the famous town, he'd been sick with a memorably horrific stomach bug that had prevented him from going on the trip, or even attending school for four days in a row.

The most melodramatic part of him had decided that it was "meant to be" and that perhaps he wasn't intended to visit Salem, ever. He'd drearily decided, all that time ago, that he probably had a few witches in his ancestry, and they had forbidden him from visiting Salem, lest he find himself unfairly charged for a crime and, quite possibly, publically executed.

All of this mythos had created a disproportionate vision of what the city might look and feel like. He'd pictured a few more dark alleys, more bloodstains on the cobblestones, more scowling old women wearing headscarves and luring young men into the aforementioned alleys.

He'd certainly imagined fewer visors.

"Where are we going?" he asked finally, rushing to catch up to Lola as she powered ahead.

"We're picking something up."

Death dodged a group of gawking tourists and some kid in a cheap witch costume. "I thought we were following a lead you had about Fashion."

"Yeah, well, it's all related."

"How's it related? Can you give me some clues? Just a few clues."

"A jar," Lola said. "It has to do with a jar."

This didn't feel so much like a clue as some cryptic reference to a conversation they'd never had. He waited for her to laugh or express some signal that she'd been speaking sarcastically, but she just continued walking.

"A jar?"

Lola nodded.

"Okay, we're back to the thing about me needing a few more clues. What does a jar have to do with Fashion?"

With what sounded like a very long-suffering sigh, Lola slowed her pace and glanced sidelong at Death. "He was last heard from while searching for a jar." She paused, as if even she realized how absolutely absurd her words sounded. "From what I hear, he was asking around about a jar that holds nightmares in it."

"Why would he care about nightmares? That's my thing. Unless he was looking for a way to contact me, maybe."

"Do you know anything about the jar?"

Death racked his brain for any information regarding important jars, but finally shook his head. "I don't think so. For some reason I feel like someone was talking about a jar around me recently, but…" He shrugged helplessly. "Never mind, I don't remember. But he was looking for a jar? What else do you know?"

He might have asked more, had a woman in a pink polka-dotted hat pointed at him and said, "You're from TV last night!" She tugged on the sleeve of the man next to her, who wore a matching visor, but in puke yellow. "Honey, that's the guy from TV, I can see his blue hair poking out from under his hat. Oh my gosh, is it true that one of those things bit your neck? Are they *vampires*? They're vampires, aren't they?"

"No, zombies," the husband said.

"Oh my *gosh*, are they zombies?" the woman asked, taking a step backwards. "Did you get bitten by a zombie?"

Death wished, for perhaps the thousandth time that week, that he had his aura. Disappearing would have been preferable just then, or even causing a bit of a scene and stepping upwards, up and up and up into the sky, walking away from these gawping fools with a grin on his face and a feisty swagger.

"You were?"

"What? What was the question?" Death demanded.

"You were bitten by a zombie?"

"No! No, I was not bitten by a zombie." Death inched back from the woman, taking note that about a zillion people had stopped what they were doing and politely turned their heads in his direction to stare. Between the embarrassment of being ogled and the countless quaint little stores called things like POTIONS AND ONE-EYED TOADS, the whole situation felt comfortably nightmarish. And that would have been great, if the agent of nightmares himself weren't experiencing it.

"They say we have a better chance of a zombie apocalypse than of the world economy improving," the woman said, in a helpful tone.

Out of the corner of his eye, Death spotted a hooded figure moving steadily in his direction. He tensed, preparing to either run or throw the annoying visor woman at the reaper, but the figure reached up and pushed its hood back. Oh. Never mind. Just some goofy-looking kid with stringy hair and a lot of freckles.

Lola tugged on Death's sleeve. "Let's go."

"If you've been bitten, you should probably quarantine yourself until you know for sure if it was something serious," the woman said. "Be safe!"

Death grinned. "And you should avoid falling into manholes, Susan! Bye!"

As Death followed Lola, he heard the woman sputtering some nervous comment to her husband about how she didn't want to talk about manholes.

"Okay," Death said, "Where is this jar that Fashion was looking for?"

"It's currently in the possession of Captain Asher," Lola said. "Are you ready for a fight?"

"Wait. A fight?"

Lola shrugged "You never know with this guy. Sometimes he hugs you, and sometimes he holds a knife to your neck until you cry."

Great.

CHAPTER THIRTY-SIX

If someone had taken two shops and managed to squeeze one between them, without really making provision for things like a proper entrance or room to breathe inside, they might have made Captain Asher's dimly lit, smoky little shop. Maybe.

Death stumbled on his way into the shop and jumped higher than he'd like to admit when something brushed against his legs. The something turned out to be a black cat, and the owner of the black cat turned out to be lounging on a chair behind a narrow counter, smoking and smirking at his guests.

"She doesn't like you."

"Cats like me," Death said, before he could stop himself.

"Well, she doesn't." The man took another long drag from his cigarette and flicked dark eyes toward Lola. "Lola Lane, Lola Lane, the lady of Boston's cheapest criminal circuit. What can I do for you? You finally want me to bump off that idiot Wellington?"

Lola's face took on a pinched quality that Death hadn't seen before. "No," she said. She cocked her head to one side, propped a hand on one hip. "Wellington tells me you're holding something for us."

"Does he?"

"We're on a tight schedule, Asher."

The man's eyes sparkled at that. "Is that right? I love tight schedules. They're great for so many things, you know?" He stood up then and slowly danced his way around the counter until he stood directly in front of Lola. He had a good five inches on her, and his wiry arms were covered in colorful tattoos of wild animals. "One time I met this pretty girl, maybe nineteen years old. Preacher's daughter. She was on a tight schedule, real tight, something to do with her daddy making a bad deal." His hand moved so quickly that Death didn't realize the man held a knife until it was poised dangerously close to Lola's cheek. "I saw her kill a man three times her size with a knife, like she'd been meant for that kind of thing all along."

Death opened his mouth to say something, but Lola spoke first.

"That's a great story, and relatable for me, too," she whispered, her hand snaking up and curling over Asher's. "But I'm not a preacher's daughter, and I prefer the subtle approach."

After what felt like a heart-pounding eternity, Asher smiled and stepped away from Lola. "I never knew Wellington was interested in interior design." He pushed aside a cloth that served as the door into his back room and disappeared from sight for a few seconds. When he returned, he held a small jar under one arm. "Why's it so important to him?"

Lola's face became impassive once again. "I have no idea. You know he doesn't tell me anything. It could be for his elderly aunt, for all I know. How much?"

"That blabbermouth Olivia called me last night and said Wellington would be looking for this." Asher held the jar in front of his face, as if inspecting it, and then glanced at Lola again. "I got my hands on it right away. Nothing passes through this town that I don't know about." He paused again. "Which makes me curious, Lola Lane. Why don't I know anything about this?"

"Because it's meaningless to anyone but Wellington," Lola said, and though her face was still expressionless, her voice sounded strained to Death's ears. "None of his jobs ever mean much of anything to me."

"That's true. You know, I just don't understand why you won't take my offer and work for me instead. There's a lot more exciting things in the world than old jars and spying on used bookstores."

"You bet. How much?"

"Paris, for instance. I've heard you want to run away to Paris. I go there all the time. Just come with me, Lola. It's a great city."

Death inched closer to Lola and, for a long few seconds, silence filled the smoky shop. Finally, with more than a little hesitation, Lola sucked in a deep breath and spoke again.

"I do want to go to Paris. But when I go, it'll be without the ownership of anyone else," she said. "Now, tell me how much I owe you so I can get back to my boring life in Boston."

For a few tense seconds, Death wondered if Asher might go bananas and kill both of them in a meticulous and supremely messy way that involved slit throats and dozens of knife thrusts into the chest, eyeballs, and other important body parts. Probably starting with Lola, to build anticipation.

And honestly, he just wasn't prepared for that kind of bloodshed.

"Yeah. Yeah, you should get back to that," Asher said then, and Death let out an audible sigh of relief. Asher slid behind the counter, settling into his chair again. "Who's your girlfriend?"

"He's a friend."

Asher chuckled to himself, the kind of chuckle that makes babies cringe, and placed the jar on the counter. "Hundred bucks," he said. "Low price today, just because you're feeling so sassy and I like that."

Lola handed over a card. "Swipe it."

"Ooooh, plastic? Wellington's moving up in the world." Asher chuckled again, successfully making Death cringe this time, and bent to swipe the card through a tiny machine. He punched some numbers in, humming to himself. "I love talking to him on the phone. He tries to act like he's got it together. But that guy's ready to piss himself every time he so much as hears my name."

"I stay out of his business."

"Do you? I guess his business gets pretty boring, huh?" He handed the card back over. "It's always such a pleasure doing business with you, Lola Lane."

"I wish I could say the same."

"You can lie to me. I know how good you are at lying," Asher said and winked at her. "Enjoy your jar. And if you ever change your mind and want a real man, you know where I'll be."

"You bet I will," Lola muttered, as she pushed Death toward the door.

"It would be sad for the little orphan girl to just wander the streets of Boston forever. Or until someone snaps her neck and leaves her broken, pretty body in an alleyway."

Lola paused as they reached the doorway and turned back to Asher. "My friend here is a psychic."

Asher laughed. "Oh, I'm sure he is. Did he read your palm before or after he tried to get into your pants? I mean, not that you'd mind, since you're such cute little lesbians."

Lola cast Death a narrow-eyed glance. "Do your thing," she whispered. "The fear thing. Do the fear thing."

Crap.

Death searched his memory, not finding anything attached to this guy. Had he ever even made a nightmare for Asher?

"Please," Lola said.

Finally, Death straightened to his full height and pushed past Lola so he stood directly between her and the lounging jerk. "Your days of modeling underwear are over. That spot on your hip is gonna get bigger and bigger and bigger. And it might be skin cancer. People are gonna be grossed out when they see it, so I'd keep that covered if I were you."

Asher's face lost its smug slant and Death and Lola made a hasty exit from the store.

"That was amazing!" Lola said. "Did you know he used to be a model?"

"No, it was a guess."

"A good guess!"

"Yeah, well, I'm good at my job. And that guy was like a knife trick and a dancing monkey away from some kind of traveling circus freak."

Lola laughed. "Well, that's Asher."

"Seriously, though, why did you tell him we're getting the jar for Wellington? I thought you said it had something to do with Fashion?"

Something felt odd, all at once, in a way that Death couldn't quite pinpoint until he realized that no one around him was moving or making any noise at all. He grabbed hold of Lola's arm to stop her and took note that everyone's attention seemed to have been diverted toward the sky.

Death tipped his head back and peered heavenward, only to see a swirl of crimson bleeding into the purple of the sky.

"What—what is that?" Lola whispered, shifting closer to Death until she was pressed against his side. "Is that them? Your agency?"

Numbly, Death nodded and watched as several strands of red streaked across the sky with a lazy, ominous bent. A shriek pierced the air and a woman pointed at the sky, words of fear and confusion tumbling from her mouth.

Death felt a shudder run through Lola and he slipped his arm around her back, folding her closer.

"Is it aliens?" someone called, and other voices, other suggestions sounded, everything from aliens to experiments to falling stars to volcanoes. Fearful clusters of mental anguish and crackling worry sounded around Death, a discordant symphony that should have distracted and deafened him.

But all he could do was study Lola's profile as she stared at the sky.

"We should get back to Boston," he said. "Things could get ugly fast, if people panic."

Lola's lips remained parted with the same contagious, wordless fear that had infected everyone in sight, and though she nodded, she made no move to heed his suggestion.

"Come on, Lola."

"Look, it stopped! It's gone!" she said, pointing.

Death tore his gaze from her and glanced at the sky. Sure enough, the red had vanished into the purple and everything looked as it might on any ordinary afternoon.

"We should go," Death said again, and this time Lola complied.

As they boarded the train back to Boston, Lola tugged on his shirtsleeve. "What were they doing?" she whispered to him.

He shook his head, sitting beside her. "It's unusual for them to change it again so soon. I think they like to wait about a hundred years before changing it again."

"Changing the color of the sky?"

"Yeah, I dunno. It's weird. But they shouldn't be doing it already. It hasn't been long enough."

"Are they trying to scare us?"

Death heard conversation after conversation regarding the changes in the sky, and all manner of possible explanations from the people sitting around them.

"Maybe it was an accident," he said finally, and felt Lola lean against him. "Don't worry, Lola. I'm sure it doesn't mean anything." With less hesitation than he would have expected, he pressed his lips against the side of her head and heard a soft sigh in response. "Maybe someone had a temper tantrum and played around with the color. Or maybe someone's pulling a prank."

But the truth was so much more troubling, wasn't it? Something had gone terribly wrong up there, and a sinister voice in the back of Death's head said it was only the beginning.

"I don't think those Sumner people were lying yesterday," Lola said, after what felt like a very long time. "What if it *was* your agency that sent that reaper after you?"

A burning sensation in Death's gut told him that Lola might be a lot closer to the truth than he wanted her to be, but he didn't dare say anything aloud. To do that might be to bring it to life.

Lola's hand fell against his cheek, turning his face toward her.

"What?" he said.

Half of her mouth turned up in a smile. "Your hair is poking out from under the hat."

"Is that bad?" he asked, reaching up to pat at his head.

"No, it's just funny, because part of it's, like, blonde, and part is blue and part of it is sort of this weird white color." Lola brushed at a wayward strand of his hair, her breath ghosting his face. "It's kinda perfect, actually, since you're so weird."

"Um, thanks?"

Lola's smile fell away. "I used to wish for a friend, when I was little. We were always on the road and I didn't have any siblings, so sometimes I made up these friends to go on adventures with. Usually, they were like Indiana Jones. One of them was closer to my age, though, and he lived in a big house on a cloud." She sighed quietly. "His name was Mortimer Vandersnout."

"Vandersnout? Wow, you had rich friends."

"Well, he had to have *some* money, if he lived in a cloud house," Lola said, rolling her eyes, but she giggled. "He was really weird, and he was going to take me on adventures and then we were going to go live in his cloud house. Which, of course, would be full of all kinds of cool things like candy and skateboards and movies and an indoor swimming pool. And a dog, maybe."

"So what happened to Mortimer? Will I get to meet him sometime?"

Lola rested her head against his shoulder. "Nah, I stopped thinking about him after Daddy and Mom died," she said, the words falling heavily one after another, borrowed from a little girl who had disappeared a long time ago.

"I used to think of places I wanted to go when I got older," Death said. "Some were going to be a little more difficult, like Middle-Earth, but some of them were concrete enough that I'd get books about Australia or Brazil and plan my trips."

"Did you go?"

"What, to Middle-Earth? I mean, as much as being hobbit-sized would have come in handy, I decided the dragons and evil rings were a bit too much for me."

Lola's arm snaked across his lap, which caused that general area to take notice as she hugged herself against him. "Australia, I mean. Did you go to all of the places you wanted to go?"

"Yeah, I guess. But it wasn't how I imagined it. A lot of things are different after you, well…die in a car accident," he mumbled, and neither of them spoke for a long time.

"Maybe I found my friend," Lola said at last.

"I don't have a house on a cloud."

"No, but you're probably the only person I've enjoyed spending time with since my parents died." She shifted, turning his face toward her again. "And you are definitely weird."

He meant to say something, but she kissed him. This time, he didn't experience the electrical charge of lust or even the frenzy of going too long without human contact. This time, he felt only a gentle buzz of contentment and a comfort in exploring his own existence.

After a long time Death realized they were still wound up in each other, and that the woman sitting in front of them had turned and craned her neck so she could shoot them a rather disapproving look.

"When we get back to Boston, I'll take this to Wellington and meet you back at the apartment," Lola said, her lips brushing against his ear. He shivered and nodded. "Do you think you can find your way back all right, without me?"

"Yeah, I'm pretty good with directions. Except in Texas, apparently. I was lost there for twelve hours one time."

"Don't get lost for twelve hours."

"I'll try not to." Death turned his head, and caught a glimpse of the purple sky through the windows of the train. The red had vanished, but thumbprints of fear remained.

Lola sighed quietly, resting her head on his shoulder again. "Don't get lost at all, okay? Things that get lost in Boston tend to stay lost."

CHAPTER THIRTY-SEVEN

Wellington was not a man to be frightened of anything except feminine hygiene products and the occasional Burger King commercial, but having Jessica storm into his coffee shop sent a cold shudder up his normally stiff spine.

"Good afternoon, Mr. Wellington," she said, in the sort of voice that made cabinet doors slam shut and children run for cover. "Do you know that today is Friday?"

Clearing his throat, Wellington nodded. "Aye, day after Thursday, same as always."

"You must know why I'm here, then?"

In that moment, Wellington fully expected the phone in his pocket to vibrate and for Lola to be on the other end, huffing and puffing and yelling that she was just down the street, on her way, moving at a brisk pace. She would, of course, reveal that she had the jar in hand, and then Wellington would just smile at Jessica and offer her a cup of coffee.

But his cell phone remained dead and still in his pocket.

"She's in Salem now."

"Who is?"

He hesitated. "Lola. She went to Salem this morning to get it. My contact found it, and, well, anyway, this other bloke called me about it because he'd heard I was looking and he has his fingers on everything in Salem." Wellington reached up to wipe sweat from his forehead, only to realize that he wasn't sweating. In fact, he felt unpleasantly cold.

"Ah, I see. And when will little Lola arrive with my item?"

Wellington felt as if he had arrived at a very important destination. This was the sort of destination that a man only arrives at approximately once in his lifetime, and usually on a battlefield or in some similarly disagreeable circumstance. He could answer honestly and risk Jessica's fury, or he could lie and risk something worse.

"She should be along soon. I can't tell you exactly when," he said. "Would you like a cup of coffee, perhaps?"

Jessica smiled, and not the pinched, fake smile that he'd seen during their dinner at Walking Turtle. "I'd like you to have my jar to me within the next three hours, Mr. Wellington. You can keep your coffee beans and your pathetic little shop. After all, soon there won't be much use for things like stores or money, so enjoy it while you can, hmmm?" Jessica leaned toward him, her eyes searching his. "When the girl brings my jar, you're going to run as fast your legs will carry you. You're going to meet me at South Station. All right?"

Wellington was certain that he intended to nod, but he wasn't certain if he actually went through with the action. His brain had betrayed him and had gone into a new mode of white-hot panic, in which all thoughts and words had simultaneously disappeared and hadn't bothered with leaving any sort of notes about when they'd be back.

"Don't disappoint me, Wellington. For your own sake."

He managed to nod and then, much to his own surprise, to speaks as well. "Just what did you mean about the coffee shop and coffee bean business? Something about no use for money?"

"Oh, did that stick in your mind?"

"A bit, yeah."

Jessica smiled. "It's not the end of the world, if that's what you mean."

"Comforting." Wellington tapped his fingers against the counter. "But picturing a reality in which money is of no importance is still disturbing. I'd rather like to hear more about that."

"I don't like to give away the climax of the story, Mr. Wellington. How boring would it be if I regaled you with tales of mass panic and fear and clamor and then, somewhere down the line, quiet streets and meditation and respect? That seems awfully unfair, doesn't it? You should never spoil the story for someone."

Jessica's hand slithered down her side, stopping at her belt.

"But I suppose I can give you a little preview," Jessica said. "Just a little one. Watch closely."

And before Wellington's eyes, Jessica transformed.

CHAPTER THIRTY-EIGHT

As Death headed into Lola's building, he nearly tripped over a homeless man. This wasn't an altogether surprising turn of events until the homeless man coughed and said, "Thank God I found you, Death," in a voice that sounded suspiciously like Mr. Right's.

"What?" Death said, because that was the question programmed into him for any situation such as this one.

"It's a good thing I had her address, from when they told me to make her fall in love with Wellington," the homeless man said, and raised his head from the Styrofoam cup cradled in his hands.

Oh. It WAS Mr. Right.

"What do you want?" Death demanded.

Mr. Right let out a miserable groan. "I've been exiled. I always thought Boston was a nice city, but it's terrible. A little girl kicked me earlier and said I have evil eyes. She couldn't have been older than five years old."

"Yeah, imagine how I felt when you left me on a train. Imagine how I felt when I managed to get *off* the train and then found myself in an underground horror show of…of…of khaki pants and cell phones and claustrophobia!" Death said, his voice getting louder and tighter with every word. He stepped back from Mr. Right, crossing his arms over his chest. "Why'd they exile you? Did you fail to get one of your *other* friends fired?"

"There are so many terrible things that I must warn you of, Death. I know that what I did to you was inexcusable, but I was working under orders. Please sit down with me, old friend, and let's talk," Mr. Right said.

"Old friend? You tricked me!"

Mr. Right stood up. "Please, Death, let's talk. I'm not sure how much time I have, considering what they've got planned." He took a step forward and Death lunged away from him. "Kelly."

"You can't just show up."

"Kelly."

"Get out of here!"

"Kelly. Please listen to me."

"Stop calling me that!" Death shouted, taking another step back.

"I was the one who brought you into the program," Mr. Right said, his voice quiet and sad. "When you died, they assigned me to test you and approve or disapprove you for placement in the agency."

Death shook his head, trying to think of something to say, anything to ease some of the burning rage building inside him. His hands trembled and twitched at his sides and, when Mr. Right stepped toward him, Death shoved him back. "Stay away from me."

"They tested you."

"I know they tested me! Don't you think I remember that? Wires and—and...all of those noises and the questions, and those bindings? Don't you think I remember being held down by ropes or cables or something, when I didn't even know if I was alive or dead?"

"Listen to me, Kelly. They tested you, and you had a high number on the aggression scale."

Oh, that memory stood out above all others. The ghost faces over him, the sensation of being alive and not alive and dead but not himself but someone, someone concrete and fluid and tingling with fear. They kept saying he was fighting too much, he wasn't ready for them or he didn't belong in the program or something. And he'd just wanted to go home.

"You didn't have a 5.0."

"No, I'm pretty sure I did. They only said so a thousand times."

"You had an 8.9. And I changed it on the paperwork, because I wanted them to keep you," Mr. Right said, in one easy sentence disrupting reality, the world, everything.

"That's...that's not true."

Mr. Right tossed away the Styrofoam cup, letting the last of his coffee spill out on the sidewalk. "Malcolm said that we needed to recruit someone for the Death position. You happened to arrive on the right day. They were going to pass on you, though, because you were so unstable and angry. I wasn't even supposed to be there, it all just happened that way, I don't know why. And I convinced Malcolm to hire you." He hesitated. "Kelly.

Do you really think I would have done that if I'd only intended you harm?"

"It doesn't matter," Death said, his hands still shaking at his sides. "Whatever you did for me doesn't matter. You betrayed me. A reaper tried to kill me. I've heard the Rattle twice. I'm hungry and I'm tired and my feet hurt and I—I'm... Things lost in Boston tend to stay lost!"

"Please listen to me. Jessica and Malcolm are up to something, and that reaper was only the beginning. Your life is in danger."

"No kidding. My life has been in danger ever since you got me fired." Death turned away from Mr. Right, glancing heavenward. "Lola's going to be back soon, and you need to go away."

"Lola? Wellington's little pawn? Kelly, she's using you. I fear her motives are darker—"

"Don't talk to me about Lola," Death ground out between clenched teeth.

"Jessica instructed her to keep an eye on you, and to retrieve a jar for her. Do you know what that jar is, Kelly?"

Death froze.

"It's Pandora's jar."

"Pandora had a box, not a jar."

Mr. Right smiled a terribly sad smile. "That was a mistake in the translation. Pandora was given a jar, and it held all of the nightmares of the world in it. It's been hidden for some time, in an ordinary spot, somewhere where we'd leave it alone and mortals would forget about it. Jessica instructed Wellington to find it, though. *And* she instructed Lola to keep an eye on you."

Death's mind ticked through random memories of the last few days. He thought of going shopping with Lola and running into the Sumner people and the trip to Salem earlier and their time together on the train ride back.

No.

"The paperwork they stole from you is connected to the jar; I'm almost convinced of it. Jessica set you up by giving you the names of the damned and who knows what else, having it stolen from you and…well, now she can keep all of it."

"But the Wings," Death said, the words falling out with a miserable punctuation.

"She's sidestepped everyone, even them. And she and Malcolm are planning all sorts of awful things. I don't know the half of it, but I do know we have to do something."

Death shook his head. "No. No, you can do whatever you want, but I'm going to get my job back."

A great sigh emitted from Mr. Right, and he reached deep into his pocket to produce three of Death's talismans. "Here," he said, holding them out in offering. "Malcolm sent your things to the incinerator. I was able to save these before he exiled me."

For a long time, neither of them spoke and neither of them moved. Mr. Right held his hand extended and Death stared at it in hesitation. Finally, Death snatched the talismans off of Mr. Right's palm and pocketed them.

"They intend to kill you, I think," Mr. Right said. "Perhaps if we work together, though—"

"Hey!" a voice called, and Death started, turned slowly. Lola approached him at a brisk pace, her arms hugged over her chest like she was cold. "What's going on, Death? Who's this?"

"I need to—I need to talk to you," Death said. He pulled her away from Mr. Right and then faced her head on. "Did someone tell you to keep an eye on me?"

"What do you mean?"

"Just tell me." Say no, say no, say no. Even as he wished for all of this to be some evil fabrication on Mr. Right's part, though, he could see the hesitation and disappointment in Lola's gaze. "Don't lie to me, Lola. Not this time. Did someone tell you to keep an eye on me?"

She nodded.

"The jar," he said. "We weren't looking for it to find Fashion, were we?"

Lola held his gaze and slowly shook her head.

"You don't even know where he is, do you?" Death asked, his voice failing on the last word.

"I do. Lillian told me where he is a couple days ago. Before we went to the bookstore," Lola said. "You're not going to like it."

Instead of the expected rage or pain, Death felt only a surge of eerie calm claim his mind and words. "Where is he?"

"He's with the Sumner people. I guess he works out of their head office. Death, listen…"

"Where's their head office?"

"Wellington *did* ask me to keep an eye on you, but that's not the only reason I've spent time with you. You're—you're really weird and—and kinda fun and…"

"Please just tell me where my friend is, Lola. Then you and Mr. Right should hang out because I really think the two of you would get along great. Both of you have gone out of your way lately to make sure I'll never trust you again."

Lola looked away from him, tore through the contents of her backpack. She offered him a folded pamphlet. "The address is on there," she said. "I can take you—"

Death shook his head. "I'll find it myself."

"Be careful," Lola called after him as he walked away and rain fell around them again. "Be careful, Death. Wellington said something's going to happen. I've never seen him so spooked. Something's happening today, and it sounds bad."

CHAPTER THIRTY-NINE

The Sumner Organization building was not at all what Death had expected. The glass door announced THE SUMNER ORGANIZATION in tacky white stick-on lettering, but he couldn't help wondering if he'd gotten the wrong address as he pushed his way inside out of the rain.

Death's eyes moved over the walls of the foyer, seeing only a few faded motivational posters and a framed award for "Most Charitable Waterfront Citizen" for someone named Neil Matherson.

Wait.

Matherson?

"Can I help you?"

Death tore his eyes from the wall and then realized with a start that he was staring at Fashion, or some version of Fashion. This version of Fashion had close-cropped hair and lines around his wide mouth. His outfit consisted of jeans and a beige polo shirt, without one bit of silk, velour, leather or fur to be seen.

"Kelly!" this strange version of Fashion said. "Kelly Gold, you've found me at last!"

Death was almost certain that he was supposed to say something, but he couldn't force his lips to move or his voice to work properly. Finally, he just threw himself at his friend, initiating a back-slapping hug like the ones they'd shared more than a few times back in the day.

"You have no idea how happy I am to see you again," Death said. "I thought maybe they killed you or—or were torturing you or something. And then Lola said you worked here. You aren't going to believe the things that happened to me. They exiled me, and then I woke up on this train because I think I fell into a coma or something or into shock, but then I was on this train and I got off the train and walked up out of the station and heard the Rattle—"

Fashion pushed him away. "The Rattle?"

"Yeah, you know. That loud, scary noise that agents hear before they get—"

"I know what it is. Did you hear it before or after the reaper attacked you?"

Death bristled. "Was it the Sumner people who sent the reaper after me?"

"We don't have reapers, Kelly, good Lord. We're not like the agency! We only employ good people, and our entire purpose is to educate and protect mortals and former agents alike from the tyranny of Them."

"But how did you know I was attacked by a reaper?"

"You're all over television." Fashion shrugged. "It's been good for us! I don't think I've ever seen as much interest in our organization as I have this week. Letters, emails, phone calls, pilgrims at the door. Everyone wants to know what we know and who you are and what's going to happen."

Right about then, Fashion ought to have broken into a grin and said he was sick of acting serious and wanted to talk about something fun. He ought to have done a lot of things, but instead he just stood in front of Death with a stiff back and a fixed expression.

"What *is* going to happen?" Death asked finally, stepping back from his friend. "You have to help me. Everything's all wrong and I don't know what to think. Mr. Right got exiled and he showed up and said all of these confusing things." He closed his eyes, shook his head, let out a long breath. "I don't know what to do, Fashion."

"You must stop calling me that, for one thing. We don't use their tyrannical labels here. Those titles are demeaning and nothing more than a part of the agency's culture of control."

Death opened his eyes.

"More importantly, though, you've come to the right place. I'm so thankful that your spirit led you here, Kelly, because we have the answers you've been seeking. We've spent hundreds of hours studying the negative impact that They've had on this planet and on us, as people, and we've researched all sorts of methods for freeing the mind and the spirit from the negative energy that exists inside of us."

"Negative energy," Death said, a uneasy laugh erupting from his throat. He squinted at his friend, waiting for the punchline, waiting for anything to signal that this was all some badly timed joke. "What are you doing here, anyway? I mean, aren't these guys nuts? Malcolm said—well, not just Malcolm. Everyone said these people liked to torture agents." He cast a nervous glance around. "Are they listening to us?"

"Who, my colleagues?"

"Yeah, the Sumner people. Are they listening?"

Fashion leaned against a wall, crossing his arms. "I'm the only one here right now. Twee and I met this morning to talk about his future, and what good he'll accomplish once he becomes an official member of the Sumner Organization. He'll want to see you, considering he stopped by because of your television appearance. Same with this older man—you just missed him, in fact! He asked me all about you."

"Have they given you a lobotomy or something?" Death asked finally, the words tumbling out before he could stop them. "You don't sound like yourself, you don't act like yourself and, good God, you do not look like yourself." Death waved his hand. "I thought you said you hated polo shirts. You are wearing a *polo shirt.*"

Fashion's expression barely changed. "Not all of us can stagnate, and not all of us can allow our minds to be carved eternally by the cruel knife of oppression. I've changed out of a genuine need for freedom and sanity."

"To be honest, you sound like a complete tool right now!"

Silence fell between them.

"What happened to you?" Death said, shaking his head. Nothing about this man signaled the cool friend who had cared more about his hair than boring office policies. Death had always thought Fashion's signature long, curly hair had looked a bit like Captain Hook's, but who was to judge? And without the hair, his friend looked older and less dimensional.

"I'm happy now, here, with my brothers and sisters."

"You used to be pretty happy at the agency with me, too, if I remember right."

"Ah, Kelly, the memory is faulty and can believe whatever it wants to believe. Do you really think I was exiled because of the clothing styles of the 80s and 90s?"

"Uh, the 80s were pretty bad. I mean, I lived through half of that decade and even I was a little embarrassed."

"Kelly. Do you think that is why I was exiled?"

Death thought of the day when his friend had stumbled, wide-eyed, into Death's cluttered office cubby and had announced in a stunned whisper that he'd been exiled. It *had* happened awfully quickly, but Death had been too caught up in trying to save his friend from getting fired to really think about "why."

"I dunno," Death said.

"No, Kelly. I was exiled because I happened to overhear a conversation that I wasn't meant to. The funniest thing about that, really, is that I never told a soul about the information I'd accidentally acquired. But they knew. They knew everything, and they sent me down here with nothing but a bag of belongings and a bullet with my name on it. I would be dead now if it weren't for the Sumner Organization."

"How long have you been here?"

"They found me about a week after I arrived in Boston. Their leader was elderly, a kind woman who knew that her days were short. She trained me and asked me to lead in her place. And here I am. It was frightening at first, but I've come to love it. Hell might have been built under Boston, but Boston has kept some strange nobility through it all. It's truly a city where anything can happen."

"I hate it."

Fashion held out his hand. "Let me show you what the city was meant to be, Kelly! A harsh place, yes, but full of opportunities to cleanse the mind, to battle those who wish to make us conform."

"Why didn't you answer my letters?"

"Letters?"

"I must have sent you a hundred of them. Why didn't you answer?"

Fashion's face softened from its grim resolve and, for a few seconds, he almost looked like the man Death had always considered his best friend. "Do you think I could have kept correspondence with someone on the inside, Kelly? It would have been impossible. It would be a betrayal of everything we stand for. I didn't read the letters, though, if it makes you feel better."

"No. Not really."

"I've had other things to think about. We're preparing. And you must join us, Kelly."

Death cast another long glance around the foyer, noting that nothing seemed intimidating or frightening or even a fraction as strange as he'd always been told. In fact, if he were being honest, it felt a bit like the waiting room of a dentist's office. "Join you doing what?" he asked finally.

"They exiled you. Haven't you come to get your revenge?"

Before Death could think of any sort of answer, he sneezed.

"Ah, you're sopping wet. Forgive me for not noticing before. This rain, it's just another part of Jessica's sick plans for the mortals. Get them all depressed and dependent on whatever she wants them to be dependent on. Who knows what that'll be," Fashion said with a heavy sigh. "Would you like something warm to drink? I have coffee, hot chocolate." He crossed the room again, stepping behind the front desk and rummaging around. "And you're in luck, I even have two clean mugs!"

Fashion had always been Death's go-to source for good ideas. Well, bad ideas too, since Fashion had been a king of pranks and dares. But the older agent had been a wellspring of advice and history, something markedly different from the cold eyes and stiff posture of the man standing in front of Death now.

A part of Death wanted to give in, but he knew that couldn't happen. Instead, Death pushed his hands into the pockets of his hoodie and shook his head. "You're just a company man for these guys now," he said. "I have to go."

CHAPTER FORTY

Death wandered aimlessly, the buildings melting into each other and the rain soaking him clear through. Eventually, his legs grew weak and he slowed down; he stumbled a few times until he stopped walking and surveyed his dreary surroundings. It appeared that he'd found his way to some sort of pond. Well, if you could call it a pond. More like a shallow body of water with a bunch of decayed swan boats floating listlessly in the middle of it, like the remains of a floating fairground funeral.

With a heavy sigh, Death sat down in slushy grass and pulled his knees up to his chest. He sneezed a few times, and his vision blurred. At first he thought it was just from the rain on his glasses, but then realized that it was actually tears obstructing his vision. Now, Death had never been much of a crier, not even back in his Kelly days. Tears were usually a last resort, saved for things like broken relationships and that one time he'd fallen off the stage during the Christmas play.

But these were tears. Real tears, the kind that burned your eyes and made you feel even sorrier for yourself than you had before.

"This is really depressing," a familiar voice said, from just beside Death. He turned his head and saw only the faint glimmer of a shape beside him. "Oh. You probably don't remember me, do you? I don't know how many ghosts you come into contact with but I'm Michael. Ohio? Baseball fan…?"

More tears crowded Death's eyes at this news. He hugged his knees closer to his chest and closed his eyes, effectively curling himself into the smallest shape humanly possible.

"That's fine. I probably wouldn't want to talk to me either, I guess," Michael said. "God, those boats are awful, aren't they? Someone really ought to repaint them or burn them or something." After a long pause, Michael spoke again. "You're not going to commit suicide, are you?"

"No!"

"You don't have to act indignant. It's not that strange of a question, given the circumstances. You're sitting in wet grass during an apocalyptic rainstorm, staring at a bunch of depressing swans. This is the moment when even the sanest man could crack."

Death groaned. "Thanks. I was completely unaware of my situation before you laid it out for me."

"No need to be snippy. I just observe a lot from my unique perspective."

"I don't want to die, okay? I just want things to be okay, and nothing is okay," Death said, raising his head enough to look at the ghost. "Why can't things just go back to being okay? I was working, minding my own business, delivering that parcel for Malcolm and visiting Boston. None of this was supposed to happen." The more he thought about it, the more miserable he was. He'd become lost in Boston, and things lost in Boston didn't tend to be found. He'd probably end up rotting here and becoming another part of the depressing scenery. Or worse, he'd apply for a bunch of mediocre jobs and end up a mailroom jockey for a law firm.

"So, I guess it's not enough that everyone's already depressed. Now they need to be terrified, too." Michael said, effectively interrupting Death's dismal daydreams of nondescript coffee mugs and mail-sorting. "Do you know what she's doing?"

Death's eyes fell on Michael again. "Who?"

"That woman with all the shadowy stuff around her. I'm assuming she's someone important, because she's surrounded by ten of those creepy things in the hoods and capes." Michael paused. "Ten isn't an exact number. I didn't do a full count. There was a lot of hoopla about a jar, though."

Jessica. It had to be Jessica.

Overhead, the clouds gathered and twisted together and an inky red permeated the horizon. Death stood up without thinking, walked away from the swan boats, past a fountain statue of a baby and through a gate. As soon as he left the park area, Death realized that many other people were doing the same thing he was—staring at the sky in open-mouthed shock. Some of them clung to friends or spouses, and some of them sat down on the ground, as if even gravity itself had betrayed them.

Somewhere across the street, on the side of a building, a sign announced FEEL LIKE THIS IS THE END? ASK YOUR DOCTOR ABOUT SMILUSET.

"Kelly?"

A shudder ran through Death, as if he'd just died and come to life again. He turned around slowly, expecting to see the long-ago image of his high school bully, Carter Reed. Instead, he saw only a gray-haired man wearing rumpled clothes.

"It *is* you," the man said, in a voice that stank of sorrow. "I followed you here from the Sumner building. I knew it was you." He stepped closer and closer until he stood over Death, his hands shaking. "God, it's you."

Death tried to force his legs to move, but found himself completely frozen. "Who...?" he asked hesitantly.

"You did all of this, didn't you? You cursed me."

Under all of the wrinkles, Death thought he could almost recognize someone else, a figure from his past, the person whose voice matched up to this voice. "Carter," he whispered, and knew he was right before he even said the name.

"Why did you curse me? I didn't have anything to do with what happened to you." Carter's voice broke and Death winced. "It wasn't my fault you died! Why can't you just leave me alone?"

Death had never quite given up his high-school image of Carter. He still saw Carter as a tall kid with a crooked, annoying smile and broad shoulders.

This Carter Reed had been transformed by time and everything that came with 24 years. This Carter Reed was an old man with bad posture and an age spot on his cheek, too many wrinkles for 50.

"Why are you haunting me?" Carter said, his words falling out in clumsy bunches. "I didn't kill you! I was at your...I-I came to the funeral. How are you still...? I saw them bury you."

"You came to the funeral?"

"I was just a kid, Kelly."

Not long after he'd taken on the position as agent of nightmares, Death had visited Carter's dreams and created such a horrific vengeance that even the superiors had been surprised. Not many nightmares registered above a 10, but Death's cruel concoction of guilt and fear had set a few records and messed Carter Reed up for life. It had been easy to justify such an action, but only until the subject stood quaking in front of you.

"Stop haunting me."

"I'm not. Not anymore."

"You told me I'd be alone."

Death shook his head, knowing the rest all too well. "Don't, Carter. You're free of it. I didn't really mean what I said; I was just stupid and abused my power."

"So was I!" Carter shouted.

Death met Carter's gaze and saw only decades of missed opportunities and accidental bitterness staring back at him. "I'm sorry. I'm so sorry. I thought you ruined my life and I just wanted to—I wanted to feel vindicated. You're free, though. None of it was even true. It was just a dream."

Carter tipped his head up. "You said the sky would turn red. You said I'd live to see the end of the world."

"No. No, this isn't what you think it is."

"You said, before the end, I'd see you again and I'd be old and you'd be young. God, Kelly. Why? Making a mistake doesn't make me a villain. And getting revenge doesn't make you a hero."

Death heard a scream in the distance and jumped, raising his gaze to the heavens. Finger-trails of red traced across the darkening sky, even more sinister than before. Lightning flashed a few times in the most dramatic manner possible, and thunder rumbled. Another scream punctured the air.

"Listen to me, Carter. You're free from all of that. You're free! Just go home. I'm gonna fix this."

"You can't stop the end of the world."

Death shook his head. "This is bad, but it's not the end of the world. The rest of your life is going to be pretty great, I promise," he said. "Just go home and forget I ever existed."

Death ran.

First things first, he needed Michael.

"I have a job for you," he said, as soon as he found the ghost. "I need you to use your ghosty powers to lead me to Mr. Right."

CHAPTER FORTY-ONE

Death found Mr. Right almost exactly where he'd left him, outside of Lola's apartment building. He all but collided with the older agent, panting from running and burning with overextended energy. "Look," he said. "Look, you're right. We need to work together and stop Jessica—" He stopped, stared at Mr. Right for a long few seconds and then quirked an eyebrow. "Are those…sugar-free cookies?"

Mr. Right let out a heavy sigh. "Yes, and they're quite rich. But I knew the craving would not go away until I satisfied it." He shot a doleful glance at the cheerful recycled-cardboard box cradled in his big hands. "They cost me most of what I had left in the way of monetary provision."

"Why are you…?"

"They're so sweet and savory. I suppose, at this point, what do the calories matter?"

"No, I mean, if there's no sugar in it, why bother?" Death asked, and then waved his hands around in the air. "Whatever, whatever, forget it. Look, I came back to find you because we really do need to stop Jessica."

"But what can we do?" Mr. Right motioned at the sky. "Malcolm said they plan to unleash reapers on the world. Without the help of the Wings, I hardly think we're much good against reapers, never mind Jessica and the powers of Pandora's Jar. The more I think about it, the more hopeless it seems."

"That doesn't mean we can't keep this from getting any worse." Death drew up to his full height, though that just made his lungs burn even more. "You and I make a pretty epic team when we need to, and I think this is one of those times."

Instead of Mr. Right straightening his tie and making some stiff comment about how they might as well get on with it and save the world, nothing but bleary silence emanated from the older man.

"Come on, Right. We'll be like—we'll be like the characters in *A Wrinkle in Time*. They were just kids, you know. And Meg. Meg was scared. She wanted someone else to step up and save everyone." Death cleared his throat, tears burning his eyes. "But she had to do it. And she did pretty well, in the end, because she used her weaknesses to her advantage for once."

"I have no idea what that means," Mr. Right said.

Death laughed, despite himself. "Of course not. Uh, never mind all of that, then."

"We are powerless here without our auras, old friend."

"Not as helpless as you think! Because we have Michael!"

Mr. Right blinked. "Who?"

"This, right here. Michael, the ghost." Death snapped his fingers. "Michael?"

Michael half-materialized.

Death pointed at him. "Michael can see auras."

"I guess they have to give you some sort of talent when you're dead," Michael said, with a heavy sigh. "Since you have absolutely nothing else going for you."

"And he can see the negative in almost every situation," Death added.

"Ah." Mr. Right cleared his throat. "If we decide to ride out for this mission, old friend, we may not come back. You do know that, don't you?"

"Yeah, by this point it's been pretty deeply ingrained. But this is all partly my fault, and I need to try to fix it." He thought again of Carter Reed. "I don't want to be the bad guy, even if by default."

"Wellington mentioned something about Jessica wanting paperwork, along with the jar, I have a feeling that's what Lola stole from you. And if it's what I think it is, it's the instructions for how to use the jar. Do you know if Lola still has the paperwork? Or has it been delivered to Jessica?"

Death sucked in a deep breath. "There's only one way to find out."

*

Death knocked on the door to Lola's apartment, stepped back, stepped forward, swayed a bit, and struggled to both catch his breath from the stairs and catch his thoughts from the nervous direction they'd run off in.

After what felt like forever, the door swung open and Lola stood in the doorway with her arms crossed over her chest.

"Can I come in for a second?"

"Did you come back for your things? Because I've already packed them for you," she said, her mouth barely moving.

For a few seconds he thought she might throw a bag in his face, presumably full of heavy personal belongings, and then slam the door. But instead he saw only a flicker of something like sadness and a slight quiver to her lip, just before she raised a hand to cover half her face.

"No," he said. "No, I came back for you."

She stared back at him. "Why?" she whispered, after a long pause.

"Remember when you said how I'm the only person you really enjoy spending time with? Or—or something nice like that. Well, anyway, you're like that. But for me." He felt as if his tongue had turned to rubber and a nervous shiver ran through him from hands to toes.

"You know, I didn't keep you around just because Wellington told me to."

Death sighed. "Will you please come with me? I have to try to stop Jessica. That jar you gave Wellington, and the stuff you stole from me? It's serious stuff. He gave it to Jessica and, well, she's the one out there changing the weather forecast."

"I don't know anything about the jar. Honest."

"The papers you stole from me. Did you ever look through them?"

"Only a little. It's not my job to care about the content."

"What did you see when you looked through, though?"

She hesitated. "Mostly names. Lists of names. But there were also some kind of instructions for something that kinda looked like a spell."

"That was probably for the jar! Apparently, I was her errand boy and you were the delivery service."

"Look, I—I talked to Wellington when I delivered everything, and I told him that I didn't want to do this anymore. I didn't want to be assigned to keep an eye on you or keep things from you."

"Oh."

"No, listen! He was in a panic, he ran off yelling that he was in a lot of trouble. But I told him. I told him that I wasn't going to…that I didn't want assignments that had anything to do with you."

"Whatever. We'll talk about that later," Death said, shaking his head. "I need to try to stop Jessica. And I'd like you to come with me."

This time Lola didn't hesitate. "Let me get my bag," she said, turning and darting back inside.

"If we needed to get across the city pretty fast, what would be the best way to do so?"

"Where is it?"

"Uh, we'll be taking directions from my…friend."

Lola snatched up her bag and turned to Death. "How much is time of the essence?"

"It's very of the essence."

"Well, if you have no idea where we're going and we have to follow directions, I guess a car would be the best choice. My roommate has a car we can use."

A car.

In Boston.

*

Cara's car turned out to be one of those little ones that made you feel a bit like a circus bear on a bicycle. Death peered into the window and shook his head. "We'll walk," he said.

"I'm afraid we don't have time for that," Mr. Right said in his supremely apologetic voice. "We must make haste to Jessica or risk failing our mission. She may have already opened the jar."

Death glanced between Mr. Right and Lola. "Can't you drive?" he asked Lola.

"I wasn't exactly lovingly raised by sweet suburban parents and given a brand new cherry-red Mustang for my sweet sixteen. I've never driven in my life."

Death let out a mighty sigh, but it ended in a note more like a sob. Ooops.

"Fine, fine," he said, hauling the door open and plopping himself in the driver seat. Memories flooded him, centering most heavily on the bizarre and inconsequential. He'd worn an unmatched pair of socks in his hurry to get on the road, it had taken three clicks to get his seatbelt to work, and the new Depeche Mode song had been playing on the radio.

"We really must hurry," Mr. Right said, shaking Death from his thoughts. "Will you be able to operate this motor vehicle?"

Lola slid into the front passenger seat, snapping her seatbelt into place. "You look like you've never seen a dashboard before," she said.

"Everything's a little different from how I remember, okay?" Death said. He pulled his seatbelt on and shoved the key into the ignition. The car roared to life and the buttons lit up, as a chirping noise sounded overhead. "Okay, this has to be pretty similar. It's the same idea, right?"

He pushed a button and the windshield wipers roared to life.

"Why are you cleaning the windshield?" Lola said.

"I like it clean!" Death said, his face burning. He managed to turn the windshield wipers off and then directed his attention toward moving the car.

After a few false starts, he placed the car in drive and inched it forward a few feet.

"You know, walking might be faster," Michael said from the backseat.

Death ground his teeth together, commanding his brain to stop bombarding him with memories of his accident. With more than a little effort, he drove the car out into the street. Good, good. Now to increase speed from…15mph….to something a bit more reasonable.

"Where are we going?" he asked as they reached a victorious 30mph. The driver behind him blasted his horn and pulled into the oncoming traffic lane to pass Death.

"She's over South Station," Michael said. "Hey, though I can see you've clearly made quite a lot of effort already, you may want to speed up a bit."

"Switch lanes," Lola said. "We need to make a turn up here."

Death held his breath and switched lanes. "I did it! I DID IT!"

"Switching lanes at five miles an hour is pretty impressive if you're riding a tricycle," Michael said. "Not to discourage you, of course, when you're making such substantial progress."

Between snarky comments from Lola and Michael, they made their way across the city and toward the column of black smoke that marked Jessica's melodramatic descent from the heavens.

"What a showoff," Death muttered, glaring into the distance. "I never liked her. I mean, I disliked Malcolm more, but Jessica was a close second." He looked at Lola then. "Where do we park?"

An explosion in the black column shook the ground.

"Never mind, I'll park here," Death said, killing the engine and jumping out of the car. "We should stick close together, I think."

South Station had become consumed by a column of sooty black smoke that shot clear into the sky. Jessica floated perhaps a hundred feet above the ground. Surrounding the column was a group of maybe fifteen, twenty reapers.

A headache crashed into Death's thoughts, scattering them like reapers fleeing a Wing.

"We'll never get past them," Mr. Right said, but Death gritted his teeth and shook his head.

"We have to try," he said, already launching himself in their direction. "They still carry those bottles, don't they? Their aura bottles?"

Mr. Right cleared his throat from somewhere behind Death. "That has always been the policy, so I would assume so, but Malcolm has taken great liberties with so many policies in the last—"

"I think they do. Look, if we get the bottles from them, they're basically powerless." Death paused. "Lola! We're going to pick their pockets!"

Lola pushed closer to him, eyeing the reapers. "More information, quick."

"The reapers carry their auras in bottles. They usually keep the bottles in the pockets of their robes, or sometimes on their belts. It's a built-in safety mechanism, in case they ever go rogue or something, because then the bosses can just destroy their reaper auras. The big guys didn't want them to just have unlimited creepy power. Only the real Reaper is allowed that."

Lola gave him a jerky nod. "Okay."

"So, we just have to pick their pockets and break the bottles! Easy!"

Well, it seemed easy until the first of the reapers clawed Death across the face, successfully breaking his skin. Death reeled back, but just as quickly he forced himself to dive forward and slip his hand into the reaper's robe pocket. With a triumphant gasp, he dashed the bottle against the ground.

The reaper howled and melted into itself, collapsing to the pavement like wet tissue paper.

Another reaper jumped into its place, slashing at Death with merciless claws. Death dove low, curled his fingers around the reaper's aura bottle and threw it to the ground.

The third and the fourth reaper were relatively easy to disarm, but a fifth rushed Death from behind, striking him hard enough to send him sprawling across the pavement and into an abandoned taxicab. A quiet whine escaped Death as he pushed himself up and surveyed his torn palms and knees.

"Kelly, Kelly Gold," the reaper said, and then another said it, and then another. Three reapers surrounded Death as he climbed to his feet again. "Kelly Gold, it is your time…"

"Leave him alone!" Lola pushed into the circle, stealing one of the reapers' aura bottles and crushing it under her boot. Death took the opportunity of distraction to disarm another of the reapers, and then moved on to the third.

Jessica floated overhead, as if blind to what was taking place on the ground.

Death stole an aura bottle from another reaper. "Where's Mr. Right?" he shouted.

Lola glanced around, leaping to one side and then another, dancing among the reapers and effectively avoiding harm from any of them. "I don't know. He was right behind me a second ago!"

Death spun around, his eyes straining to spot his friend. All at once, he realized that a group of maybe five or six reapers had circled Mr. Right. He dodged a pair of especially menacing claws and then sprinted toward the other reaper group.

Disarming one of them was relatively easy, but Death quickly found himself trapped by several reapers with no wiggle room. "Right!" he yelled. "Mr. Right, get their aura bottles!" He took another brutal blow to the head and staggered sideways into a reaper. After a few seconds of blinking and attempting to push away the darkness that threatened to crowd into his head, Death dove forward and snatched another aura bottle.

Mr. Right hesitantly stole one of the aura bottles, and Death thought for a brief second that the older agent might actually apologize, but then he crushed the bottle in one of his hands. Lola threw herself into the fray too, and Death was able to stumble away, toward Jessica.

Jessica floated downward, slowly, landing on the ground in front of Death with a gentle thump.

"You're still alive," she said. "I'm not surprised. Rodents and roaches are hard to kill." Jessica spread her hands and the ground shook again, setting off screams.

"What are you doing?"

"I'm doing my job, Kelly. It used to be your job, if you'll remember correctly, but you lost it when you betrayed your friends and sold us out to the Sumner Organization."

"You have no right to scare everyone like this. They don't know about us. They don't need to see this!"

"And why do you care so much about mortals all of a sudden? If I remember right, you quite enjoyed making nightmares."

"Nightmares are different," he said finally.

"Different from what? From physical death? From fear?"

"Yes, because you wake up from them and everything is normal," Death said. "That's the fun in nightmares. They're not real."

A voice rang out from one of the clusters of terrified bystanders. "It's that guy from TV!"

Jessica smiled. "Nightmares aren't real? Well, that's news to me." She tugged at one of the holsters she always wore and tossed it aside. The smooth skin of her face changed, slowly, as if someone was painting it over with a glowing darkness. Her eyes changed too, fading into a full yellow color that Death had only seen once...the night of his promotion. She tore off her other holsters, and transformed fully. "The nightmares you make might not be real, but mine are the most famous nightmares in the history of the world. Wars, diseases, broken hearts, genocide... You might have been some pathetic little stand-in for Death, but I am the *real* Death. I am the Reaper, Kelly Gold, and your time is up."

Death struggled to regain use of his tongue, to think, to keep his knees from buckling. He felt as if all of his energy had drained away, but he fought against it. So that was why she always wore the holsters. Unlike her cronies, who had to carry their auras on their persons or lose their power, she had to carry some sort of charms at all times to keep her *true* form from showing.

Oh God, he'd always hated her.

"Battle me," he said finally. "Battle me with nightmares."

"Battle you?" she repeated, her voice filtered through whispers and screams and bells and static signals. "Why would I bother doing that?"

"I'm a better Death than you. You only work in the physical realms. You're no good when it comes to anything else. Give me my aura back and battle me. Prove how good you are at nightmares."

Jessica considered this, her new form strangely elegant in its evil grace. Finally, she smiled.

Stay strong! Stay strong. He held his chin high and stared back at her. "Go on, unless you're afraid you'll lose," he said, and she bowed her head slowly forward, toward her chest. One of her hands extended. Her fingers brushed against the wounded skin on his neck and it felt as if he'd just been torn into all over again.

But wait! He felt the familiar buzzing in his hands, in his feet, up his spine, sizzling in his head. Death sucked in a deep breath and looked at Jessica with something akin to confidence this time. He had his aura back.

"Follow me," he said, and created an invisible series of steps stretching into the sky. He climbed them without looking back, knowing Jessica would follow. Yes, she would probably kill him, but he intended to go out with style, so he strutted up those steps, making sure to wiggle his hips once or twice and even turn a fancy spin at the top.

Jessica followed him, though with considerably less flair. She had taken her human form again, mercifully.

"All right," she said. "Now what, Kelly? Are you going to crash a car into me?"

He shook his head. "I wouldn't waste a car that way. You go first. Create the strongest nightmare you can."

At that, Jessica raised an eyebrow and cocked her head in his direction. "You want me to go first? Do you really want to die so soon? I was rather looking forward to seeing what you came up with."

"My mother taught me to be a gentleman and always, always let ladies go first."

"How sweet."

Death took two steps backwards in the sky, crossing his arms over his chest. "Go on. If I give in to the nightmare, if I can't see that it's a dream, you win."

"Hmmm. Such a simple challenge. But then, you always *have* thought small, haven't you? Small body, small brain."

"But if I create a nightmare, and you don't know that it's a nightmare, then I win, and you have to give up your position and your aura."

She smiled. "Deal."

Jessica raised her hands with a dramatic flourish, and smoke danced between her fingers. The world around Death shifted, gently, and he felt as if he were being pulled through threads of lives and dimensions that were not his own...

...and then he was walking, hands shoved deep in his pockets, in a city of night tones, of shadow people and broken fluorescent signs. He felt older and then, somehow, saw himself as if from the outside. He *was* older, years older, and his hair was a dull sort of blond, approximately the blond of a man who has given up his personal appearance, his reading habits and most of his dreams.

He ran inside a grimy building, through hallway after hallway of graffiti messages and shouting inhabitants. Eventually, he let himself into an apartment and knew right where everything was, even though he'd never been there before, and walked to the sink before remembering that he had that thing to take care of. The baby. Where had he left it?

Oh right. The couch. The baby was still all wrapped up in blankets and gurgling and wiggling and staring helplessly around, waiting to be taken proper care of. But what do you do with a baby? Feed it, burp it. Take it for walks. He had no idea how to do any of those things and, come to think of it, didn't have any bottles or anything. How had he gotten himself into this mess? He couldn't even remember the girl who had brought the baby over.

He carried the baby out into the street, fully intent on handing it over to someone more capable of dealing with it. After all, he had work in the morning, always work in the morning, and come to think of it, work was at about 5AM and it was at the ominous black building at the top of the hill. Now that he looked at the building, it looked a bit like an evil octopus with tentacles that reached down into the midnight city below and controlled everything by a Lovecraftian power.

And it wasn't that surprising, really, that he couldn't remember the girl who had brought him the baby. It was hard to remember any faces, lately. It was hard to think ever since he'd started taking Smiluset. And Happinex. And Grinposa. He couldn't quite remember why he was taking all of them at the same time, since it wasn't recommended, but he had taken maybe 10 pills last night and then a few more before work that morning, hadn't he?

He dropped the baby off with a friend who knew a lot about kids because she used to have one, or maybe she still had one, but whatever, the important thing was that he got rid of it, and then he wanted to walk home but was always walking in the direction of the octopus building and really hated it, but he was searching his pockets for that bottle of Smiluset because maybe taking all of them would be a good idea on a night like this.

This is me, he thought. This is me now, this is me without the accident. This is me without Jessica, without the agency. This is Kelly Gold, 33 or maybe 34 or something, something in the 30s. Kelly Gold without an aura.

The thought was so heavy that he sat down on the ground and watched as the octopus building loomed ever closer and closer.

But wait. Wait, this couldn't be true.

"Poor Kelly. This is your future without us. Look what we saved you from!" Jessica said, from somewhere close by. He couldn't see her, but he heard her voice in his ear. "We saved you from all of this."

No. No, before his accident he'd finally gotten up the courage to apply to a job in Massachusetts, and had even looked at an apartment outside of Boston. He was sure of that. He'd made some progress. And he'd certainly decided that it was time to get out of New Hampshire, to do something with himself.

"No, you would have ended up alone and depressed in a place you hated," Jessica said. "Look what we saved you from! Endless turmoil and useless suffering."

Wait. No one used Smiluset in the 90s! "This is a nightmare," he said, sitting up. "This is just a nightmare. I was about to be awesome, before the accident!" He stood up. "This is a nightmare! This is a *nightmare!*"

And suddenly his eyes opened and Jessica towered over him, scowling.

"Go on, then," she said, drawing back from him. "See if you can do better."

Death hesitated, still breathing too hard from the lingering unpleasantness of the nightmare. He cleared his mind as best he could and focused on only one thing—Jessica.

And so he created a room, a simple bedroom. He created a modern vanity table, a mirror, a chair. He pushed dream Jessica into the chair, and coaxed her to gaze at herself. The reflection smiling back at her was the beautiful, intimidating form that Jessica usually wore. Her brown hair was pulled neatly back in a tight bun, her eyes were lined with black and her lips were a soft pink color. She smiled at her reflection and blinked.

Her reflection's eyes didn't reopen.

Dream Jessica stared at the mirror for a long few seconds, becoming more and more uncomfortable with each passing second. "Stop it," she said. "Stop it!"

Her reflection went on moving as she did, but with its eyes still closed.

"Stop it!" dream Jessica screamed. "Stop it, stop it, STOP IT!" She screamed louder and louder until she finally carried the screams into reality. Her body jerked and shuddered and her eyes finally flew open, just as another scream left her.

"I win," Death said.

Jessica shook and twitched from the dream, but finally she turned her angry gaze on him. "You little fool, you're no hero. You're only a coward who runs away from his problems and cries when he fights with a girl." She waved her hands and produced the one thing Death was not prepared to face.

Pandora's Jar.

CHAPTER
FORTY-TWO

Death wasn't sure if Jessica even opened the Jar entirely, or if she barely cracked the lid on it. All he knew was that it sent him tumbling backwards, falling, and burning from some unknown and undefinable pain that ripped through him, weakening his aura to almost nothing.

He couldn't hear himself as he howled from pain, because he was falling too quickly, and because the sky was exploding along with him. The heat and hurt ate into his eyes, forced his arms over his face in some pathetic attempt to block it all out, but nothing proved any solace.

The ground. Death was vaguely aware that he was going to hit the ground. Perhaps it would be better, though, because that way he'd be dead long before the world burned. He felt sorry for Lola, sorry that he hadn't been a little nicer to her. And he was even sorry for the guy who'd stolen his wallet. He was sorry for everyone, because he'd failed.

But then he felt hands grab him, stopping his descent so quickly that his neck hurt. He gasped and struggled and kicked, daring to open his eyes against the brightness overhead. "Michael?" he said. Michael had caught him and held him suspended above the ground.

Death gasped and covered his face again as the burning pain flooded him a second time.

"You have to do something," Michael said. "Come on, we're friends, remember? I don't really want to see you get fried."

"It's the Jar!"

"Okay, okay. So?"

"It's *the Jar*. It's not supposed to be opened, ever!" Death said, barely able to keep his feet as the ghost righted him. "This isn't a dream. There's no waking up from this." Flames fell around them in a chaotic symphony of destruction and Death's eyes brimmed with tears. "She won. The Jar won't stop until there's nothing left."

"Death! Death!"

Death turned slowly and saw Lola with Mr. Right on her heels. Lola looked as if she'd been burned, and Mr. Right's face was dark with ash. "Get away from me!" Death shouted. "You have to go away. It's not safe!"

And, sure as anything, he heard Jessica's voice over him, descending slowly from her lofty perch. The Jar was still open in her hands, spewing out its curses and spells and sickness and fire and smoke.

"Kelly Gold," she said, stepping down one last invisible stair and standing next to him. "The stupid little boy who dreamed of destruction but was too afraid to commit it. Aren't you happy you lived just long enough to see this?"

Death looked at his friends, his gaze lingering on Lola. "I have to go," he said, quietly, because he'd never gotten to say that before his car had run off the road all those years ago.

And he threw all of his slight weight onto the Jar, knocked it out of Jessica's hands and fell on top of it.

Everything went dark.

Dark.

Dark.

Silence.

Pain.

Dark.

Dark.

Dark.

Pain.

Dark.

Dark.

Dark.

Dark. Dark. Dark.

Dark...

"Kelly?"

Death became vaguely aware of voices, of someone prodding and pulling on him until he uncurled from the ball he'd ended up in. He felt them pry the Jar from his fingers, and felt pain explode through his hands because he'd been holding onto it so tightly that his fingers had gone stiff.

He felt warmth, the kind of warmth that usually kept company with something good, like sunshine or a toasted marshmallow, rather than something bad, like a fireball or an explosion.

And then he opened his right eye, just a little.

Wings! A couple of Wings were crouched around him, all glowy and bright with their golden wings and perfect skin and freaky weird eyes. Death felt like hugging every single one of them around the neck.

"Good. You're all right," one of them said.

No, he was not all right. In fact, Death was certain that his back was broken, his skin had been burned off, and his fingers were useless, but any attempt to argue this point was cut off when his voice decided not to work. Oh, well. He attempted to question them about what had happened through a complicated series of moans, groans and soft mewing noises, as well as a little twitching.

One of the Wings offered a rather joyless smile. "You closed the Jar. Not without more than a little threat of harm to yourself, Kelly. We stepped in to help."

Death coughed appreciatively and, after a little more of the moaning, groaning and mewing, he managed to sit up.

The world was no longer burning, but damage was still visible in every direction Death turned his eyes.

And Jessica.

Jessica and the remaining reapers stood close by, surrounded by a flock of Wings. Jessica seemed to know that Death had spotted her, because she turned her eyes on him and smiled.

"You've said I have to give up my position. Someone has to be the Reaper," Jessica said. "Give it to him! Give it to Kelly Gold!"

It seemed as if all of the Wings were looking at Death, questioning him with their weird eyes, but then a few of them took Jessica by the arms and hauled her out of sight.

"Where are my friends?" Death managed to say, finally. He coughed so hard that his internal organs threatened to escape. "Where's Lola? Where's Mr. Right? Where's…" He paused for more catastrophic coughing. "Where's Michael? Michael is a ghost."

"Someone will tend to them. For now, you need time to recover," one of the Wings said, and Death felt as if he were being lifted by a score of invisible hands. "You have done quite enough, Kelly Gold."

Chapter
Forty-Three

Death was kinda hoping for one of those luminescent rooms with a giant bed and a bunch of pillows, like in *Lord of the Rings*. Instead of photo-retouched faces and scads of flowers and soul-stirring music playing in the background, he got an uncomfortable cot in a cold room with only one window.

Even so, he slept for about a million hours and woke up feeling a lot less achy. A few Wings stepped into the room only moments after he woke and one of them, a particularly huge and intimidating one with red hair, eyed him a bit too closely.

"How do you feel?" the Wing asked, in a rumbling voice.

"Uh, okay. Where are my friends?"

"You will be able to see them very soon, Kelly Gold. First, I need to ask you some questions about Jessica."

"I think Malcolm has a lot to do with all of this too, just so you know. He's the one who sent me to the mail room for the papers in the first place. And he's really slimy, once you get to know him." Death paused, and couldn't resist adding, "Have you seen his mustaches?"

The Wings all froze and turned their eyes together, as if speaking amongst themselves.

"We have conducted a thorough investigation into matters involving both Jessica and Malcolm," the red-haired Wing said finally. "As well as several other staff members. We have already taken action against them."

Death hoped that the actions taken involved hanging them up by their toes and dipping them into a water tank full of hungry sharks, but he wasn't sure if he should share that idea aloud.

The Wings asked him a series of rather boring questions about Jessica's habits in the agency and her history of aggression against agents. Death made sure to recount, in great detail, the time that Jessica had yelled at him during one of the holiday parties and accused him of only attending for the food. (Which had been true, but none of her business, in his opinion.)

"Thank you for your help, Kelly Gold," the Wings said, all at the same time. Death shivered and shot them a nervous smile. "We have spoken to Them, and They would prefer that we promote from within, now that Jessica and Malcolm have been removed from their posts."

"Oh." Death leaned back against his pillows, pulling his blankets a little tighter around himself. "You should have Mr. Right do it. He knows all the rules. He's really old and stuff."

"Mr. Right has chosen to step down from his position. He has expressed a certain concern that he might become unstable if he continues in the vein he's in."

Mr. Right, stepping down? Death wondered for a brief second if the Wings might burst into uproarious laughter and slap him on the back and reveal that they did actually have a sense of humor, but had kept it hidden for so long that no one believed it anymore.

But they didn't.

"Wait, he really did? He stepped down?"

"We think you would make an excellent Head of Agent Resources, Kelly."

Ooooh. That didn't sound so bad, after all. "Will I get my own office?"

"You'll have a sizeable office, yes."

"Can Mandy be my personal assistant?"

The Wings stopped and stared at each other again for a long time. Finally, one of them nodded. "She may," he said.

"Cool. Okay!"

"You will begin work next week, Kelly. Is there anything else you need at the moment?"

"My friends. I'd really like to see Mr. Right and Lola and Michael. Michael is a ghost."

"Yes, we're aware of Michael. He is quite talkative." All of the Wings winced at approximately the same time, which was creepy. But then they shuffled toward the door, one by one, their magnificent wings fluttering behind them. "Enjoy your recuperation, Kelly," the red-haired one said, and then they were gone.

A few seconds later, Lola entered the room with slow, hesitant steps, as if she were walking on a boat for the first time. "Are you all right?" she asked, in a whisper.

"It's okay, my ears don't hurt. You don't have to whisper."

She glanced over her shoulder. "It's not you I'm worried about. It's those…"

"The Wings? Yeah, they're pretty cool, huh?"

Lola hugged her arms across her chest. "Cool? Not the first word that popped into my head, but okay. Cool works, I guess." She slipped closer and closer to his bedside, until she stood close enough to reach out and place her hand on his forehead.

"What're you doing? I don't have a fever," Death said, unable to keep from grinning.

"Well, you did. I think someone said you had a fever of 158 or something. And if I remember correctly, Mr. Right said that your aura was the only thing that kept you from melting like the Wicked Witch of the West."

"Oh." That was a troubling thought.

"But you feel all right now. You don't remember that?"

"It's all sort of patchy."

"Do you remember when you flirted with my mom?"

Death blinked. "Wait, what?"

"My mom. One of your finely feathered friends claims that my parents were agents a long time ago."

Once again, Death found himself waiting for the laughter that signaled a prank, and once again no laughter followed. "Who is your mom? Who are your parents? You're not kidding?"

"No, I'm not kidding. I guess they were called Drama and Muse when they were here. And you asked my mom on a date."

Death considered the merits of pretending to faint. A lot of the heroines in his favorite fantasy novels fainted at convenient times like this.

"Errrrrrr…"

"It's okay. I guess that's a risk you run when you date an old man," Lola shrugged. "You probably don't remember saying you love me desperately and want to marry me as soon as possible either, huh?"

"I… What? I…"

Lola pressed a kiss to his forehead. "I'm kidding, you didn't really say that. But you did say a lot of very strange things about cardboard, telephone poles and bubblegum."

Death let out a heavy sigh. "Well, that's okay, my brain was scrambled from fever and the Jar and whatever," he said, and then felt his face heat up. "I do kinda like you though, uh, speaking of that. You tend to be there when it matters." As he waited for her answer, he felt almost as nervous as when he'd faced off with Jessica.

"Well, you said you didn't have a cloud house," Lola said, leaning down so their faces almost touched. "But this? This HQ building is pretty close to a cloud house, in my opinion."

"Close enough?"

"Close enough." Lola kissed him and Death forgot that he was still sort of in recuperation, and eventually Mr. Right knocked on the door and a great deal of throat clearing and embarrassment ensued as Lola unwound herself from Death and rolled back off of the hospital bed and Death attempted to fix his hair and wipe pink lipstick off his face. "I'll let you boys talk," Lola said, and left the room with a smile.

Mr. Right approached Death with a certain confidence to his step that Death had never seen before. The older agent still wore a full suit and tie, but the tie was ever so slightly loosened.

"Wow, Right, you're really letting yourself go!"

"I am no longer Mr. Right, Kelly. I have decided—"

"Yeah, the Wing told me! What are you gonna do? I mean, haven't you been working for the agency for, like, six million years or something?" Death asked, frowning.

Mr. Right straightened to his full height. "I have not conducted myself in the moral way that a gentleman should. And for that, I truly apologize. I've not been a worthy friend and, for quite some decades, I've held a grudge against the very establishment that employed me." Mr. Right shook his head. "It's time for me to become a better man."

For a long time, Death just stared at his old friend. "Well, you should go golfing, first of all. I hear that's fun," he said at last.

"I think I will. And perhaps I will go skiing. And hiking. Perhaps I will even ride a motorcycle."

Death laughed. "Yeah, sure, good idea." With more than a little effort, he propelled himself out of bed and managed to stand up. As soon as the dizziness cleared, he hugged Mr. Right. It was a bit like hugging a bear in a suit, but that was a comforting sensation. "Go be that guy. Go be someone cool," Death said.

Mr. Right patted Death on the back, but not too hard. "You are a good friend, Kelly. Not just to me, but to many people. Don't let anyone take that from you." With one last pat on the back, Mr. Right pulled away and walked to the door.

"You should eat, like, three boxes of those weird cookies!" Death called after his friend.

Mr. Right turned in the doorway and smiled. "Oh, I should think it is time to try some cookies with real sugar. With coffee, of course. Lots of coffee." And with that, he was gone.

AFTER

Well, the sky was fixed, so that was good.

And according to Cara, Boston seemed almost back to normal. Part of that was memory-wiping, of course, but part was just good old cleanup. As long as people were honking at each other and driving like lunatics and flipping each other the bird, things were pretty much fixed.

Kelly Gold's office door never really closed, because everyone had a question for him. In his three weeks as Head of Agent Resources, a lot had changed around HQ, starting with the top floor. All of the annoyingly cheerful decor and exotic plants had been cleared out and replaced with a dreary color palette that set everyone at ease. And that said nothing of his policy regarding a small feast served at every mandatory meeting.

"Kelly? Brian's here to talk to you," Mandy said, successfully interrupting Kelly's analysis of the week's progress reports.

Brian nervously shuffled into the room, sat down when instructed. "I really hope I'm not bothering you—"

"Not at all. Mandy says you would like to transfer from Literature to Fitness."

Brian nodded. "If it's not too much trouble. Well, I mean, I tried to do it before, but Malcolm said…well, he didn't think anyone should transfer."

"In my opinion, you're far more qualified for Fitness than Literature. So we'll give it a try."

"Thank you so much, De—err, Kelly." Brian paused. "It's exciting to finally get to meet you, sir."

"Uh, we've met, like, four hundred times. We pushed the bubbler over together one time."

"Well, we haven't met since you became a hero," Brian said, and coughed politely behind his hand. "Do you think you'll make your hair blue again?"

Kelly glanced up, catching Mandy's inquisitive gaze on the other side of the room. Her gossip supply had increased greatly since she'd become Kelly's assistant. Just the night before, he'd overheard her telling someone else that everyone wanted Kelly to have blue hair again, "just because."

"Maybe at some point," Kelly said at last. "For now, though, my girlfriend likes it how it is."

Brian nodded. "I'm thinking of making my hair blue, actually. If you wouldn't mind."

About a dozen agents had switched to blue hair already, but Kelly just smiled. "Sure, go for it. It's a good color."

Brian climbed to his feet, all long limbs and nervous excitement. "Thank you, sir. Thank you for everything. I'll do a good job, I promise!"

"I believe it! Have a good evening, Brian."

The second Brian left, Kelly sprang from his chair and gathered his belongings into a bag. He always enjoyed hiring days, because they had a sort of electric charge in them, a potential for a little bit of much-needed inner-office drama. Would someone work out, or wouldn't they? Would Mandy catch the new guy visiting Wendy's office and enjoying some locked-door time?

But he had somewhere to be.

Considering that Wellington had shut down his coffee shop and moved back to England to live with his mother, Lola had a bit more time on her hands. Lola had still never been to Paris, and tonight seemed as good a night as any to pop over to the city of romance and explore. Even if some of the exploration was just a fancy hotel suite and Jacuzzi.

When Mandy swung by the office a few minutes later, with another potential hire in tow, she found Kelly's office quite empty and a note on his desk that read, "TOMORROW IS AN UNSCHEDULED MARCH 32ND. I'LL BE BACK IN A FEW DAYS. PS—HAVE FUN."

Acknowledgements

Writing is such a weird, hidden, secretive, insane sort of thing. Most of the people who hang out with writers are also hidden, secretive or insane. That being said, they deserve thanks anyway.

Dusty Alexander, thank you for walks in Boston, doodling Matt at 3am, Stella in sketchy bars, Arrested Development references, cupcakes/cakes, 60s French cinema, AoB, and, mine god, BABES. You're the best friend I could ask for.

Megan Cullity, thank you so much for being so great. I've never known someone so effortlessly chic, so Parisian, so loyal and straightforward. I truly don't deserve a friend as awesome as you. Thank you for the Boston trip, the beautiful teakettle, the Russian Christmas card and those boozy cupcake recipes!

Steph Usis, you are the true NYC lady in every way. Thank you so much for letting me make a spontaneous trip to NYC and crash with you. You make people's dreams come true (sometimes literally). You're an inspiration to us all, and I'm beyond humbled to call you my friend.

Ricky and Luna, thank you for welcoming me into your world and sharing cheap noodles, aspirin bottles, hair products, makeup tips and queen size beds with me. You guys have opened my eyes to a colorful gypsy lifestyle that I'd only ever dreamed of before. I hope you love Death and Lola, because they are my gift for you.

Kate Edler, where do I even start? From Mr. Right's health food to Death's fascination with "frog week", you really helped make these people jump off the page. Thank you so much for that. And seeing you in your home element, in the greatest city in America, was truly one of my favorite memories. Ever.

Megan Hebert, I've said it a zillion times but that pep talk in your car has stuck with me to this day. I love you, lady.

Karmen, you've been one of the greatest things to happen to me in the last year. If I've ever had anything to thank CC for (and that's a list all on its own) you would be the top of the list. You're one of the most supportive, sweet and empathetic people I've ever known. Thank you for your love, support and 3am conversations about people who don't exist.

Dr. Jason Mangiardi, thank you for trying to fix my head. You're the only person I'd ever trust to poke things around my brain. You're basically a superhero in my eyes!

Thank you Fabio and Rebecca for that wonderful summer evening you spent with my sister and me. Sometimes I think back to our wheeling, rambling conversation about designers, NYC, feet, ice cream, and Bjork and it seems like a beautiful dream. Let's do it again!

Thank you to Josh Hough, Audrey Grieve, Nicole Clark, Amanda Tarlton, Kim Taton, Stephanie Manzione, Raina Kirby-Jones, Paige MacDougall, Isaac Tyler, Megan Robertson, Emily White, Darby Karchut, Karen Rock and Joanne Rock, Marimonster, Matt Connarton, Kale Howard, the Concord NH Starbucks crew, the ladies of TAM, the folks of IO, Jennifer Allis-Provost (for phone conversations, gossip sessions, Russian phrases, and making BEA the best day of my life), Vikki Ciaffone (fearless editor and namer of "tb chic"… probably the coolest phrase of all time) and Kate Kaynak (for the NYC trip, letting me pitch this to you and even letting me come up with the crazy cover idea!)

Thank you to my tumblr and twitter followers! I love you guys!

Thank you, Dmitry Sholokhov, for your ongoing kindness and inspiration. You made BEA a lot of fun for all of us and I'm totally planning to wear your dresses to every major event in my literary career. Let me know when you need more maple syrup!

Janice Janostak, thank you for being my muse and for being such a great friend. You're the real life Matilda (but a lot nicer, of course).

Thank you to those who contributed to my fundraiser, namely: Sherry Ficklin, Eric Taylor, Marcelle Liemant, Anthony Caroto, Suzanne Reynolds-Alpert, Kim Taton, David Joseph Clarke, Greg Brown, Kaitrin Acuna, Celtic Moon Books, Kaitlyn Abdou, V is for Villains, Eric Letendre, and Rachel Patrick.

And finally, to my wonderful parents and five younger siblings… I love you guys. So much. Thanks for letting me choose a career that makes almost no money and involves me crying about people that don't exist.

THE OTHER TREE

It's been four years since Chris Arlin graduated with a degree that most people think she made up, and she's still no closer to scraping up funding for her research into rare plants. Instead, she's stacking shelves at the campus library, until a suspiciously well-dressed man offers her a lucrative position on a scientific expedition.

For Chris, the problem isn't the fact that they're searching for the Biblical Tree of Life. Nor is it the fact that most of the individuals on the expedition seem to be fashionably lethal mercenaries. The problem is that the mission is being backed by SinaCorp, the corporation responsible for a similar, failed expedition on which her mother died eleven years ago.

However, when Chris's father is unexpectedly diagnosed with inoperable cancer, Chris sees only one solution. Vowing to find the Tree of Life before SinaCorp's mercenaries, Chris

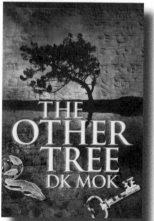

recruits Luke, an antisocial campus priest undergoing a crisis of faith. Together, they embark on a desperate race to find Eden. However, as the hunt intensifies, Chris discovers growing evidence of her mother's strange behaviour before her death, and she begins to realise that SinaCorp isn't the only one with secrets they want to stay buried.

SPENCE CITY • spencecity.com

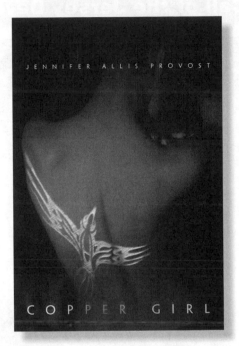

JENNIFER ALLIS PROVOST

COPPER GIRL

Sara had always been careful.

She never spoke of magic, never associated with those suspected of handling magic, never thought of magic, and never, ever, let anyone see her mark. After all, the last thing she wanted was to end up missing, like her father and brother.

Then, a silver elf pushed his way into Sara's dream, and her life became anything but ordinary.

SPENCE CITY • spencecity.com

Call of the Jersey Devil

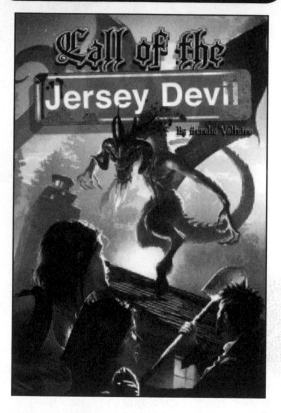

Four Goth teens and a washed up musician get stranded in the Pine Barrens and discover that New Jersey really is a gate to Hell--and if they don't do something, being banned from the mall is the least of their worries.

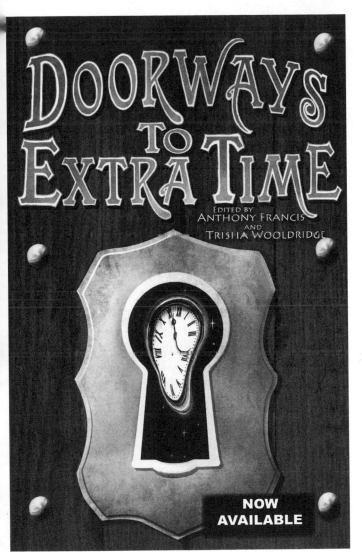

DOORWAYS TO EXTRA TIME

EDITED BY
ANTHONY FRANCIS
AND
TRISHA WOOLDRIDGE

NOW
AVAILABLE

Also available as an ebook • **SPENCER HILL PRESS** • spencerhillpress.com

ABOUT THE AUTHOR

Photo by K.L. Saunders

Kendra L. Saunders is the author of the magic realism novel *Inanimate Objects*, short story collection *Overlapping Visions* and the dark comedy *Death and Mr. Right*. She has been published in *Snakeskin Magazine* and *Premier Bride Magazine*, and has conducted interviews with NYT Bestselling author Jennifer L. Armentrout, goth rocker Aurelio Voltaire and fashion designers Dmitry Sholokhov and Fabio Costa for ipmnation.com, The New England Horror Writers and Steampunk Magazine. She reports regularly for Pure Textuality and writes helpful writing articles for NerdCaliber's Pages of Note.

In her spare time Kendra likes to daydream about boys with dark hair, drink too much tea, read fashion magazines, listen to records on vinyl, plan her dream trip to England and attempt to travel back in time to the Jazz Age. She also snaps some pretty amazing black and white photography. Find her online at www.kendralsaunders.com or on twitter at @kendrybird